DEATH *of a* SCAM ARTIST
BY MIKE BEFELER

DEATH *of* *a* SCAM ARTIST

BY MIKE BEFELER

Encircle Publications, LLC
Farmington, Maine U.S.A.

ISBN-10: 1-893035-38-7
ISBN-13: 978-1-893035-38-6

Library of Congress Pre-control Number: 201 7940054

Editor: Cynthia Brackett-Vincent
Book design: Eddie Vincent
Cover design: Beth MacKenney
Cover photographs; car © tournee/stock.adobe.com; building © cb34inc/istock.com

Published by: Encircle Publications, LLC
PO Box 187
Farmington, ME 04938

Visit: http://encirclepub.com

Printed in U.S.A.

Publisher's Cataloging-in-Publication data

Names: Befeler, Mike, author.
Title: Death of a scam artist / by Mike Befeler.
Description: Farmington, ME: Encircle Publications LLC, 2017.
Identifiers: ISBN 978-1-893035-38-6 (pbk.) | 978-1-893035-72-0 (ebook) | LCCN 2017940054
Subjects: LCSH Retirement communities--Fiction. | Old age--Fiction. | Swindlers and swindling--Fiction. | Murderers--Fiction. | Magicians--Fiction. | Mystery fiction. | Mystery and detective stories. | BISAC FICTION / Mystery & Detective / Cozy
Classification: LCC PS3602.E37 D43 2017 | DDC 813.6--dc23

For all the wonderful people I've met while visiting and speaking at retirement communities

Acknowledgements

M any thanks to Wendy Befeler, Laura Froisland, Chuck Heidel, Donnell Bell, Michael Schonbrun, Eddie Vincent, Cynthia Brackett-Vincent and members of my critique group.

Chapter 1

Reginald Bentley sank into a swivel chair previously compressed by a much larger derriere than his. As the new executive director of the peeling white behemoth known as Sunny Crest Retirement Community, he realized the challenge ahead. After detecting a musty smell emanating from the bottom drawer of the worn, wooden desk, he spent thirty minutes removing a grimy coffee mug, disposing of Jolly Rancher wrappers, throwing away a half-eaten, moldy Twinkie, filing poorly written reports and discarding gnawed pencils.

The framed photograph on the wall of a snow-covered mountain pass would have been the one item of quality here, except for what looked like a bullet hole in the lower left corner and a knife slash on the right side. Below the picture, the once white walls displayed charming brown handprints, possibly the remnants of the previous executive director trying to escape the barely livable workspace. Reginald hoped it was mud or chocolate, and nothing worse.

He shook his head, wondering what he had gotten himself into. Perhaps he should call in Special Forces with a flame thrower to torch the office. He eyed a bent paper clip that appeared to have a dollop of earwax attached and pitched it into the wastebasket.

A woman who resembled a large red gummy bear in a white nurse's uniform burst into the office, dragging a tiny, twitching woman by the arm.

Ms. Gummy Bear skidded to a stop in front of his desk. She reminded him of a tank sliding through slime. "We have a dire emergency!" she said.

Visions of suicide, murder or terrorist attacks ran through Reginald's mind. The veins on the forehead of the larger woman pulsed as though ready to explode at any moment. If that happened, he didn't know whether blood or gummy bear juice would flow. The smaller woman shivered as if caught unprepared in a snowstorm on a high mountain peak.

1

He tapped his desk with the tip of a pen that looked like it had been manufactured around 1960. "Ladies, please give me a calm report on what's going on."

The nurse squeezed the arm of her companion, causing the smaller woman to wince. "Helen here went to Jerry Rhine's room this morning to give him his medication as she always does right before breakfast." The large woman paused to gulp air, like a struggling swimmer. "And . . . and Henrietta Marlow was in bed with him. You know . . . the two of them alone. Whose children should we notify first?"

Reginald relaxed, pushing aside images of a crazed prison escapee ready to rake the dining room with an AK-47 or ISIS holding all the residents for ransom. Not that he figured the old fussbudgets living here would be worth much. He focused on Helen, who wore the insignia of a certified nursing assistant. "Tell me exactly what happened."

"Like Rita said, I . . . I." She gasped and turned red, then purple.

Reginald feared she had swallowed her tongue. Finally, Helen took a deep breath and continued. "I . . . I was making my rounds this morning. I entered Mr. Rhine's apartment to give him his cholesterol pill like I do every morning."

"Did you knock first?" Reginald asked with his most direct corporate CYA stare.

"Yes. But he's a little hard of hearing. That's why I went inside. He has a single room suite and the bed sits right off the kitchen entryway. Once inside the door, I discovered he and Mrs. Marlow were in bed together with . . . with their clothes in a heap on the floor." She covered her eyes as if the scene would haunt her forever.

"And their marital status?"

Helen lowered her hand from her face, and her lower lip quivered. "Neither is married. He's a widower, and she's a widow."

Reginald directed his gaze for a moment toward the dirt-streaked window, which looked as if it hadn't been washed in the last ten years. Two dogs were humping in the open field beyond the retirement community property line. Maybe it was something in the water around here. "Did anyone appear to have been coerced into this situation?"

"Oh, no." Helen shook her head so vigorously that her bobby pins appeared poised to fly out and pierce the wall. "They both had huge grins on their faces."

"Then what's the problem?" Reginald asked.

"We . . . we . . . we can't have that kind of behavior here," Rita, the gummy bear RN, spluttered.

Reginald pushed aside the memory of the nursery rhyme his mom used to recite to him about the little piggy who cried, "Wee! Wee! Wee! " all the way home. "They do reside in an independent living facility."

"But . . . but . . . but . . ."

Reginald ignored the sound that reminded him of a misused Briggs and Stratton five horsepower outboard engine and held up a hand. "Leave this to me, ladies. I'll speak with Mr. Rhine."

After they'd scattered from his office like rodents abandoning a sinking barge, Reginald sat with his head in his hands, wondering why he had traded in his corporate controller role at Cenpolis Corporation in Chicago to take this position at one of their financially struggling retirement communities in the wasteland of Boulder, Colorado. One thought occurred to him. He picked up the phone and called his boss, Armand Daimler.

Daimler's admin put him through.

"Mr. Daimler, this retirement home where you sent me is going to need some work."

"That's why you're there, boy. You're my Benihana Chef of slashing expenses. Get that facility back in the black."

Reginald gulped. "It may take some time."

"Don't go soft on me. Fix it or fry it." The line disconnected.

Reginald had been around Daimler long enough to know that this blunt delivery translated into a directive to turn around an uncertain investment or face the alternative to pop and scrape the building to sell the land for residential lots. If the latter, Reginald's only involvement would probably be as a real estate agent, having been forced to change careers. Once Daimler made up his mind, Reginald knew there were only two alternatives—genuflect and follow the order or pack his bags to join the unemployment line.

This assignment in no way fit into his picture of a sound career path. Reginald had never held any fondness for the unholy triumvirate of seniors, kids and animals, and here his sorry behind had been plunked down right in the middle of one of that trio—old people. At least in this place, the geezers were too old to have little runts squirming around in the hallways and the facility allowed no pets. He still had to put up with a building full of aging, creaking, disheveled senior citizens.

He shook his head, remembering the low points of his childhood.

When his friends in elementary school raved about their kind and loving grandparents, he thought they were delusional. His own grandparents smelled like rotten fish and had the dispositions of surly wolverines. And when an old hunched crone in the neighborhood would tweak him under the chin, he felt like spewing his lunch on her high-laced shoes.

Reginald looked out the window of his office at the large, uncultivated field, displaying a mixture of green and brown. Green pine and aspen trees amid long, brown grass, dried out from the summer heat. The dogs had finished doing their thing and had disappeared. When it cooled down in the autumn, he'd have to explore this open space. If he lasted here that long.

*****

"Call me Reginald." That's the first thing he said to Jerry Rhine and his two geezer buddies at their lunch table in the corner of a noisy, sour-smelling dining room.

Jerry adjusted his hearing aid. "Thanks for the profound statement, Reggie." He gave an octogenarian smirk.

Reginald met his eyes. "Reginald or Mr. Bentley."

"You've got to be kidding. What are you? All of forty years old?"

Reginald squared his shoulders and stuck out his chest. "Forty-one, to be exact."

Jerry threw his spaghetti-spattered napkin down on the table and glared at him. "Why don't you remove that corncob stuck two feet up your butt and come join us common folk?"

Reginald gave his most polished corporate smile. "Don't mind if I do." He pulled out the fourth chair at the table and settled down on the hard surface, which did nothing to help the corncob. "In fact, I want to discuss a little event from last night." He leaned closer to Jerry and whispered, "I have something we should discuss in private."

Jerry tweaked his right earlobe. "You'll have to speak louder, Reggie. I'm a little hard of hearing."

Reginald cleared his throat. "Can we go somewhere by ourselves to talk?"

"Look, I'm willing to listen to any palaver from you and your corncob in front of my friends. Fire away."

Reginald took a deep breath and almost gagged on a burnt smell permeating the air. He couldn't exactly place the aroma. Somehow it

4

reminded him of camping rather than being in a retirement home. "It seems there has been a complaint regarding where Mrs. Marlow woke up this morning."

Jerry guffawed. "That's rich. I don't think Henrietta has any concerns. But I wouldn't bring up this subject with her. I'm a gentleman, but she's apt to poke you in the eye."

The two other men at the table chuckled.

"But if you want to endanger your life, she sits right over there, the cute gal facing us." Jerry pointed two tables away to an attractive older woman with a silver page boy. She appeared no worse for wear as the result of her visit to Jerry's apartment. "As long as you're imposing on us, I might as well introduce my companions. Reggie, meet Al Thiebodaux, retired photographer par excellence, and Tom Balboa, the army colonel who kept the Ruskies from invading us during the Cold War."

Al Thiebodaux clasped Reginald's hand with both of his and gave it a warm, weak shake. Tom Balboa grabbed his hand, almost crushing a couple of knuckles with his viselike grip, and then glared. "Don't mess with my friends Jerry and Henrietta."

Reginald met his eyes. "I wouldn't think of it."

Tom wrinkled his nose and gave a nod.

Jerry adjusted his hearing aid and tapped the table. "Reggie, since you're new to this joint, I have a piece of advice for you."

Reginald had a piece of advice for him as well but decided to bite his tongue. "Okay."

Jerry leaned forward and stabbed a finger into Reginald's chest. "We have a big problem here, and you need to do something to fix it." He leaned back and folded his arms. His two friends' chins bobbed in agreement.

When Jerry said nothing else, Reginald took the bait. "Don't keep me in suspense. What's the problem?"

Jerry's eyes twinkled. "That's good. You know how to listen. Not like the jerk who preceded you. And I'm supposed to be the one who can't hear well."

Reginald gave a start at the sound of a dish crashing to the floor and saw an attendant rush to help a woman who had dropped a full plate of spaghetti. He returned his attention to Jerry. "I take it you didn't think much of the previous administration."

Jerry exhaled, sounding like a bus releasing its brakes, and his lower lip puffed out. "Damn right. That guy was as popular as a fart in a candy factory.

He locked himself in his office, picked his nose, and avoided decisions." Jerry bent forward and again jabbed his finger at Reginald. "Now you need to act on what he completely ignored. We have a big problem in this place with a scam artist."

"Scam artist?"

"I'm glad you heard it. Too many residents have lost money to some guy who sneaks in here and preys on old people who don't know any better. He's a wily cuss who figures out ways to convince residents here to fork over hard-earned cash. Your predecessor took no action to rid our facility of this blatant and despicable act of elder abuse."

Reginald watched a woman using a walker clomp up to a table, select a sweet roll, wrap it in a paper napkin and stuff it into her purse. "Have the police been notified?"

"Sure, but they think they have better things to do than patrol our hallowed halls. They've taken reports and done a cursory check, but no follow-through. It's up to the retirement home director to deal with this, and the previous guy ignored the issue completely."

"But there's a facility manager here on my staff responsible for security."

Jerry rolled his eyes. "Dex Hanley knows how to replace light bulbs and paint rooms but doesn't know diddly about preventing unwanted visitors from sneaking in. Tom here could do a better job."

"If I get my hands on that scammer, I'll throttle him," Tom said, tearing his paper napkin in two.

Reginald had visions of bloody body parts flying through the hallway.

"Reggie, you need to beef up security and rid our home of this menace. Otherwise, we'll have to do something to handle it ourselves."

Tom's mouth formed a snarl, and Al bit his lip as both of their chins bounced up and down again.

"I'll look into it."

"You damn well better do more than that." Jerry punched his right fist into his left hand. "We need results, and we need them now."

"Duly noted." Reginald gave them a tolerant smile and rose from his chair. "It's been a pleasure, gentlemen. Now I must continue my rounds to meet more of the residents."

Only after he had introduced himself at the next table did Reginald realize that Jerry Rhine had omitted in his introductions one specific piece of information. He hadn't mentioned his profession before retiring.

Chapter 2

As Reginald worked his way around the room, he stopped at Henrietta Marlow's table and met her two companions, Karen Landry and Belinda Davenport. After introductions he said, "I spoke a little while ago with Jerry, Al and Tom over there." He pointed to Jerry's table.

Laugh lines appeared around Henrietta's eyes. "Our gentlemen friends. I couldn't see it clearly, but Belinda says she saw Jerry haranguing you. He comes across gruff but is really a teddy bear underneath." She glanced in approximately Jerry's direction, and her lips curled upward. Reginald thought he saw something hidden in that smile.

"Are you referring to his hairy chest?" Karen, the thin, matronly woman, asked as she sipped from a cup. The coffee gave off the same aroma Reginald had sniffed at Jerry's table. A vision of camping in the woods popped into his mind. That was it—the smell of wet socks smoldering on a campfire.

Henrietta waved her hand. "Oh, Karen, you know what I mean."

Henrietta's two companions giggled.

"Do you and the trio of men go places together?" Reginald asked. He wanted to know about their relationships but wasn't sure why. They had to have some sort of life beyond this dingy yellow room, the smoldering-sock coffee and the layer of crud accumulated on the tabletops. Maybe with her eyesight problems Henrietta didn't notice all of this. She seemed happy enough. Strange.

The slightly plump Belinda Davenport perked up. "Yes. We stay very active and attend most of the Sunny Crest events as well as plan some trips of our own. The six of us went to a Rockies baseball game last weekend." Her hand shook as she pushed aside a strand of hair.

"Does one of you drive?"

Henrietta put her cup of smoldering-sock coffee down on the table.

"No, Jerry lined up a taxi van to take us to the bus stop. A bus runs to and from the game. We had a great time."

"And they gave us something as a memento," Karen Landry said, scrunching up her nose. "Y'all remember what it was? I've forgotten."

"Those little souvenir bats, dear," Belinda said, patting her hand. She returned her attention to Reginald, who knew exactly the type of bat she was talking about. He had received one at a Cubs game a month ago, one of the few times he escaped from the office on a weekday. "We each have them on display in our rooms. Now, Mr. Bentley, did you know that Henrietta serves as the official greeter for new residents here?"

"No, I didn't."

Belinda leaned toward Reginald and cupped her hand to her mouth. Her breath smelled oddly of both onions and peppermint. "She gives tours and is the best salesperson you can imagine."

"That's good to know. By the way, your gentleman friends told me a scam artist keeps coming into Sunny Crest to take advantage of the residents here."

Henrietta wrinkled her brow and paused as two women in bright red hats hobbled past as if trying to overhear the conversation before moving on. "This has become a major problem. Some man either stole or reproduced a staff badge. Most recently, he snuck in and accosted people in their rooms, claiming to be collecting money on behalf of the staff for some orphans fund. He showed a picture of a pathetic child, and a number of the women here gave him all their cash. I don't know how many times I've warned other residents, but they continue to be sucked in by this jerk. He's clever. The bugger keeps changing his approach."

"For example, Mrs. Booth wrote him a check for ten thousand dollars as a service charge for a hundred thousand dollar sweepstakes he convinced her she had won," Belinda added.

"Can we have her bank stop payment on the check?" Reginald asked.

Belinda shook her head. "Too late. By the time she mentioned it to anyone, the scam artist had already cashed the check."

"Jerry indicated the previous director didn't deal with the problem," Reginald said, as a brown handprint similar to the one on his office wall caught his eye. It was on the side of a counter littered with coffee cups, sweet roll crumbs and an apple with a bite missing.

Henrietta let out a snort. "That's an understatement. For some reason he ignored our request to beef up security. He was as useless as tits on a—"

"Now, now, Henrietta." Belinda held up her shaking hand. "Let's not offend the young man."

Henrietta's eyes flared. "Security here needs your immediate attention."

"I'll look into it." Reginald pursed his lips. The previous director was worse than useless. The guy should have addressed this situation.

"You be sure to do that," Henrietta said, a smile reappearing on her face. "Do you have a family, Mr. Bentley?"

"You can call me Reginald, and no, my career has kept me too busy to marry and raise a family."

Belinda raised an eyebrow. "My, my, a single man." She elbowed Henrietta. "That's interesting."

Henrietta brushed Belinda's arm away. "Well, yes. Now, Reginald, we're going to hold you to your promise to do something to catch this intruder."

"I'll speak with my staff this afternoon."

Karen squinted at Reginald and then gazed toward her friends. "Y'all notice Reginald is taller than most of the people we see here."

"Six foot one," Reginald said.

"Oh, I didn't think you were quite that tall," Karen said. "I never trust people over six feet."

"Let's give the gentleman the benefit of the doubt," Belinda said.

Karen looked puzzled. "The benefit of the doubt about what, y'all?"

"Oh, never mind," Belinda said.

Then Reginald remembered the question he had forgotten to ask at the men's table. "By the way, what did Jerry do before he retired?"

Henrietta flicked at a speck on the sleeve of her blouse. "He had a career as a professional magician."

9

Chapter 3

That afternoon, Reginald experienced a sinking feeling in the pit of his stomach as he contemplated what he had learned so far. In addition to being stuck with a building full of old people and facing the task of ridding the place of a scam artist, he had to figure out how to make this facility financially solvent again. It was obvious that cost-cutting measures had to be undertaken, including an assessment of staffing levels, outside services and the basic expenditure run rate. He tapped the desk with a finger then jerked his hand away to avoid a splinter. He scrolled through his mental checklist of opportunities to save dollars. He'd jump into that when he held the first meeting with his staff in a few minutes.

At exactly two p.m. he entered the small conference room adjoining his office. He looked around at the bare walls, large wooden table and institutional chairs. Four people sat there. As he prepared to close the door, a young woman dashed in. "Sorry I'm late. I had to finish planning for the dance tomorrow night."

"You must be Vicki Pearson, our activities manager."

She brushed aside a loose strand of blond hair. "That's right."

She plopped into an open chair, and Reginald shut the door. Then he scanned the faces—three women and two men. They all looked up expectantly like children on the first day of kindergarten. To their credit, no scowls appeared.

He cleared his throat. "I've been asked to step into this position for one main reason. Sunny Crest has been losing money. Our mission as the management team is to turn that situation around." He paused to peruse the faces. No change of expression or obvious emotion. Tough crowd.

"This will entail some hard decisions, but the first step will be to stem some of the excessive expenditures. I'd like to go around the room and have you each introduce yourself and tell me what can be done to cut expenses in your department." He pointed to a stocky man on his left. "Let's start here."

"Dex Hanley. Facilities and Security." He stuck a finger in his ear and then removed it like he had extracted a diamond. "Cutting costs will be a problem. We only have a minimal staff, and the place needs to be repainted."

"But his department definitely spends too much money," a tall, slim man with a pencil-thin mustache interjected.

Reginald squinted at the new speaker. "And you are?"

The guy patted his chest. "Hector Lopez, Health Services and Housekeeping."

"That's the place to really save money," Dex said. "Housekeeping is way overstaffed and inefficient to boot."

Dex and Hector glared at each other.

"Gentlemen, I'm not asking you to make suggestions in other people's departments. I want to know what each of you can do yourself. Dex, before the interruption you started saying something in regards to painting."

"I'm sure you've noticed. The exterior paint has started to peel. We need to repaint immediately."

"That's something we'll have to defer for the time being." Reginald's eyes bore in on Dex. "How can you cut ten percent from your budget?"

Dex scratched his head. "Well, besides staff, our big expenses are electricity and natural gas."

"That's all he's good for," Hector said under his breath. "Gas."

Vicki, sitting next to Hector, leaned sideways and elbowed him. "Sshh."

Reginald glared at Hector and then looked back to Dex. "See what you can do to reduce utility expenses. How do you handle trash collection?"

"We're contracted for pickup twice a week. Monday and Thursday."

Reginald jotted a note on a pad. "Cut it back to once a week. Next."

A middle-aged woman in a neat brown skirt and white blouse said, "I'm Alicia Renton of the business office. I'm short one staff person as it is. The only thing that would save money would be if I could get more volunteer assistance from the residents instead of filling that one headcount."

Finally some progress. Reginald bestowed his best executive nod of encouragement on Alicia. "Good idea. We can save money, and it involves the residents and gives them an additional activity to participate in. Do you have responsibility for our insurance?"

"Yes."

"I want you to review all the policies today. My experience says that with a little scrutiny, you can reduce the premiums. Renegotiate a cost decrease right away."

Alicia cast her eyes down. "Yes, sir."

Reginald pointed to Hector. "Okay. Let's hear not what Dex can do but what your department can accomplish in the way of cost reduction."

Hector waved his hand. "We provide a lot of free over-the-counter medication. You know, Advil, Tylenol, aspirin. I suppose we could cut back some on that."

"He's probably selling them on the side," Dex muttered.

Reginald leaned toward the table. "If you two keep fighting like this, I'll replace both of you. Dex and Hector, do you understand?"

Dex gulped, and Hector riveted his stare at the table.

"Well?" Reginald looked back and forth at the two of them.

"Okay," Dex said.

"Yeah," Hector added.

"All right. Now Hector, you have the floor. Medication."

"As I was saying before being so rudely interrupted." He shot a dirty look at Dex. "We buy a lot of over-the-counter medicine for our residents. I can try to cut back on that or buy generic drugs rather than name brands."

"Or charge a modest fee," Reginald suggested.

Hector's eyes grew wide. "We've never done that before."

"And see what you can do with housekeeping supplies. That may be an opportunity for further cost savings." Reginald looked around the room, making eye contact with each individual in turn. "I have one main message for all of you—look for new approaches to save money. Think of ways to cut expenses and boost revenue. Remember, we have a business to run here."

"Yes, but we also have residents to serve," Hector added.

"That's correct. We have to provide the best service possible, but we need to do so by spending less money than in the past. Vicki, your thoughts."

"Hmm. We have a full program of exercise, art, excursions and concerts. We wouldn't want to cut back on any of those."

"You mentioned a dance tomorrow night. How much do you have budgeted to spend on that event?"

Her eyes darted from side to side. "Not very much, except for the band."

"In the future use a CD player instead of live entertainment."

"But the residents like the band."

"Vicki, think cost reduction. Do the residents pay for activities?"

"No. It's part of the basic service we provide."

Reginald scrunched up his nose as the aroma of smoldering-sock coffee permeated the room. Then he realized that the conference room was right next to the dining room. "Take a look at a minimal charge for events. And last but not least." He opened his hand toward a woman in her thirties with neatly curled brown hair, who wore a designer suit.

"I'm Mimi Hendrix, marketing manager. I have to respectfully disagree with the focus on cutting expenses."

So he had one staff member with gumption. "Please say more."

"With due respect, our problem isn't expenses. Our focus should be on occupancy rate and keeping residents from leaving."

"Well, some do die," Alicia said.

"True," Mimi replied. "But we should invest in promoting Sunny Crest. We have a good facility here, and we should let prospects know what we have to offer. Rather than cutting back, we should instead increase our level of service and advertise throughout the Denver area. We need more residents."

"And how many vacancies do we have?" Reginald asked.

"Too many," Mimi replied. "Twenty-eight rooms."

Reginald did a quick calculation. Worse than he expected. "This is a critical issue, but we must also emphasize cost reduction." Reginald gave her his best penny-pinching stare. "I'll be reviewing your marketing budget. I'm not a fan of advertising. Find ways to implement less expensive promotional programs."

She glowered at him and said no more.

Reginald leaned forward. "Now to address our expenditures, I'm instigating a new policy. All purchase requisitions need my approval."

Alicia raised her hand. "But we often have office supply reqs for ten or twenty dollars."

"I want to see all purchases, no matter how small. This will also be a good way for me to become familiar with our spending patterns. Now, aren't we missing someone?"

"Maurice Casotti, who heads up Food Services, is out ill today," Alicia said.

"I hope it wasn't something he ate." Reginald snickered, but no one on his staff seemed to share his sense of humor. "Well . . . ah . . . one final item. It's been brought to my attention that a scam artist has been roaming free here, and residents are concerned. Dex, how can this guy be circumventing our security system?"

"We don't have anything elaborate, only a receptionist at the front desk, and at all times a roving guard checking the hallways."

"So how does an unidentified man get past the front desk to wander into residents' rooms?"

Dex shrugged. "I suppose the receptionist has to take restroom breaks."

"Someone should be manning the main entrance at all times. Find a way to cover that and have your security guards on the lookout for strangers."

"Yes, Chief."

Hector waved his hand.

"Yes, Hector."

"Maybe Dex should work longer hours and check on things himself."

"I'll leave it to Dex to work out a solution here. Now, there must be some information on this scam perpetrator."

"Several reports have been filed," Dex said.

"I want a copy of everything you have on my desk by the end of the day." Reginald paused to survey the faces. They had turned from eager kindergarteners to sulky teenagers. "Do any of you have other subjects we should address?"

Mimi Hendrix's hand shot up like a flag on the Fourth of July.

"Yes, Mimi."

"We've all introduced ourselves, but you haven't said anything about yourself."

Reginald shrugged. "Not that much to say. I've been in finance during my whole career. I started at Cenpolis ten years ago in the accounting department and rose to my most recent position of corporate controller."

Mimi gaped at Reginald. "So you've never run a retirement home before?"

Reginald met her scrutiny without backing off. "No, but I've been involved in the acquisition of twelve retirement properties and the divestiture of three."

"What do you mean by divestiture?" Vicki Pearson asked.

"In two cases we sold the facilities to other corporations. In one case we shut down the poorly performing retirement home and sold the property for residential real estate."

The room grew as silent as a morgue at midnight. Then Dex Hanley raised a hand. "What happened to the residents and staff when that place was shut down?"

"The staff had to find new jobs, and the residents had to move elsewhere."

"And you let that happen?" Alicia Renton gasped.

"Yes. It's a matter of making the numbers. We have a business to run here, folks. The Board of Directors of Cenpolis and our CEO Armand Daimler expect the company-owned retirement communities to be profitable. Cenpolis acquires sound properties and gets rid of ones that don't meet financial targets."

Hector Lopez shuddered. "Is that what we are—a property?"

"Yes. And right now Sunny Crest is a poorly performing property. Our job is to fix it."

"And that's why you're here," Mimi said. "To shape us up or get rid of us."

Reginald forced a smile this time. "Yes. Daimler expects results. Sunny Crest has not been delivering, so I'm here to work with all of you to change that situation."

"And why were you specifically selected?" Mimi pressed again.

"I wanted to move into line executive management at Cenpolis. Daimler thinks this is a good opportunity for me to demonstrate my leadership skills."

From somewhere in the room came a mumbled, "Guinea pigs."

"And your management philosophy?" Mimi asked.

"It's quite simple. I want all of you to work hard, do your best for Sunny Crest and produce the results commensurate with a financially-sound retirement home. I expect you to come up with creative means of improving our performance. We'll have regular staff meetings for communication of what's working and what's not." Reginald looked at his watch. "Is there anything else we should discuss before we adjourn?" He engaged each pair of eyes, but no one said anything. "Now, each of you review your areas of operation and come back with your implementation plans for further cost reductions. We'll meet here at nine tomorrow."

"In the morning?" Hector gasped.

"Not much time to work miracles," Alicia added.

*****

After the meeting, Reginald returned to his office, closed the door and sat there with his stomach churning over the magnitude of what he needed to accomplish. His staff seemed competent, but clearly had not thought in terms of cost containment before. It would be an uphill battle with them and would require reinforcing the steps necessary to keep this place solvent. But did he really want Sunny Crest to stay open? Two hundred smelly, limping, decrepit old fogies. And on top of it a smart-aleck like Jerry Rhine. He pressed his fingers against his temples. He had no love for anything or anyone here, but he had a job to do. He couldn't give up on his first day. He had been sent here to turn it around. In spite of all the old people, he'd do what he could to find a solution, to reduce the expenditures and to keep Sunny Crest financially viable. Besides, if he didn't, his boss Armand Daimler would have no qualms tossing him out on his fanny.

Then a spike of rage surged through Reginald's chest. He snapped a pencil in two and threw the pieces against the wall. He didn't think much of old codgers like the irascible Jerry Rhine, but these old farts had become his responsibility now, and no one would get away with scamming paying customers on his watch. He had a job to do in keeping this place open, and he needed to make sure his residents lived in a safe place where some jerk didn't invade their apartments and steal their social security money. What to do, what to do? First, he had to learn more about what steps had been taken to track down this scam artist. He called the non-emergency number of the police department and asked to speak to anyone who handled white-collar crime. After a short wait, the dispatcher put him through.

"Detective Mallory here."

"Detective, I'm Reginald Bentley, the new executive director at Sunny Crest Retirement Community. I took over responsibilities today and have discovered that an unidentified individual has been scamming my residents."

"Yes, I've been called in on several occasions."

"I consider this very serious and would appreciate an update on what the police department plans to do to catch the perpetrator."

"We've taken reports and interviewed the staff at Sunny Crest. We're pretty sure the scam artist is an outsider and not one of your employees."

Reginald almost tapped a finger on his left-over-from-a-garage-sale desk before remembering to pull his hand away to avoid splinters. "That's reassuring, but how do you plan to catch this man?"

"So far, he's proven illusive. I've dispatched a police officer on four occasions, but we haven't been able to spot the perpetrator."

"Could we have an officer assigned on a regular basis while this threat remains at Sunny Crest?"

There was a sigh. "I wish we had the staff to do that. Unfortunately, the department remains overworked with two murder investigations, a series of bank robberies and a major car theft ring we're trying to crack."

"This is pretty major as well."

"I agree with you, but right now my hands are tied. We did make some security suggestions to your predecessor, a Mr. Edwards. Do you know if your staff implemented those recommendations?"

Reginald remembered the scant amount of useful material he'd found in this office. "I doubt it, but I'd appreciate it if you would provide me the same information. I don't expect I'll be able to find anything left over here from what you previously provided."

"I can email you the recommendations."

"Let's start with that."

*****

Thirty minutes later, Reginald read the document he had received from Detective Mallory. It contained much of what he expected and suggested changes that the previous administration had never implemented. He picked up the phone and called the facilities and security manager, Dex Hanley.

"I need you in my office, right now. And bring your files on the scam artist."

"Yes, Chief."

Right now turned out to be fifteen minutes. When Dex stepped heavily through the door, he gave Reginald a stack of papers, which Reginald put aside to read later.

Reginald handed him the printed email from the police. "Dex, I want you to implement each of these recommendations from the police department. Have you seen this before?"

He shook his head.

"You need to reinforce with all your staff that catching this scam artist and preventing any further thefts from our residents is now your top priority. Let's review the list."

By the end of the meeting Dex had agreed to meet with his employees to discuss the problem and alert them to the description of the suspect. The specific recommendations to be implemented included assuring that someone would be on the front desk at all times, double-checking all emergency exits to prevent unauthorized entry, posting notices on the residents' bulletin board warning people of the mode of operation of this scammer, working with business manager Alicia Renton to put an article in the resident newsletter and increasing the amount of time the security guards patrolled the hallways.

"That will require overtime," Dex said.

"Find a way to do this within your current budget."

*****

At dinner Reginald made a pass through the dining room, and Jerry Rhine waved him over. "What brings you down here to the low rent district?"

"I want to let you know that we're taking action to catch the scam artist. I've contacted the police and put new security procedures in effect."

"Well la di da. It's time someone in authority here did something constructive." Jerry pointed his fork at him. "And we need some quick results."

Reginald almost answered, "Yes, sir," but then remembered he was in charge.

*****

Reginald had the option of living elsewhere, but had decided that if he intended to turn Sunny Crest around, it would require his around-the-clock involvement. Consequently, he now resided in an on site apartment. Opening the door, he surveyed the blank walls and meager furnishings and contemplated all that had transpired during his first day on the job.

*****

Reginald arrived at his office at seven the next morning to get a jump start on the day by preparing the agenda for the staff meeting scheduled at nine. He tapped his pen on a notepad and considered how to enlist his managers' buy-in to his new ideas. He listened to the sound of rain pelting the window and looked out to see the trees shaking in the wind of an early morning storm. In his first few days in Colorado, he had noticed how dry it was. The place could use the moisture. The squall passed quickly, and he returned his attention to the work at hand.

He had begun condensing several pages of notes into a dozen bullet points when the phone rang.

"This is Dex. I tried your apartment, and when you didn't answer, I figured you might be in your office. We have a major problem."

After Reginald's first day on the job when the big problem turned out to be Jerry and Henrietta in bed together, Dex's statement didn't cause a blip on his worry scale. He answered Dex calmly. "Which is?"

"Moments ago I received a call from the security guard. The authorities have been contacted and should be here soon. There's a dead body in the loading dock bay."

Chapter 4

Not bothering to wait for the elevator, Reginald took the stairs two at a time and pushed his way through the heavy door to the loading dock. The scene made his stomach tighten into a knot as thick as the work of a berserk Boy Scout.

A man's body lay splayed in the bay where delivery trucks would be pulling in later in the morning. His limbs sprawled akimbo. Blood spotted his face and black hair. A Rorschach blob of brownish red mixed with rainwater and spilled oil spread around him. His windbreaker beaded water from the rain blown into the open bay from the early morning storm. He appeared too young to be one of the residents, and his brown slacks and wing tip shoes indicated he didn't work on the maintenance crew at Sunny Crest.

The security guard stood on the dock, looking as dazed as if someone had whacked him on the head.

Accompanied by a fire fighter, Dex crashed through the door and shouted, "Right down there."

A burst of static grated from a radio on the fireman's uniform, and he grabbed the device to report his arrival to dispatch. A siren wailed in the distance. Within minutes a white medical van pulled up. Two EMTs jumped out and dashed to the body. One of them checked for a pulse and the other tried moving the man's arm, which appeared as stiff as a tree limb. "He's dead," the first paramedic said, removing his finger from the man's throat. "Make sure there's a police officer on the way."

"Roger," the fireman responded. He began speaking into his radio, which squawked replies in staccato bursts. Within ten minutes representatives of the fire department, police force and EMT squad were all huddled together on the dock like members of an all-star football team. Reginald never realized a retirement home could be so popular.

A police officer began roping off the dock with yellow tape.

"We have trucks that'll arrive here with food deliveries in thirty minutes or so," Dex said.

The policeman wound the crime scene tape around a pole. "The trucks will need to park outside. It'll take several hours for the coroner and crime scene investigators to check everything. We'll have to keep the dock area blocked until they're finished."

"Okay, I guess we'll have to find a way to haul things through the side entrance."

"Who found the body?" the policeman asked.

The skinny security guard half raised a hand. Reginald wondered why Dex hired him rather than someone with enough beef to fight off an intruder.

The policeman adjusted the bill of his cap. "Anyone else with you?"

The security guard shook his head.

"Okay, tell me exactly how you found him."

"I'd completed my rounds and checked the door, which had been locked. Then I came out on the loading dock. When I looked into the bay, I saw him." He pointed at the body and gulped.

The officer wrote a note on a pad and then looked up. "Any reports of fights or disturbances last night?"

"This happens to be a retirement home, not a bar," Reginald said.

The policeman gave him a steely stare. "I'm not asking what type of establishment this is. I want to know if there were any altercations."

Reginald tried to maintain his calm. "None that I'm aware of."

An unmarked car pulled up, and a man with a black bag marched toward the bay. He put on latex gloves, ducked under the yellow tape and bent over to examine the body. Once he had finished his inspection, a woman appeared and took photographs.

Fortunately, none of the residents showed up. They had no reason to be in the loading dock area, and the dead body certainly wouldn't have added to their breakfast-time enjoyment. Reginald could just picture some little old lady prancing out, seeing the body and fainting away or dying of a heart attack. That wouldn't help with his need to increase the occupancy rate.

In half an hour, a man in a crumpled suit stepped out of an unmarked blue Crown Victoria and came over to speak to a policeman who pointed to the little group consisting of the security guard, Dex and Reginald. The suit strolled over to them.

"I'm Detective Aranello. I understand one of you found the body." He stood several inches shorter than Reginald, average build, full head of black hair and tanned face. His gray eyes scanned from Dex to the security guard to Reginald.

The security guard gave a limp wristed raise of his hand.

"Your name?"

"Seth Kenyon."

"At what time did you find the body?"

Seth looked back and forth at Dex and Reginald.

"Just answer the gentleman's questions," Reginald prodded. "We need to help the police get to the bottom of this."

The corners of Detective Aranello's lips curled. "I can't remember the last time someone called me a gentleman." Then he regarded Seth. "As the man said, I need you to answer the question."

Seth shuffled his feet. "A little over an hour ago."

Aranello looked at his watch. "That would make it approximately seven-fifteen. Did you see anyone else nearby?"

Seth shook his head.

"I'll take that as a no. Why were you in this area?"

Seth looked like he would rather have wild dogs chewing on his toes than be standing here talking to the detective. "I came out to get some fresh air."

"Do any of you recognize the dead man?"

The three of them shook their heads.

"He's too young to be a resident," Reginald said.

"He doesn't work here," Dex added.

Detective Aranello stared at Dex. "Why are you so sure he doesn't work here?"

Dex stepped forward. "I'm Dex Hanley. I manage facilities and security. I know all of our staff, and I can assure you he's not one of us."

"Mr. Hanley, who might have checked the loading dock in the last six hours?"

Dex gritted his teeth. "Probably no one. No reason for anyone to come out here this early. Trucks don't start arriving until after eight-thirty."

"What kind of security system do you have?"

"A receptionist at the front desk and Seth who makes the rounds from eleven p.m. until eight a.m."

"Any alarm system?"

"No. Only Seth checking the halls."

Aranello tapped his notepad with his pencil. "And do you monitor the grounds of the facility?"

Dex looked at his shoes as if inspecting for creepy crawlies. "No one patrols outside the building."

Reginald stepped forward. "We're currently reassessing our security program."

"And you are?"

"Reginald Bentley, executive director of Sunny Crest."

Their eyes met. "Here early, aren't you?"

Reginald stuck his finger under his suddenly tight collar. "I started this week and have a lot to catch up on."

"And why are you reassessing your security?"

Reginald took a quick look at the woman photographing the scene and returned his gaze to the detective. "We've had problems with a scam artist getting into our facility. I spoke with Detective Mallory yesterday. Do you work with him?"

"He's in the financial and family crimes unit. I handle major crimes."

"This scam situation is major," Reginald said.

Aranello gave him a look like he thought Reginald was mouthing off. "Just department lingo, Mr. Bentley. I'll follow up with Detective Mallory. Now, I'll need to interview other members of your staff and some of the residents."

"Please do," Reginald replied. "I'd appreciate it if you would stop by my office before you leave. It's inside the business area on the second floor."

Aranello nodded and pointed at Dex. "Mr. Hanley, I'd like to have the names of all the employees on duty last night."

Dex and Detective Aranello headed inside, and Reginald remained for a moment to watch the activity around the body. Finally realizing he could do nothing but get in the way, he returned to his office.

With all the confusion, he decided to cancel his staff meeting as he knew Dex would be consumed in helping the police investigation. And besides, everyone would want to talk about the corpse in the loading bay, and he wanted their full attention on cost reduction.

Reginald sat in his office with images of the dead guy surging through his head. He didn't need this on top of everything else. In addition to the necessity to turn this place around and deal with a scam artist, he now had a mysterious death to add to the problems. An accidental fatality would be bad enough, but what if a murder had occurred? Had a staff member or resident killed this unknown man? And if so, how would that affect Sunny Crest's reputation? He could imagine a banner in front of the building: "Come live in the retirement home where murders take place." How would that be for an advertising tag line? Mimi Hendrix would sink into a deep, dark depression if she had to promote around a murder. Still, he would have to keep working on plans to increase the occupancy rate and cut expenses. He couldn't let this derail his efforts to make Sunny Crest financially solvent.

He had difficulty focusing on the purchase requisitions on his desk. He heard a scraping sound out in the hall and jumped. Nothing. Then his nose started to itch. He scratched it and looked at a requisition for increasing the supply of towels. He rejected it. There had to be plenty of towels in use right now. He looked up at the ceiling. A fluorescent tube flickered. He thought of calling Dex to have someone on his crew change it. No. He'd get by without the expense of a replacement. He scratched his arm, hoping there weren't lice or fleas left from his predecessor. He regarded the phone receiver with its layer of grime as if it were in a lube shop. His predecessor wasn't much of a neatness freak.

Fifteen minutes later, a large man with curly hair, a handlebar mustache and eyes that looked like they had just been dilated by an ophthalmologist interrupted Reginald's lack of productivity. "Uh . . . I'm Maurice Casotti. I'm responsible for food services and was out sick yesterday."

Reginald scrutinized him. "Yes, you missed the staff meeting."

"I'm sorry. I heard the meeting today was called off, so I thought I'd stop by to catch up on what was covered yesterday."

That's the attitude Reginald wanted. "Good. The main thing is, Maurice, we need to tighten our belt here at Sunny Crest. I'd like your ideas on cutting expenses."

He looked from side to side and then let out a deep sigh. "Our residents like the food here. I wouldn't want to change that."

"There have to be some opportunities for savings. New suppliers, less food served, inexpensive meals." Reginald stared at him. "Focus on smaller portions. I saw a lot of wasted food sitting on tables yesterday. And don't serve steak when you can get by with hamburger. I want your expenditures cut ten percent immediately."

Maurice lowered his eyes. "I'll see what I can do."

"Anything else you want to discuss with me?"

He cleared his throat, looked up and held his thumb and index finger an inch apart. "One little thing."

Reginald waved his hand to continue.

"Over the last week some of our silverware has disappeared."

"Go on."

"We wash the silverware after each meal and count the pieces before returning them to the drawers. After lunch last Friday we discovered a complete set of a knife, fork and spoon missing."

"Are you sure you counted correctly?"

"Yes, sir. I planned to notify Mr. Edwards. He's the one who insisted that we check the silverware. But by then he had disappeared and never showed up again. When I came in this morning, I heard that another set of silverware went missing after lunch yesterday, so I felt someone should know. That's why I'm informing you, Mr. Bentley."

"I want this tracked," Reginald said, scratching a note on his pad. "Tell your people to watch for anyone leaving the dining room with silverware."

"We can't search them," Maurice said.

"I understand. But please alert your staff to look for anyone acting suspicious. And let me know if any more silverware goes missing. We can't allow thievery to occur at Sunny Crest. And, Maurice, look into using a different brand of coffee."

*****

More inspired to jump into his work responsibilities, Reginald leafed through the stack of paper about the scam artist that Dex had left the day before. Out of approximately two hundred residents, twenty-three had submitted complaints of being victims of a fraud, or in some cases, the relatives of residents had submitted complaints. Amounts were noted. The most recent one involved a fake charity for starving African children. Pictures of pathetic, malnourished babies had been flashed in the faces of elderly ladies, and they had opened their purses and dispensed wallets full of cash to the scam artist.

Another example—a "nice, clean-cut young man" who wore a Sunny Crest badge and said he had been asked by the retirement home director to help them with their credit card statements had approached several other residents. The young man reviewed their most recent charges and made suggestions on how to save some money. A month later unexpected large charges appeared on the residents' credit card statements.

One woman, who had a thirty thousand dollar limit and hadn't driven a car in fifteen years, discovered that she had been charged for the down payment on a new Honda Civic!

Another time the scam artist claimed he'd been sent to help a resident balance her check-book. Later the victim's daughter discovered half a dozen blank checks were missing. Fifteen thousand dollars worth of forged checks showed up on the next bank statement.

As Reginald continued to read the reports, he tapped on his desk calculator. By the time he had only one document left to review, the readout showed this scammer had earned over a hundred thousand dollars at the expense of geezers and little old ladies.

Someone had perpetrated a series of serious crimes in his establishment. How could this creep take advantage of old people like this? When Reginald read the final report, his mouth fell open. He couldn't believe what else this guy had done.

Chapter 5

Reginald jotted down the name of the victim of this audacious swindle and looked up her room number in the Sunny Crest directory. Then he stashed all the reports in his file cabinet before he marched off to knock on the door of Mrs. Klausner.

He had to pound on the door a second and a third time. Finally, after shuffling sounds inside, the door rattled and opened a crack. A wrinkled face topped by frizzy gray hair that looked like the result of a lightning strike peered through the opening.

"I'm Reginald Bentley, the new executive director of Sunny Crest." He thrust out his identification badge. "May I come in and have a few minutes of your time?"

She squinted at him but made no move to fully open the door. "I paid my bill. I don't owe you anything this month." The door started to close.

Reginald reached out to hold it open. "Just a moment, please." He smiled, trying to use all his charm. "This has nothing to do with your account. I want to talk to you about the large charge to your medical insurance."

She opened the door a foot wider and peered at him as if inspecting vegetables at a farmer's market. "Oh, that. My son said something funny showed up. Come in." She ushered him into a primly decorated living room where a white throw rug covered the floor.

He sat in an easy chair with embroidered cloth doilies on the armrests. His nose wrinkled at the smell of Epsom salts and vinegar that permeated the room. Old people.

She looked wildly around and then stared at him. "Who are you and why did you say you're here?"

"As I mentioned, I'm the new executive director here at Sunny Crest. I just started this week and am in the process of meeting all the residents. I came to discuss your medical insurance charges."

"Oh, that's right." She licked her lips. "May I offer you some tea, young man?"

Reginald envisioned an all-day tea party, eating those bite-sized cucumber and cream cheese sandwiches with no crusts and a mouse jumping out of a teapot. "No thank you. Let me get right to the point. I understand a man came to your apartment and offered to help with your medical insurance. What did he look like?"

"Let me see . . . That was some time ago . . . He had on overalls? . . . No, I'm confusing him with the maintenance man." She put her hand to her cheek, and then her face lit up. "Now I remember. Yes, that's the one. He was dressed neatly in slacks and a white shirt. Nicely combed black hair. Even white teeth."

"How old did he appear?"

"Very young. Maybe in his forties."

Reginald leaned forward in an attempt to prevent himself from sinking too far into the soft cushion of the easy chair. "Please tell me what the man did when he came to see you."

"He knocked on my door, and when I opened it, he showed me his Sunny Crest badge. I checked and sure enough it showed his picture. You can't be too careful, you know. Can't let just anyone come into your apartment. He was very polite. Even admired my Japanese vase." She pointed to a blue and white vase sitting on an end table. "He asked to see my medical insurance statement and after looking at it explained that I had been charged too much. He wrote some notes and said he would fix it."

"But instead your insurance later showed a large charge."

She sucked on her lip for a moment. "Yes. That was very strange. My son says my medical account showed a charge for an appendectomy." She touched her abdomen. "I still don't recall going to the hospital, and I can't find any scar."

*****

At 11:30 a.m. Reginald jerked his head up from his paperwork at the sound of a knock on his open office door.

Detective Aranello loomed in the doorway. "Mr. Bentley, I've completed my first round of interviews and want to speak with you before I leave."

"Sure. Take a seat. What are your conclusions so far?"

Aranello lowered himself onto a padded chair that gave off the sound of a whoopee cushion. He ignored the sound and stared at Reginald. "We're treating this as a suspicious death. We've uncovered no conclusive evidence that points to either a homicide or an accident. The victim has major trauma to the right side of the head. That could have been caused by a blow from another party or from the victim falling and hitting the cement floor of the loading dock bay."

Reginald picked up a requisition and tossed it into his reject pile. "Wouldn't the exact cause be determined by the coroner?"

"Possibly. But it might be hard to distinguish a blow to the head from hitting his head due to an accidental fall."

Reginald thought about the recent crime scene shows he'd seen on TV. "If he had been bashed on the head first, wouldn't there be some blood spatter?"

"Not necessarily from the first blow. And any signs of spatter would be hard to analyze given the brief rainstorm that soaked the scene. The wind blew enough rain through the loading dock to confuse the issue. The crime scene investigators collected all the evidence possible."

"Any idea who the victim is?"

"We found no ID on him other than a Sunny Crest staff badge with the name Ken Fetterman. Mean anything to you?" Aranello removed a badge from a paper bag and held it up by its edges.

Reginald pushed aside his stack of requisitions and stared at the picture and name. "No, but this is only my second day here, so I don't know many staff members yet."

"Your security man, Mr. Hanley, reported there is no staff member here named Ken Fetterman."

"As I mentioned before, we've had problems with a scam artist getting in and conning our residents. He apparently wore a phony Sunny Crest staff ID." Reginald pointed to the badge. "This could be a counterfeit badge."

"We'll be checking it out. Also, I'll have a photograph this afternoon to show around and see if we can get positive identification of the dead man. We've taken fingerprints of the victim, and we'll see if we can get a match in the IAFIS database from a prior criminal record. We found something interesting on him. He had burglary picks in his pocket."

Reginald tweaked his chin. "So a stranger had access to our building by breaking in, probably through the loading dock door." Then it clicked. "That further supports that the victim might be the scam artist. It would explain how he was able to easily access our residents. Let me pull the reports I have." He sprang up, stepped over to his file cabinet, thumbed through the manila folders in the top drawer and extracted the one that had the names of residents who had been victimized by the scam artist. "Here, borrow this. You should show the picture of the dead man to these people as a start." He handed the folder to Detective Aranello.

"Besides the burglary picks, did you find anything else of interest on him?" Reginald asked.

"Only a wet, crushed cell phone."

"A possible scam artist skulking around our premises with burglary tools, a cell phone and a phony Sunny Crest staff badge. Then he dies suspiciously."

"That's the situation, Mr. Bentley." Aranello looked at his watch. "I need to get moving."

"Keep me apprised, Detective."

"I will, Mr. Bentley."

After watching Aranello stride out of his office, Reginald called Dex and suggested they grab a bite to eat and discuss several topics. Reginald walked to the dining room where he and Dex selected a table by themselves in the corner.

Reginald scanned the room full of old, bent geezers and crones. If he ever reached the age of some of them, he'd be miserable. Yet there seemed to be a background of lively conversation as the throng masticated their food. There, but for a doubling of his age, went he.

He turned toward Dex. "The detective told me some disturbing news. The dead man had burglary picks and could have broken into our building through the loading dock door."

"Yeah. He told me that, too."

"If the dead guy was the scam artist, this would explain how he entered our building without being detected."

Dex scowled. "And I thought the scammer had snuck past the receptionist."

Reginald ripped open a plastic bag and sprinkled some croutons on his salad. He pushed aside a piece of brown lettuce. "Look into a means to prevent anyone from forcing their way into our building in the future."

"That would require an alarm system . . . and money. And you want me to cut my budget not add more expenses."

Reginald gritted his teeth. "Take a look at alternatives. We need a better security setup. Find a cost-effective solution."

Dex nodded. "I know several companies who can do the work. I'll start pulling information together right away, Chief."

"Do a first pass, and let's talk again late this afternoon. We need to implement new security provisions immediately. We can't have anyone else picking locks into our building."

"Okay." Dex took a spoonful of clam chowder. "Not much clam in the chowder today."

"One other item. What's with the constant bickering between you and Hector?"

"We don't get along too hot."

Reginald buttered a roll and pointed the knife at Dex. "I want your commitment to work effectively with him."

"He's awfully difficult—"

Reginald held up his hand. "I don't want to hear his deficiencies. I want to know what you'll do to get along with him."

Dex let out a deep breath. "I guess I can try harder."

"You do that. You're both good men, and I want you as part of my team. But I'll follow through on what I said earlier. If you two don't patch things up and cooperate, I'll fire both of you. Do you understand?" Reginald gave him an unwavering stare.

Dex visibly sagged. "I'll do my part."

Reginald scraped his chair back, stood up, threw his napkin on the table and slapped Dex on the back. "Good."

After leaving Dex to finish his mystery meat, Reginald decided to stop by several tables. First, he made an appearance with Henrietta, Karen and Belinda.

"How are you ladies today?"

"The portions are awfully skimpy at lunch today, Reggie." Henrietta said. "You responsible for that?"

He adjusted his tie. "Are you going to misuse my name, too?"

A glint shone in her eyes. "Of course. Jerry said it would irritate you. I thought I'd test it out. Obviously it gets your goat."

"Oh, dear," Karen said. "Before this man arrived, y'all were discussing something bad that happened, but I can't remember exactly what it was."

"The dead man, dear," Belinda said.

"Oh, that's right." Karen lifted her gaze to Reginald. "Gracious sakes, did you know they found a dead body out in the loading dock this morning?"

31

"Word gets around fast."

"Oh, yes," Henrietta said. "We may be old, but we're informed. Rumor has it that the scam artist met his maker."

Reginald winched. "How do you figure that?"

"After all he's done, I imagine he tried to scam the wrong person and ended up dead."

"The police don't know for sure if the victim was the scam artist. They consider it a suspicious death but haven't determined yet if it was a homicide or an accident."

"I'm sure it was the scam artist," Belinda said. "He received what he deserved."

Henrietta arched an eyebrow. "So, Reggie, are you going to join us for lunch?"

"Thanks for the invitation, but I've already eaten with Dex. Just wanted to stop by to see all your smiling faces."

He said good-bye to the ladies and wandered over to speak with Jerry, Tom and Al. As he approached their table, Jerry bounced in his chair and waved. "Hey, Reggie. I hear you had the place hopping with police this morning."

Reginald scowled. "I suppose you're as current as your lady friends on the news."

"Damn right. Don't look so glum. We're all well-connected around here."

"It's just that this won't reflect well on Sunny Crest."

Jerry gave him a wink. "Yeah, first week on the job, and a dead body shows up. The corporate honchos won't appreciate that. They'll wonder if Reggie was asleep at the switch."

"It certainly won't help our public relations campaign."

"Don't worry your corncob over it, Reggie. As they say, there's no such thing as bad PR. Besides, rumor has it that the scam artist won't be hassling us anymore. One good result."

"Yes, that may be the case." Reginald paused as an idea occurred to him. "Did any of you gentlemen see a stranger skulking around here last night?"

Jerry's eyes narrowed, Al scraped his spoon in his empty ice cream dish, and Tom cleared his throat.

Finally, Jerry said, "We were each too happily occupied with a female companion. None of us had time to be checking out the hallways."

The other two men bobbed their heads.

"Well, if you happen to remember anything let the police or me know."

Jerry saluted. "You betcha, Red Ryder."

Reginald returned to his office with the distinct impression that these geezers knew something that he didn't.

Chapter 6

After wrestling with requisitions for two hours, Reginald took a mid-afternoon break. He retrieved a soft cloth stored in the dresser drawer of his fourth floor apartment and meandered out to the parking lot to admire the love of his life.

There she stood, off in a corner where no one would dent her sides by parking too close—his gleaming silver 1965 Jaguar S Type 3.8. With loving care, he ran the cloth over her svelte right front fender and dusted her right front chrome wire wheel. He took a step back to admire her again. She had been completely reconditioned five years ago, her facelift giving her the look of a beauty queen. And after his two-day drive from Chicago over the weekend, he had given her a luxurious bath Sunday night to remove all the dead bugs and road grime.

Uh-oh. He spotted a speck of bird dropping on the hood. That had to be eliminated. He spit on the offending spot and gently rubbed it away with the cloth. Ah, back to perfection.

"Just the conservative look for a corncob owner," drawled a voice from behind him.

Reginald whirled around to see Jerry Rhine standing there with his arms crossed.

"This isn't conservative. This is a work of art."

Jerry let out a hack that sounded like a cat about to disgorge a hairball. "In contrast to your absurd name, Reggie. I'm just surprised you picked a Jaguar and not your namesake car."

Reginald returned to his task and dabbed at a small speck of dirt. "A Jaguar is the perfect vehicle for Reginald Bentley III."

"It even has one of those doodads on the hood."

Reginald ran his cloth over the gleaming chrome hood ornament. "Yes. The Jaguar leaping cat."

"You'd never be able to leap like that, Reggie. Not until you remove your corncob. You seem awfully attached to this car."

Reginald gave the front grill a pat. "It's dependable, not like people."

"Figures you'd feel that way, Reggie." Jerry flicked his fingers in a half-hearted salute and ambled back toward the building.

Good riddance. Reginald continued his inspection along the right side doors, right back fender, trunk and left side, checking for the slightest spot or smudge, which he duly erased with a puff of hot breath and a flick of the cloth. Satisfied with the confirmed perfect appearance, he gave his love one last endearing glance and returned to his office.

*****

Later that afternoon Detective Aranello trudged into Reginald's office like Columbo minus the trench coat.

"Any old geezers confess to murder?" Reginald asked.

Aranello didn't seem to be accompanied by his sense of humor and only scowled. "A few last things to discuss, Mr. Bentley." He pulled out the chair he had sat in earlier and was about to drop into when he caught himself and instead lowered his body slowly onto the cushion, which gave a subtle whoosh. "I have a positive identification of the dead man."

"Excellent." Reginald smiled at hearing a piece of good news. "Who is the guy?"

"One Willie Pettigrew. A record as long as the Colorado River. Assault with a deadly weapon. Multiple burglary counts. More recently, financial fraud. Last held in the Weld County jail and escaped. Three of your residents identified him as the man who has been running scams at Sunny Crest."

"You'll let Detective Mallory know?"

"I've already left him a message." Aranello eyed Reginald. "Some might say that Pettigrew's demise has saved the courts a lot of time and expense."

"I suppose I should be relieved to have him out of the way, but substituting a suspicious death for a scam artist isn't the best tradeoff."

"We also found the Sunny Crest badge Pettigrew wore to be of interest. The name on the badge, Ken Fetterman. Pettigrew must have had a sense of humor. We checked and discovered that Kenneth Fetterman was an infamous scam artist in California who bilked people out of money on phony art."

"Must have been Pettigrew's idol."

"Something like that. One of our technicians inspected the badge and found that Pettigrew had laminated his picture and the Fetterman name over a real Sunny Crest badge. The original belonged to Victor Zimmer. Ring a bell?"

"No, but Dex Hanley would know." Reginald held up his index finger. "Wait a second." He reached for the phone, punched in Dex's extension and asked him to come speak with Aranello.

Seconds later when Dex galloped in, Reginald said, "Do we have someone named Victor Zimmer working here?"

"Yes. He handles maintenance service."

"Detective Aranello found out that the ID the scammer used originally belonged to Victor. Do you know if he lost a badge sometime in the past?"

Dex quivered with excitement. "I can find out."

"Go check it. Let Detective Aranello and me know."

Dex turned and bolted from the office.

"Any new indication whether it was a homicide or accidental death?" Reginald asked.

The detective stared at his fingernails. "The coroner has initially ruled death from head trauma. There's still nothing to confirm if death resulted from a blunt object blow or from the victim's head striking the cement floor of the loading bay."

"Anyone around here report anything from last night that would point to a potential murderer?"

"Not yet. No one claims to have been up last night, and no one saw or heard anything."

"Too bad. Maybe the hearing aids were turned off."

Aranello scowled again. "We'll keep searching for a possible weapon."

"I assume you looked in the dumpster."

The detective wrinkled his nose. "Yeah. We scoured your trash. That stuff stinks."

"What else would you expect with the building crammed full of old people."

Dex stuck his nose back in the office. "I had a chance to speak with Victor, Chief. He lost a badge a year ago."

Aranello scrunched his eyebrows together. "So Pettigrew found or stole that badge and altered it for his own use."

"And he used it to help convince residents he was legitimate when he wandered around Sunny Crest," Reginald added.

Aranello reached into his pocket and brought out a photograph. "As long as I have both of you here, take a look at this picture to see if you recognize this man."

Dex clomped over to Reginald's desk, and they both scrutinized the photo.

"Doesn't look familiar to me," Reginald said.

Dex squinted. "It looks a little like Danny Jenson."

"Who's Danny Jenson?" Reginald asked.

"Heads up laundry service for Hector."

"Can you go find him for me?" Aranello asked. "Don't mention my interest in him."

"Get right on it." Dex galumphed out of the office.

"What's the significance of the man in the picture, Detective?"

Aranello picked the photograph up and returned it to his pocket. "This guy in the photo, Harold Sykes, had an altercation a year ago with Willie Pettigrew. No love lost between the two of them. At the time, Sykes worked for a retirement home in Fort Collins. I'm pursuing the outside chance that Sykes might be working here under an assumed name and killed Pettigrew."

Dex reappeared. "Danny Jenson didn't show up for work this morning. I called his home, and no one answered."

Aranello looked thoughtful. "Interesting. Give me his contact information. I'll have to track him down and see if he's really Harold Sykes."

Dex gave a huge toothy grin and handed Aranello a piece of paper. "I figured you might want that. I wrote it down for you."

"Thanks." Aranello put the note in his pocket. "I have to be going."

"Me too," Dex said. "I have work to catch up on." He charged out of the office.

"Let me know if I can support your efforts in any way, Detective." Reginald watched as Aranello exited, his black wingtips beating a staccato on the linoleum of the hallway. He felt a headache coming on. Too much excitement for one day.

In one sense it was a relief to have this scam artist out of the way. He shook his head in disgust. What kind of person could take advantage of old people? All the money the scammer had taken from the residents and the resulting pain he had caused these unwary victims. Then Reginald sat bolt upright in his chair. Since the suspicious death might still be ruled a homicide and one of the Sunny Crest employees met the description of a man holding a grudge against Pettigrew, would this be another nail in the coffin for Sunny Crest?

Chapter 7

After another hour of administrivia, Reginald heard a noise. He jerked his head and spotted Dex, standing in the doorway again.

"Ready to discuss security, Chief?"

"Sure, why not? Come in."

Dex plopped his bulk down in the non-whoopee cushion chair.

Reginald could imagine the chair groaning.

Dex thrust some papers across the desk. "Here's the plan. First, we'll need to add one receptionist to provide better coverage. Then another patrolling security guard and finally, I have three preliminary estimates for alarm systems."

Reginald looked at the numbers, his headache increasing fifty decibels. How could he afford this when Daimler wanted him to turn the place around quickly or shut it down? "How long would it take to hire the additional staff?"

Dex rubbed his chin. "I'd guess a month or so."

By then they'd most likely be out of business under Daimler's order to fry the place. "Let's hold off for two weeks. What can you do with some overtime to boost the coverage?"

Dex's face beamed. "Hey, my folks always respond to a little overtime pay, but it's rare to have it authorized."

Reginald gave Dex the accountant's evil eye. "Work that angle, but keep the additional expense reasonable."

"Yes, Chief."

"Now let's look at the alarm systems. Talk me through it."

Dex described the three alternatives. One definitely exceeded the price range Reginald considered reasonable, but two fell within the ballpark.

Reginald picked the one that looked to provide the best combination of protection and price performance. "Timeframe if we go with this?" He tapped the proposal of choice.

"Probably start within a week and be ready in two weeks."

"Go back and ask for a final quote. I want you to negotiate this number down by a minimum of ten percent. And I want it implemented next week."

Dex's large shoulders sagged. "I'll try."

After Dex left, Reginald juggled some budget numbers to cover the overtime expenses for the increased security. By deferring several non-essential maintenance items and some pending supply orders, they could squeak by.

But he had to rest his financial acumen when the receptionist called to say a reporter wanted to speak to him. "Send him up to my office."

"Actually it's a woman."

"Oh. Send her up."

Reginald had a few extra minutes because of the slow elevators, so he surveyed his office to make sure he had nothing out that would raise the interest of a press snoop—nothing related to the scam artist, the suspicious death or the stolen silverware. By the time there was a knock on his door, his desk was populated with only innocuous purchase requisitions.

A woman who looked like she might be ready to join Sunny Crest appeared. Her arm shot out. "Marjorie Alsecian of the *Boulder Daily Camera*."

He shook her hand. "Reginald Bentley of Sunny Crest."

She gave him a long, searching look. "I'm here in regards to the dead body found in your facility this morning."

Reginald gave her his most press-endearing smile. "Actually it was found outside our facility in the loading dock area."

She wrinkled her nose. "Would you care to make a statement about what happened?"

"I'll tell you what I know, which isn't much. I received a call this morning and saw the body of a dead man lying on the floor of the loading bay. The authorities arrived, and the situation is now in their capable hands. For more details I suggest you speak with the police."

"I've already spoken with Detective Aranello."

"Good. He should be the accurate source for any information regarding the investigation."

"I'd like to get a little background on Sunny Crest."

Reginald reached in a drawer and extracted a color brochure. "Here's our marketing flyer. Gives all the relevant facts."

Marjorie accepted it as if she had been given a piece of spoiled liver. "Yes, but I want to ask a few questions about Sunny Crest."

"I'll be happy to answer anything I can, but this is only my second day on the job."

She cocked an eyebrow. "Interesting. You just get here, and the cops find a dead body. Now according to Detective Aranello, this dead man is also suspected of being a scam artist."

Reginald's eyes widened at hearing the police had released that information. "Yes, apparently so."

"Were there problems at Sunny Crest with scams?"

"Before I arrived. I don't think that will be a problem any longer."

"Do you mind if I speak with your staff and some of your residents?"

This was a lose-lose question. "The only person on my staff who has been involved is Dex Hanley. He handles security. Just don't take much of his time. He's very busy with our new security provisions."

"Beefing up security after the incident?" she asked.

"We're always looking for improvement. Now, if you'll excuse me, Ms. Alsecian, I have some work to complete."

*****

No dead bodies showed up the rest of the day, so Reginald headed to the dining hall to grab some dinner. As he entered the room, he listened to his charges slurp, chomp, hack and spew. When he closed his eyes, he imagined feeding time at the zoo. Then he began to pick up a subtle background cadence to the noises. These old folks had music of their own.

Before availing himself of the food, he stopped by to chat with Jerry Rhine, Al Thiebodaux and Tom Balboa.

"Hey, Reggie." Jerry waved a forkful of meat loaf at him. "You tried this dog food yet? Tonight it sucks. Anything to do with you taking over?"

Reginald didn't think Maurice Casotti had been able to reduce the cost of food yet. "I had lunch here today. I thought it tasted pretty good."

"Maybe you have a problem with your taste buds like Al here."

"What do you mean?" Al said. "I think the food tastes fine."

"You just proved Jerry's point," Tom said.

Jerry dropped a dinner roll back on his plate. "Reggie, you make sure we have high quality food and enough of it or you'll have a riot on your hands."

On that happy note, Reginald retreated to find an empty table in the corner. When the meatloaf arrived, he took a big bite. It had the texture of cardboard. Had the quality of food degraded this much since yesterday?

*****

Reginald's second day at Sunny Crest wasn't over. He had agreed to attend the dance that activities manager, Vicki Pearson, had organized for the residents. Dressed in his corporate attire, he stood next to Vicki and watched a dozen couples shuffle around the dance floor while Perry Como tunes belched from a boom box. Reginald experienced the warm glow of fiscal success knowing she had taken his cost-cutting suggestions to heart and eliminated the expensive live music. But his reverie was interrupted by a firm thump on his shoulder. He turned around to see Jerry Rhine glaring at him. "What's with the canned music? We used to have a band for these events."

"New world, Jerry."

"Cut the crap, Reggie. Are you one of those buttholes who thinks he can save money by degrading services?"

"I don't know how much business experience you had, but this place needs to make money to survive. We can't operate like a nonprofit endeavor."

Jerry's gaze narrowed. "So that's it. The corporate bigwigs won't make their bonuses unless you turn things around here." He wagged his right index finger. "Remember this. If you have no residents, you have no profit." He grabbed Henrietta's hand, and they traipsed onto the dance floor.

As the couple picked up momentum, they were joined by Jerry's two tablemates, Al Thiebodaux and Tom Balboa, dancing with Henrietta's eating companions, Karen Landry and Belinda Davenport.

"Those six always hang out together?" Reginald asked Vicki.

"Yes. They're the social committee. They refer to themselves as the Jerry-atrics."

Reginald snickered. "With Jerry as the official ringleader?"

"Exactly. They're led by Jerry and are always acting up. Henrietta is the first resident to volunteer to help out with any event even though her eyesight continues to decline . . . macular degeneration."

"Jerry seems pretty spry. The only problem I've noticed seems to be some hearing loss."

She patted a curl on the side of her head. "And he plays that very effectively. He hears everything he needs to, but when he wants to ignore you, he'll claim his hearing aid isn't working."

"Tell me more about the other four."

Vicki's eyes sparkled. "Just like Jerry and Henrietta, they show up for all the social events. And the six of them are best friends. Each has individual medical challenges, but nothing seems to slow that crowd down. You'll notice that Al doesn't move very well due to arthritis."

"Jerry told me Al used to be a photographer."

"Yes, he has wonderful photographs in his apartment. When you visit him be sure to have him show you his pictures of New York City in the late 1940s. He has an incredible collection of street scenes. I've tried to convince him to take photos around here, but he claims it's too painful with his arthritic fingers."

Reginald pointed toward Karen who supported a stumbling, stiff-legged Al on the dance floor as if holding him afloat in a stormy sea. "And Karen Landry?"

"It's sad. Karen suffers from short-term memory loss and needs her companions to keep her oriented. She used to be a legal secretary. She tells wonderful stories of lawyers tricking witnesses during trials. Her memory of long ago remains excellent, but she can't remember things consistently from the recent past."

Tom steered Belinda around the dance floor while other couples catapulted out of their path as though ducking for cover from a runaway truck.

"And Tom Balboa?"

"Tom has heart problems, but his pacemaker seems to allow him to be as active as the rest of them."

"I understand he has a military background."

Vicki reached out and consolidated two bowls of chips into one on the snack table. "To the core. Rumor has it that he had experience in the demolition line. Can you imagine him blowing things up?"

Reginald had a brief image of a huge crater showing up in the front lawn as dirt, grass and prairie dog parts from an explosion pelting the side of the Sunny Crest building. "He almost threatened me when I met him at lunch yesterday."

A twinkle appeared in Vicki's eyes. "He comes across gruff, but he's basically kind-hearted."

"I notice that Belinda shakes a little."

"Yes, Parkinson's," Vicki replied.

"Did she have a career?"

"The hardest. She raised three kids and loves to relate stories of her six grandchildren. I've met several of her grandkids when they've come to visit. Quite a collection of towheads."

Reginald pictured a mob of young commandos with Uzis blasting sunflowers to smithereens in the Sunny Crest garden area.

Jerry and Henrietta pirouetted in front of him.

"Those two seem like live wires," Reginald said to Vicki.

"Yes, indeed. Jerry is a natural entertainer, and Henrietta is a born social butterfly. She used to be a teacher and won all sorts of awards. She had quite a positive impact on several generations of elementary school students. Some adults who were once students of hers still stop by and visit her."

The song came to an end, and everyone left the dance floor except for the Jerry-atrics.

"Those six lead the residents at Sunny Crest. They look after each other and have become the unofficial spokespeople for the rest of the residents." Vicki strolled over to the boom box, leaned over and put in a new CD.

Reginald followed her. "Jerry is definitely the most outspoken."

Vicki gave an eye roll. "You don't want to cross swords with him. He can rally people either for or against you."

Perry Como began crooning, "Catch a Falling Star," and the dancing resumed.

Reginald leaned toward Vicki. "I already seem to be on his hit list. On another subject, what can you tell me about Edwards, the guy I replaced?"

She let out a deep sigh. "He wasn't the most effective director."

"How did he get the job in the first place?"

"I heard a rumor that he had connections through some relative high up in the Cenpolis organization."

Reginald watched Jerry give Henrietta a twirl on the dance floor. "That's strange. High up usually means Armand Daimler, and he isn't loyal to anyone. Making money is all that counts with him."

"There have to be other big-wigs back in Chicago," Vicki said. "Maybe Edwards had an influential relative other than Daimler."

"That's possible. Daimler doesn't make the staffing decisions at the remote locations unless he has an agenda."

"Like with you?"

Reginald chuckled. "Correct, Vicki. I've been personally selected to turn this place around."

Vicki swiveled her head toward him with a thoughtful expression. "If you can spare the time tomorrow, I'm taking a group of residents on a field trip. It would be useful for you to experience another resident event, and I know they would appreciate your involvement."

"I don't know. I have a lot to come up to speed on."

"It will only take two hours. We leave right after lunch at one-thirty."

Reginald weighed the pros and cons. "I'll see what I can do."

Jerry headed over to the refreshment table, extracted a flask from his hip pocket and emptied the contents into the punchbowl.

"What's the current policy on alcohol?" Reginald asked Vicki.

"The residents can stock liquor in their rooms, but we allow none at community events."

"Figures," Reginald said.

*****

After watching Jerry and his pals become the last residents standing, Reginald departed for his room. He had a sinking feeling he would have a long uphill battle to be successful at Sunny Crest—running the gauntlet of quirky residents, staff infighting, dead bodies, scam artists and silverware thefts. And who knew what other excitement awaited him? It would take at least six months to regain financial stability, during which time he'd have to put up with these old people. He wondered if Jerry Rhine would cause him to regret having accepted the job.

*****

The next morning Reginald went down for breakfast, after which he continued his rounds through the dining room, introducing himself to residents. Out in the lobby, he greeted an elderly woman holding the hand of a little boy. "Hello, I'm Reginald Bentley, the new retirement home director."

"It's nice to meet you, Mr. Bentley. I'm Patricia Newbury and this is my great-grandson, Tyler. Say hello to Mr. Bentley, Tyler."

The little kid glared at Reginald, who took a step toward him. "Hi, Tyler."

Tyler wrinkled his nose and gave Reginald a vicious kick in the shin.

Reginald bent over in pain, and Tyler whacked him on the head with a tiny fist.

"Tyler, that's not nice," Patricia Newbury said.

"I don't like him," Tyler retorted.

Reginald resisted the urge to say how he felt about Tyler.

"I'm sorry, Mr. Bentley. Tyler has always been a little high-strung. Tyler, apologize to the nice man."

"He's not a nice man. He's mean."

"Tyler, he hasn't done anything to you."

The kid glared at Reginald again. "He's mean, mean, mean!" Then he stuck out his tongue.

Reginald had to restrain himself from grabbing the little pink tongue and giving it a good yank.

"Tyler, that's not the way we act," Patricia Newbury said.

Tyler moved his leg back like a placekicker preparing to score a field goal, so Reginald decided to cut his losses and limped away. Once safely out of striking distance, he rubbed the knot on his head, wondering if his epitaph would read: "Mean, mean, mean."

*****

Things went downhill from there. Reginald stepped in some green and black gunk outside the door to his office and found that the wind or some stray passerby had knocked a bunch of his requisitions to the floor. After he cleaned up the mess and sat at his desk, the phone rang.

He forced a pleasant voice. "Sunny Crest."

"You're a week overdue."

"Who is this?" Reginald asked.

"You know who. You need to make the payment by midnight tonight."

The phone clicked off.

What did that mean?

Reginald had no further chance to consider the strange call, because a woman approximately his age stomped in. She put her hands on her well-formed hips and said, "What the hell has happened to your medical service here?"She was attractive in a deranged sort of way with long, black, glistening hair and azure eyes that were currently sending daggers at him.

"It's nice to meet you, too. I'm Reginald Bentley." He held out his hand.

She didn't make any effort to reach for his hand. "I know who you are."

"Then I guess I'm at a disadvantage since I don't know who you are."

She ignored his hint. "My mother hasn't been sick a day in her life, and now she's suffering up in her room with no one helping her. What are you going to do about it?"

"What's her room number?"

"Six-twenty-four."

Reginald picked up the phone and rang for health services. "Hector, please have our RN go immediately to room six-twenty-four. . . you say she's on her way? . . . thanks."

The woman turned on her heels and stormed away. In spite of her anger, her derriere waggled provocatively.

Reginald shook his head. This place would drive him to drink some of Jerry's punch yet. Picking up the in-house directory, he scanned down to find that room 624 belonged to Henrietta Marlow. He'd had the pleasure of being accosted by Henrietta's daughter.

He headed down the hallway to Hector's office. The facilities manager Dex Hanley stood inside, and he and Hector were shaking their fists at each other.

"Gentlemen, remember my warning."

They both looked toward Reginald with wide eyes.

"He-he was. . ." Dex stammered, then caught himself.

Reginald held his hand up as if to ward off a bad dream. "I know both of your departments might have conflicts, but you've got to find ways to support each other rather than to waste energy undermining the other group."

Dex turned and pushed past Reginald and out of the office.

Reginald regarded Hector. "I'm serious. I want you to take the initiative to work effectively with Dex."

"I can do that, but I'm not sure he'll put in the same effort."

"You pay attention to what you can do to improve relations between your departments. I've already spoken to Dex. Understand?"

He pouted. "Yeah."

"I came by because I want to thank you for dispatching the R.N. Henrietta Marlow's daughter was on a rampage this morning."

Hector closed his eyes and shook his head. "That woman constantly complains that we don't clean her mother's apartment thoroughly. If the laundry pickup runs an hour late, she's on the phone to harass me."

"What's her name?"

"Rebecca Downing. I call her Dragon Lady. She's divorced, probably drove her ex-husband away. The Dragon Lady comes across very different from Mrs. Marlow, who's a dignified lady."

Reginald thought of Jerry and Henrietta being found together in carnal bliss in bed and Jerry's warning to not provoke Henrietta by any reference to the romantic tryst. These old people certainly didn't live up to his preconceptions, but he still didn't know if he liked this new picture any better. Old people owed it to the world to get out of the way and prepare for death—not be cavorting around like randy teenagers.

Half an hour later the Dragon Lady sashayed into Reginald's office. The storm clouds seemed to have receded.

"Is your mother okay?"

"Yes. Someone came to assist her, and she's feeling better." Rebecca Downing turned up her nose at him as if inspecting a piece of fish to determine if it was fresh or should be relegated to the trash. "You dress awfully formal. Why the suit during summer in Colorado?"

Reginald fidgeted with the sleeve of his suit coat. "I guess it's a remnant of my Chicago corporate life."

"Business casual would be more appropriate."

"I'm sure you're right. Since I'm new here, I'd appreciate some feedback from you."

She blinked. "Oh?"

"We're working on improving security. Has this been a concern to you?"

The storm clouds reappeared, followed by a flash of lightning from her eyes. "Damn right!" She shook a bright red fingernail at him. "Your security is atrocious, and if my mother didn't have her friends here, I'd move her elsewhere."

Reginald raised his hands, fearful she might actually rake his face. "Why don't you have a seat and educate me on what you've heard?"

She paused as if trying to decide between bodily harm and acquiescence. Sanity won out, and she avoided the whoopee cushion chair and settled into the chair with the silent cushion, wrinkling her pert nose as a lightning bolt shot from the storm clouds. "Anyone can walk into this facility without identifying themselves. I'm surprised that no one has been kidnapped or had their apartment looted."

"We're changing the procedure to make sure a receptionist remains at the front desk at all times and that all visitors sign in and wear a temporary badge."

Her eyes flared again. "Well that's obviously not working! No one appeared at the front desk when I arrived, and I'm not wearing a badge." She pointed to her chest, and Reginald couldn't help but admire her well-shaped breasts forming two breathtaking bulges under her tan sweater.

"I understand your concern. It will take us several days to implement the new procedures. Please bear with us as we make the necessary changes."

"And in the meantime any criminal can march in here to take advantage of the residents. That's completely unacceptable."

"Guard patrols have been increased already."

She stood suddenly. "I've had enough of this." The red razor-claw pointed at him again. "I'll be back to check on my mother tomorrow. I expect to see those improvements in security by then!"

As she turned her back, Reginald said. "It was nice meeting you, Rebecca."

She hesitated for a moment, then straightened her shoulders and completed her exit.

Reginald imagined speaking into a public address system: "Attention everyone. It's safe to relax. The Dragon Lady is now leaving the building."

Chapter 8

Reginald looked at his watch. His staff meeting would start in five minutes. With a sigh, he headed into his conference room to see what blood he could extract from the Sunny Crest turnip. The troops arrived at exactly nine o'clock as if part of a military maneuver staged outside the door.

Once they'd settled in their seats, Reginald scanned the room, displaying his most severe scowl. All eyes turned to him as if drawn by a magnet. "Cost cutting, ladies and gentlemen. Let's go around the room. Vicki?"

The activities manager swallowed and brushed away a stray strand of hair from her forehead. "Per your instructions, I took one measure yesterday. As you saw last night, I eliminated the band. That saved five hundred dollars, although I received numerous complaints."

"They'll get used to it. What else?"

"I've added a five dollar charge for the aerobics, water aerobics, watercolor, pottery classes and any excursions."

Reginald leaned back in his chair and steepled his fingers. "Good. People will hardly notice, and it will boost revenue."

Vicki furled her brow. "I don't know. I heard grumbling this morning, and it might reduce attendance. Many of our residents are on fixed budgets because of social security and pensions, so any increase is a direct hit to their pocketbooks and wallets."

"I don't see this as a problem if fewer people attend."

"But we'll have fewer satisfied residents who may either leave or pass their negative feelings on to prospective clients," marketing manager Mimi Hendrix interjected.

Reginald held up a hand. "Okay, Mimi, we'll suffer that risk. What plans do you have to reduce expenses?"

She pursed her lips. "I intended to hire a graphic designer for our new brochure, but I suppose I could put one together myself by using my computer. It won't be as professional, but I guess it will have to suffice."

Reginald clapped his hands together. "Excellent. You all need to eliminate outside expenditures. Keep thinking of ways to get by without hiring contract services."

"In this case it will work," Mimi said. "But I wouldn't recommend it for all situations. You wouldn't want Dex carting trash to the dump, would you?"

"Actually that's a good idea for our facilities organization," Reginald replied. "What do you think, Dex?"

"Uh . . . uh . . . uh."

"I'm only kidding," Reginald said.

Dex let out a sigh as if a big weight had been removed from his large shoulders.

"I want all of you to use your good judgment. The message for each of you to memorize and keep foremost in your thoughts is to cut costs, but do so in an intelligent fashion. So what will you implement for cost savings, Dex?"

"My budget had money earmarked for repainting this month. I'm going to defer that for a month or so."

"Don't wait too long, Dex," Mimi said. "We can't have this place looking like it's falling apart. Prospective residents notice things like that. The first impression when they see the building could make or break their decision to come here."

Muttered agreements circled the room. Maurice Casotti waved his hand.

"Yes, Maurice?"

"I bought cheaper hamburger for the meatloaf and tried reducing food portions yesterday, but I don't think that's cutting costs in an intelligent fashion."

Reginald winced at the memory of the meatloaf and almost agreed with the statement, but he had to keep the pressure on. "I think we can go with smaller amounts of food served. Experiment and see what seems most appropriate. What else do you have?"

"I found a less expensive supplier for lettuce."

"Good. Other things?"

"I could buy bulk cookies rather than fresh from the bakery every day. That would save several hundred dollars a week."

"Do it. Other ideas?"

Maurice removed his chef's hat and scratched his head. "I had one assistant cook resign yesterday. We could try to get by without replacing him."

"That's another good example of what I'm looking for, ladies and gentlemen. Let's reduce our staff through attrition and effective allocation of personnel." Reginald turned toward the Sunny Crest business manager. "Alicia?"

"First, I posted a notice in the elevators asking for volunteers to come work in the business office. As we discussed on Monday, this is in lieu of hiring a new staff member. Next, I renegotiated the insurance policies as you ordered. That will save us several thousand dollars a month."

"Well done."

"And I've found a new office supplier who has quoted me ten percent lower prices than the current vendor."

Reginald nodded and pointed to Hector Lopez. "Reductions in health services and housekeeping?"

"I've located a supplier who charges less for generic over-the-counter drugs. As you suggested, I will start imposing a small fee for these drugs as well. We can save twenty percent on our cleaning supplies with another new supplier and cheaper cleaning products."

All was silent for a moment, except for Hector tapping his finger on the table. Maurice tweaked his moustache. Dex fidgeted in his chair. The three women sat motionless, like stone statues.

Reginald let a smile creep across his face. "That's what I'm after, people. When you look at your departments, you can always find ways to chip away at some of the expenditures. It's too easy to be lulled into complacency and spend more than necessary. Our efforts here require constant diligence. Keep at it." He pointed to each of them in turn. "You can find creative ways to save money." With that pep talk he asked what other subjects needed to be covered.

Maurice's hand shot up. "I'm working on trying to find out who stole the silverware. No leads yet."

"Anything else?"

"Yes," Mimi said. "Did you see the newspaper this morning, Mr. Bentley?"

"No, I didn't."

She pushed a section of paper forward. "Read that article on the top of page one of the local news."

Reginald picked it up and read an article by Marjorie Alsecian titled, "Mysterious Death at Sunny Crest Retirement Home." The article quoted Detective Aranello saying that an investigation into the death continued. A quote from Reginald said: "We need to beef up our security process." The article went on to mention concerns from residents that security was not adequate. The article closed with a quote from Jerry Rhine, "This used to be a good place to live, but since the new director arrived, in addition to security problems, the quality and quantity of food has gone downhill." Reginald assumed that Jerry probably said something to the effect that the quality of the food had gone in the crapper.

Mimi stared at Reginald. "Well?"

"As they say, Mimi, there's no such thing as bad PR. Other topics."

Dex thrust his meaty hand in the air. "No word yet from Danny Jenson. He's still AWOL." He looked toward Hector. "You hired a possible criminal to head up your laundry service, and now the guy has disappeared. How could you let that happen?"

Hector's face turned bright red. "That's not my fault. If your incompetent security department had done an adequate background check, we'd have known if Danny was a problem. You're the one to blame."

Reginald felt like a referee in a boxing ring. In spite of his cost-cutting program, he wondered if he should invest in buying a bell to use between rounds. "Gentlemen, quit the accusations. We don't know for sure if Danny is a suspect or not. We don't even know if the death was an accident or a murder."

Dex and Hector glared at each other.

"Any other items to discuss?" Reginald scanned the surly faces, but no one raised a hand. "I have one other thing to bring up. A little while ago I received a strange phone call. Someone asked me to pay up and threatened me. Any idea what precipitated that phone call?"

Their gazes turned downward as if an ant circus were entertaining on the floor of the conference room.

"People. What aren't you telling me?"

Dex cleared his throat. "Did you know the previous director?"

"No. I've only seen his detritus in the desk."

"Do you know why he left?" Mimi asked.

"No," Reginald replied. "It all happened quickly. My boss, Armand Daimler, called me into his office last Friday and told me to be here on Monday."

Dex looked around the table, and the others gave him nods of encouragement. "Your predecessor, Mr. Edwards, had a little problem."

"Define problem."

Dex fiddled with his collar. "He . . . uh . . . liked to go up to Central City and Blackhawk on weekends and gamble."

Reginald slapped his forehead. "So he must have accumulated debt owed to some unsavory types of characters."

"Yes," Alicia said. "He left a letter of resignation and poof—" She snapped her fingers. "He disappeared last Thursday. Didn't say good-bye to any of us. No one knows where he went."

Veiled eyes around the table turned toward Reginald. He couldn't decipher if they hid concern or relief. "But someone thinks he's still here at my phone number."

"I guess he didn't bother to inform his debt collectors of his change in employment," Alicia said.

*****

After the meeting adjourned everyone dashed out of the conference room like they had roman candles up their butts, except for Hector. Holding his hands behind his back and scraping his foot, he stood near the door.

"Hector, do you have something on your mind?"

"I didn't want to bring this up in front of everyone, but we have a problem, Boss."

"We've had nothing but problems the two plus days I've been here. Now what?"

Hector brought his hand out from behind his back and handed over a sheet of paper. "Did you see this? Someone taped it up in the elevator. Actually, each elevator had a copy."

"I used the stairs this morning," Reginald said as he looked at a poster with his picture on it. Superimposed around his face was a drawing of a vicious Indian wielding a tomahawk. The caption underneath read: THIS MAN WILL SAVAGE YOUR HOME AND YOUR SCALP!

He recognized the photo of his face as the one posted on the Cenpolis corporate website.

"And you discovered this poster this morning, Hector?"

"One of the housekeepers found the first one. She told me, and I removed all of them."

"Someone went to a lot of trouble to make this. Any idea who?"

"I don't think a staff member would do this. More likely a resident."

"I'd suspect a creative person who knows how to use Photoshop. Do we have many computer-literate residents?"

"Maybe twenty percent."

"Tell your staff to be on the lookout for someone putting things up in the elevators. Try to catch the culprit."

*****

Reginald returned to his office, wondering if for the first time in his career he might be getting an ulcer. He dropped the poster in his drawer.

Maybe he could start a portfolio of his experiences as a retirement home director. He mentally pictured himself approaching a future employer. *Here, take a look at what my residents thought of me in my last job. They loved me so much they posted thank-you notes in the elevators.*

He slammed his fist down on the desk. Reginald Bentley the Third never shied away from a challenge, no matter what the circumstance. Nothing had happened here that he couldn't resolve. It would only take intelligence and perseverance. He knew he could handle the task.

With renewed resolve, he prepared to reject a requisition, when the phone rang with a call from the receptionist's desk. "There's a Detective Aranello here who wants to interview some of our people."

*****

Downstairs, Reginald shook hands with Aranello. Today he wore a crumpled brown suit, white shirt and a tie with pictures of Dalmatian dogs on it.

"You a dog fancier, Detective?"

Aranello pointed to his tie. "Oh, you mean this. Nah. Just a present from my kids. A gentle reminder that they want a dog. I haven't given in yet."

"I share your lack of interest in animals. What brings you back to our fine establishment?"

"I'd like to show Willie Pettigrew's picture to more of your residents to determine if anyone saw him the night of his death."

"I hope it's not too grizzly."

"No, we have one taken after a little cleanup at the morgue." He held it out.

Reginald scrutinized a face that looked pasty but not bloody. He recognized the man he had seen sprawled out on the floor of the loading dock. "I guess that shouldn't push our residents over the edge. Any word on whether Danny Jenson is Harold Sykes?"

"No. We haven't been able to locate Jenson yet. I'm also checking to see if there is any record of Sykes elsewhere. Now, if you'll excuse me, I'll show Pettigrew's picture around."

"Have at it, Detective. Let me know what you find out."

When Reginald returned to his desk, he found a stack of mail had been left for him. He began sorting through it, noting with satisfaction that letters had been forwarded to his new address. The Chicago post office had acted quickly.

As he thumbed through the unending pile of mostly unwanted correspondence, he found a notice from his health insurance company. Gingerly opening it, he found that once again Xbest Medical Service had denied paying his last eye doctor's bill. He slapped the letter down on his desk and reached for the phone.

A sing-song recorded female voice asked for his name, date of birth and member number. After a brief pause the voice started going through a litany of options including everything but visiting a veterinarian. Knowing the drill Reginald repeated the word "representative" every five seconds. After several minutes and reaching option twenty-three, his electronic girlfriend agreed to transfer him to a customer service representative.

A recording described how Xbest Medical Service prided itself on outstanding customer service before a real human voice identified himself as Hal. Reginald wondered if this was really the computer from *2001 Space Odyssey*, but Hal exhibited a slight stutter that probably hadn't been programmed in. Hal politely asked for his name, date of birth and member number. Reginald refrained from pointing out that he had already done this and instead provided the requested information before saying, "Please put me in touch with one of your rapid resolution representatives."

"First, tell me the nature of your call."

Reginald sighed. "Hal, I've been through this routine every six months for the last three years. You won't be able to help me, so let's cut out the middleman. Transfer me to the rapid resolution representative, who can continue the process of slow resolution."

This time Reginald waited five minutes while he heard how Xbest Medical Service could help with prescription drug orders, locate a specialist or even provide advice on prenatal care. That's just what Reginald needed.

Finally, a pleasant sounding woman identified herself as Jennifer and asked for his name, date of birth and member number.

"Didn't Hal give you that information already?" Reginald asked.

"Who's Hal?"

Reginald looked heavenward and repeated the information for the third time.

"Now, how may I help you Mr. Bentson?"

"It's Bentley, and here's my problem. Every six months, I go to my doctor for an eye pressure exam because I have ocular hypertension. When the doctor's office submits the bill to Xbest Medical Service, your clerks always reject paying it, claiming that it's a normal eyesight examination and not covered. Then I call up and have this conversation with one of your colleagues, usually requiring three phone calls until someone finally admits that my bill should be covered. In the meantime I receive monthly letters from the doctor's office asking for my payment because my insurance company has refused to pay. How about if we resolve it right now rather than going through all the rigmarole?"

"Let me bring up your account, Mr. Bantley."

The sound of rapid keystrokes could be heard across the phone line.

"I found your record, Mr. Banley. I'll have someone look into it. You'll receive a letter in the mail."

Reginald hung up, resisting the urge to heave the phone into the wall. The only thing worse than old people was dealing with insurance companies.

To calm his nerves, he reviewed a number of purchase requisitions, rejecting one from Dex Hanley to add a second staff plumber with a reminder note to be sure to cut trash pickup to once a week. Then he revised the amount of potatoes Maurice Casotti wanted to purchase for the week and approved miscellaneous office supplies for Alicia Renton but denied a request for a new laptop computer. Then remembering some information needed from Mimi Hendrix, he called to ask her to come to his office.

When the marketing manager arrived, Reginald tapped a blank sheet of paper lying on his desk with the back end of his pen. "Tell me what the trends have been for occupancy rates and the waiting list."

She scrunched up her nose. "Not good. Occupancy has dipped from ninety percent six months ago to eighty-five percent currently."

He jotted down some figures "And what happened?"

"Several new competing facilities have opened in Broomfield and Louisville. That's why I mentioned to you the need to advertise. We have to stay ahead of the competition."

"I'm not ready to approve a new advertising campaign. What kind of waiting list do we have?"

She adjusted the jacket of her neat, gray business suit. She gave off the aura of the consummate professional marketing type. "That's part of the same issue. It's a good-news, bad-news situation. We used to have twenty or so people waiting for an average of two months. Now the list consists of less than a handful of people with a two-week waiting period. People can get in as soon as we clean and repaint the rooms. I like that we're able to move people in quickly, but a larger backlog would certainly help us maintain a higher occupancy rate."

Reginald said, "Look at inexpensive ways to promote Sunny Crest. Figure out how we can get an article into the local newspaper—"

"Unfortunately, that already happened."

He cleared his throat and dropped his gaze to the sheet of paper where he had scribbled some numbers. "Well . . . uh. . . we'll forget about that one." Then he looked back at her. "On the positive side, there have to be some human interest stories here for press coverage. Something that would attract attention and make people say, 'Wow, I want to live there.' Do we have any celebrity residents?"

"Not unless you consider Jerry Rhine who was a professional magician."

Reginald resisted the urge to make a sign of the cross to ward off old people. "That's probably not what we want to emphasize. Anything else that might be newsworthy?"

"Only the dead scam artist, and we don't want to revisit that."

"You give it some thought and get back to me by the end of the week with a marketing plan. I want to see creative ideas that require minimal or no expenditure. Guerilla marketing, word-of-mouth, viral campaigns, reaching the tipping point—all those low cost alternatives."

She stared at him as if he had spouted words from some marketing guru's popular bestseller, which he had.

"Nothing's free," she muttered.

*****

After Mimi left, Reginald felt a sinking feeling in the pit of his stomach.

It would take more than cutting costs to turn this place around. For Sunny Crest to survive, he now realized he'd have to invest in services and programs to attract new clients. That would be a tough message to sell to headquarters. He'd need a few weeks to formulate a plan. If he could just train his managers to make wise investment decisions—to go after "A" priorities and defer less important expenditures while figuring out ways to increase the occupancy rate—

The phone rang, and he picked it up to hear his boss Armand Daimler on the line. "You hacking costs out there, Reginald?"

"I'm working on it, sir. There's been something strange going on here. I received a threatening phone call intended for my predecessor, a man named Edwards. Do you know much about him?"

"Nope. His uncle used to be our operations officer. Edwards had good recommendations, but he up and quit. That's why you, my boy, are now fixing the situation out there in the wilds of Colorado."

Reginald looked around the office, noticing the smudged evidence of where Edwards had left his DNA. "Apparently he had a gambling problem and accumulated debt to some mob types."

"No longer our problem. He's history. He certainly didn't manage the expenses down. But you're the one who's going to fix it, right?"

No sympathy from Daimler. Reginald had to at least keep his boss on the phone long enough to broach an important matter. "I also have another subject to discuss with you."

"Anything as long as it isn't increasing our investment in Sunny Crest."

Reginald swallowed hard as if trying to consume a horse pill. "Actually, a small, intelligent and well-placed increase in capital improvements may be necessary."

"Don't go soft on me, boy."

"Look, Mr. Daimler. The occupancy rate has dropped. I think some minimal strategic investment would increase revenue and return the facility to profitability."

"We've covered this ground before. Fix it or fry it." The line went dead.

So much for a rational exchange with Armand Daimler. At least he didn't mention having heard of the suspicious death. Reginald would have to see what Mimi recommended and continue to trim expenses. He'd keep the heat on his staff and get this place financially solvent if it was the last thing he did.

His morning continued to cascade downhill when moments later Henrietta

Marlow charged into his office. "This situation continues to be completely unacceptable and can't go on!" she shouted.

Reginald recognized the same flashing eyes and determined expression that her fiery daughter exuded. Dragon Lady and Dragon Mum. Quite a pair.

"You seem to be feeling better, Mrs. Marlow."

She gave him a blank stare and then caught his reference. "Yes, I'm fine now. But don't sidetrack me. We have a big problem!"

He exhaled. "What now?"

"The food here sucks! In the last two days the quality has gone to hell." She shook a finger with accompanying pointed red nail at him in the same manner that her daughter had. "You need to do something, Reggie!"

"I'll . . . I'll work on it."

She lowered the red dagger and put her hands on her hips. "I understand you met my daughter."

Reginald let out a sigh of relief, aware that he wasn't going to have his face slashed after all. "I didn't exactly meet her. She invaded my office. Quite a woman."

"She seemed impressed with you, Reggie. Most men shrivel up, too intimidated to stand up to her. Her first husband bailed because of that."

"She definitely expresses her feelings."

"You can say that again. By the way, you can call me Henrietta. Mrs. Marlow makes me sound too old. Now when are you going to improve the quality of the food?"

*****

Soon after Henrietta left, Reginald was assessing what steps to take next in his turnaround efforts, when Detective Aranello appeared in his doorway.

Reginald waved him in. "Have you discovered anything else?"

"Nothing new. No one saw anything unusual the night of Willie Pettigrew's demise. No one except scam victims recognized his picture."

"And the missing guy from our laundry service?"

"We still haven't been able to locate Danny Jenson. The only additional relevant information—I received a phone call a few minutes ago that Harold Sykes was reported to be in Boulder two months ago."

"I wonder when we hired Danny Jenson," Reginald said.

Aranello tapped his foot. "You're not very familiar with your personnel, are you, Mr. Bentley?"

"Give me a break. I've been here three days."

"Danny was hired two months ago."

Uh-oh. "So Danny could be Sykes and could be involved in the suspicious death."

"Yup."

Reginald considered the repercussions if one of his own staff members had killed Willie Pettigrew. That wouldn't bode well for turning this place around quickly. "So how do you proceed in a case like this?"

"First order of business is tracing the Harold Sykes-Danny Jenson connection. Regarding Pettigrew, there will be the coroner's final report. That might shed more light on the cause of death. We'll keep speaking to people here and track down any leads we get. And let me know if your staff reports anything else."

"Okay. Does a case like this stay open for a period of time?"

"If it's ruled an accident, we close the case. I'm not going to believe it was an accident until I find Danny Jenson and Harold Sykes. With homicide, we never close the case until it's solved."

Reginald wondered if Aranello would be visiting his office every week until the place closed. "That must put a strain on your workload."

"We put the most effort on a homicide during the forty-eight hours after it occurs. Over time we'll have to redirect our attention, but that doesn't mean we forget it."

Chapter 9

Having succumbed to Vicki Pearson's invitation, at 1:30 Reginald climbed aboard the white mini-bus festooned with the Sunny Crest name in blue script and the distinctive logo of an orange half-sun radiating from behind a gold shield. They were headed to the Butterfly Pavilion in Broomfield. The Jerry-atrics plus some other residents sat on the bus yakking while Reginald plunked down next to Vicki. Jerry padded over and placed a paw on his shoulder, "Slumming today, Reggie?"

"Yeah, I thought I'd see how the other half lives."

Jerry chuckled. "Good for you. You're getting in the swing of things. What'd you think of the article in the newspaper this morning?"

"Nice of you to give such a positive quote, Jerry."

"Hey, only calling a spade a spade. Both the security and the food are the pits. Those are things you should fix rather than make worse, Reggie."

"We'll get things back on track. Just stay away from reporters."

Jerry ruffled Reginald's hair before returning to the back of the bus.

Reginald wanted to more than ruffle Jerry's hair.

When the van arrived at the Butterfly Pavilion, Vicki and Reginald got off and waited for the rest of the group. They moved at a fast pace except for Al Thiebodaux whose arthritis had flared up. He had a little trouble getting down the steps and once clear of the vehicle leaned heavily on Karen Landry as he had on the dance floor last night.

Reginald had a flashing image of Al's arthritic limbs spread over Karen in bed. He shook his head to rid himself of the mental picture. Old people.

Vicki took care of the admission fees, and in short order they all entered a large atrium full of tropical plants and colorful butterflies. In the warmth and humidity, Reginald plucked at his tie as Jerry ambled up. "Reggie, you need to loosen up more than your tie. Dump the suit. No sense overdressing. This is summer in Colorado." In contrast, Jerry wore Bermuda shorts and a Hawaiian shirt. He elbowed Reginald in the ribs before disappearing around a curve in the pathway.

Reginald wondered why he had agreed to come on this trip. He figured all he would accomplish would be collecting butterfly poop on his shoulders and head. Following the concrete path through the lush setting, he came upon Henrietta who squinted at him. "Isn't this amazing?"

"Quite a place." Reginald dusted something off his shoulder that he hoped was only a piece of leaf.

Henrietta put a finger to her cheek. "It's too bad Rebecca had classes today. She would have enjoyed this. She sometimes accompanies me on excursions."

The image of Rebecca flashed into Reginald's mind. A pleasant memory followed by the recollection of the anger in her eyes. "Did you know that some people refer to your daughter as the Dragon Lady?"

Henrietta laughed. "Oh, yes. She has quite a reputation at Sunny Crest. But that's her tough exterior. People who get to know her find her warm, friendly and caring." She winked at him.

The wink caught Reginald by surprise as he tried to regain his composure. "I—I don't know. She seems pretty lethal with those long red fingernails."

Henrietta made a pretense of clawing her nails at him. "That's right. You don't want to mess with the Marlow women. Treated right, we're gentle as lambs. Rebecca doesn't get mad without a good reason. If you improve the services at Sunny Crest, I dare say she won't be in your face."

Unexpectedly, Reginald experienced a pleasant vision of Rebecca's face meeting his.

Henrietta must have seen the faraway look in his eyes. "You have to admit that she's an attractive woman, Reggie."

Reginald brought his eyes back into focus. "Yes, she is."

Henrietta gave him a knowing smile.

At that moment, Jerry came prancing around the bend in the path. "Look what I have here." He held out an open hand to display a bright yellow and black Swallowtail. Then he smashed his other hand into the hand with the butterfly and ground them together.

Henrietta gasped.

Jerry opened his hand and the healthy butterfly took off in graceful flight.

Reginald's jaw dropped. "How'd you do that?"

Henrietta punched Jerry in the shoulder. "More of your stupid magic. You love performing these silly tricks, especially making things look gross—

63

like pretending to squash a butterfly." She swatted him again. "I don't know what gets into you sometimes, Jerry."

"I can also make things disappear." In a lightning fast move he reached over, removed Reginald's tie tack, put it in his palm, closed his hand to form a fist and then opened it to reveal—nothing.

"Only a matter of a little sleight of hand." Jerry chuckled as he clapped Reginald on the back. He grabbed Henrietta's hands. "Come on. There's a side room with all kinds of spiders."

Henrietta wrinkled her nose. "That sounds so appealing, Jerry."

"What did you say?" Jerry asked, placing his hand to his ear.

"You heard me. I don't want to see spiders."

"Hell, you don't see that well anyway. You'll love them."

She shrugged, and they sauntered off together.

Moments later, Vicki came up behind Reginald. "You have something shiny on the back of your suit. Here." She plucked at the back of his shoulder where Jerry's hand had been moments before and handed him the tie tack. "You don't see many of these."

Reginald's cheeks became warm. What the heck? He didn't really enjoy dressing so formal. He decided he could change a little. At the very least, he wouldn't be wearing a tie or tie tack again any time soon.

*****

Back at the big house, Reginald continued to plan his cost-cutting attack. A knock on the open door caused him to look up and find Maurice Casotti of food services standing there, his chef hat in his hands.

"What's up, Maurice?"

His mustache drooped. "Another set of silverware went missing after lunch today. We've never had this problem before. I just don't know what to do."

"So let me make sure I understand. Last Friday, this Monday and today a set of silverware disappeared."

Maurice continued to wring his toque as if a solution would pour out. "Correct."

"And each time an exact set of knife, fork and spoon. No more, no less."

"Yes."

Reginald pushed aside his stack of requisitions. "And this has only happened at lunch, not breakfast or dinner?"

"That's right."

Reginald thought for a moment. "I can't see why a resident would suddenly start collecting silverware. And why did the culprit skip Saturday, Sunday and Tuesday?"

He shrugged. "Maybe the person missed lunch those days."

"Or it could have been a staff member. Any new hires added last week?"

Maurice shook his head. "No turnover in the last month. Besides, we have a trustworthy group of people in food services. They wouldn't steal anything."

"Do we sign people in for meals?"

"Not residents. Only guests."

"Ah, ha." Reginald rubbed his hands together. "That's a place to start. Why don't you check to see what guests we had during lunch those three days? See if a common name pops up."

Maurice's eyes lit up. "Good idea. I think it's more likely to be someone from the outside than one of our residents or staff. I'll check with Renee, who keeps the visitor meal sign-in logs."

"As long as you're here, Maurice, I have a question to ask."

Maurice reduced his eyes to slits.

"Don't look that way. I want to enlist your assistance in helping me understand the bad blood between Dex and Hector. Take a seat for a minute and explain the hard feelings."

Maurice plopped down in the non-whoopee cushion chair. Apparently the staff knew what seat to avoid. "That goes back a long way. There have always been disagreements between facilities and housekeeping. Whenever problems occur, they tend to blame each other."

"But I didn't pick up that kind of animosity among other members of the staff. I don't see Mimi, Alicia, Vicki or you arguing with your peers."

He dropped his chef hat into his lap. "Dex and Hector both take pride in their work and feel they've hired good people. When a resident reports a problem that could be either housekeeping or facilities, they each get a little defensive and then blame the other department. Like we had a resident concerned over a frayed rug in her apartment. Hector told Dex to fix it, and Dex told Hector to have his housekeepers be more careful with the vacuum. That kind of thing."

"I understand those disagreements can happen, but after working together so long, I'd think Hector and Dex would have resolved their differences."

Maurice shook his head and his mustache wiggled. "Things calm down for a while until one of them does something to irritate the other. It's an ongoing feud."

"Well I'm glad there isn't that kind of animosity between food service and another department. I'd hate to see you go after one of your peers with a meat cleaver."

*****

While taking a stroll around the large white building to view the extent of his new domain, Reginald came up with an idea for saving money on grounds maintenance— they didn't have to plant as many expensive flowers as currently decorated the pathway. Satisfied with one more opportunity for cost reduction, he headed into the parking lot to check on his love. There she rested in the sunlight, gleaming in all her silver glory. He stepped up to the hood to give her a pat. His body shuddered.

She had been raped!

Reginald stood there in disbelief, his fists balled at his sides, his arms shaking with rage. The Jaguar leaping cat hood ornament had disappeared.

Who would violate a thing of beauty? What dastardly villain had perpetrated such an act of depravity? And where had this thug taken the Jaguar leaping cat? Would it be held for ransom or tossed unceremoniously in a trash bin? He couldn't believe what he was seeing.

Reginald extracted his cell phone and called the police. "I want to report a heinous infraction of the law!"

"What type of crime?"

"Some thief stole the hood ornament from my Jaguar!"

There was a pause on the line. "A hood ornament?"

"That's right."

"Give me your name, address and phone number, and I'll have an officer come by to take a report."

"You do that." Reginald gave the necessary information. "How soon will someone be here?"

"We have quite a number of calls today with the University of Colorado students moving in. I expect an officer will be there in one to two hours."

Reginald signed off his cell phone, stormed into the building and jabbed the elevator button to go up to his apartment on the fourth floor to collect a picture of his pre-violated car to give to the police. After an inordinate wait, he dashed into the elevator, noticing on one interior wall a calendar of events and a letter from Alicia asking for volunteers in the business office. Then he saw a poster taped next to the other two notices. A computer-generated composite showed a gangster with Reginald's face pointing a Tommy gun at the Sunny Crest building. The caption read: THIS HIT MAN WILL DESTROY YOUR HOME!

*****

Back in his office, Reginald kicked the wastebasket and took his revenge by rejecting a dozen requisitions.

An hour later his cell phone rang. "This is Officer Hughes. I'm in your lobby. I understand you have a theft to report."

"I certainly do, Officer. I'll be right down."

He grabbed the photograph and raced down the stairs, taking them two at a time. A young man in his late twenties in blue police attire, a blond mustache and a thin build stood there. He didn't look capable of wrestling a hood ornament thief to the mat.

"Come with me." Reginald strode past the officer, waving to follow.

Out in the parking lot, Reginald pointed. "There. Someone stole the hood ornament."

The police officer bent over and inspected the two holes in the hood where the ornament used to be attached. "Ah, this was one of those thingamabobs with the chrome cat."

"That was a Jaguar leaping cat hood ornament. Violently removed and resulting in the desecration of my beautiful car. Here's what it looked like." Reginald handed him the photograph.

The policeman squinted at the picture, took out a note pad and made a note. "What does one of these cost?"

"Probably sixty to seventy dollars. But that's not the point. Someone flagrantly damaged my lovely vehicle. The perpetrator must be punished."

His mouth dropped open as he stared at Reginald. "That only would be a Class 3 Misdemeanor."

"I don't care what class. Just find the culprit, lock him up and throw away the key."

The policeman shook his head. "You should be aware that the punishment consists of a fine of fifty to seven-hundred-fifty dollars and up to six months in jail."

"Lock the vandal up for the full six months. He doesn't deserve to be wandering free in society."

The police officer returned the notepad and pen to his pocket. "Rarely happens. Usually just a fine and a suspended sentence if it's a first offense. Do you know who could have done this?"

Reginald threw his hands in the air. "I have no clue. It happened sometime in the last two days."

"I'll ask around, but unless you have anything specific, I'm not sure what more I can do."

"Why don't you dust for fingerprints?"

The policeman leaned close to the hood. "It looks like this surface has been wiped clean."

"I keep it that way."

"I'll notify you if I find anything, Mr. Bentley."

As Reginald stomped back toward the entrance to the building, he spotted Jerry Rhine sitting on a bench.

"You seem awfully heated today, Reggie."

"Damn right. Some jerk stole the Jaguar leaping cat hood ornament from my car."

"Man, you sure have a way of making friends around here, Reggie."

*****

Reginald called a special staff meeting that afternoon. Once his troops had assembled, he pounded his fist on the conference room table. "Someone is out to get me."

"Yeah, we've seen the artwork in the elevators," Vicki Pearson said. "Good picture of you, though."

Reginald glared at her. "No, this new event far exceeds the sleazy posters. Someone stole the leaping cat hood ornament from my Jaguar."

"That one of those chrome thingamajigs?" Maurice asked.

"That's right. Some thug committed a serious crime. Have any of you noticed anyone messing around my car?"

They all shook their heads.

"Well, be sure to let me know if you see or overhear anything."

"Yes, Boss," Hector answered.

The rest of the group remained mum.

*****

Reginald had stacked his paperwork in a neat pile in preparation to leave his office after his third fun-filled day on the new job, when the phone rang.

"Sunny Crest."

"This is your last warning. Payment tonight by midnight or else."

"Or else what?"

"Or else you go on a little one-way trip."

"This isn't Edwards!" Reginald shouted, but the line had gone dead.

Adrenaline surged through his body. If he were Edwards, he'd be scared out of his mind. But given that he happened to be Reginald Bentley the Third, he would suck it up and get on with life and figure out how to turn this place around. He had reached one conclusion, though—retirement homes weren't for the faint-hearted.

*****

Day four on the job at Sunny Crest began on a better note. Vicki stopped by and reviewed her plans to reduce expenses for some of the resident activities.

"These cost reductions you propose are exactly what I'm looking for," Reginald said. "By the way, I received another threatening phone call late yesterday afternoon."

"Someone calling for Edwards?"

"Apparently. Could the guy have been that stupid to get in debt to mobster-types?"

She shrugged. "He wasn't the most effective director."

Reginald regarded the empty bookshelf on the other side of the room. "What exactly did he do around here, anyway?"

"Mainly stay out of the way and let each of us run our departments." Vicki gave him a smug smile.

Reginald opened his mouth to make a profound pronouncement on effective management but thought better of it.

After Vicki left, the Dragon Lady sauntered into the office, this time without the thunder cloud over her head and the lightning bolts shooting from her eyes.

Reginald looked up from his stack of requisitions. "Hello, Rebecca."

"Reggie, you look better in a short-sleeved shirt and no suit."

He twiddled the top button on his shirt. "Well, I decided to go native."

"And I owe you an apology."

He gave a start and almost knocked over his pile of reqs. "Oh?"

"Yes, I want to thank you for the quick action you took to have someone help my mother yesterday."

Reginald blinked at this second reconciling statement. "She seems to have bounced back nicely."

Rebecca crinkled her nose. "Yes, one moment she appeared on death's door and within an hour she returned to her usual feisty self. And I do appreciate that you had someone see her so quickly after I spoke with you." Her full red lips separated like two rose petals, and her even white teeth sparkled. "And your security has improved." She pointed to her impressive chest. "They made me wear a visitor's badge this morning."

Before he could control himself, he blurted out, "Rebecca, we're holding a family dinner here Saturday night. Would you be able to join me?"

"You asking me on a date, Reggie?"

"Well . . . uh . . . I'm sure your mother would like seeing you, and we could sit with her and her friends."

She gave him a studied look. "Sure, why not?" She held out her hand, claws sheathed, and he clasped her warm palm. "Thanks, again." She turned and sauntered out, leaving a lingering fragrance of lilacs.

To say that the day went downhill from there would have been an understatement. Unfortunately, rather than concentrating on the image of Rebecca, Reginald chose to recount the incidents of the day before—the kidnapped hood ornament and the poster in the elevators—and since again he had not used the elevator first thing that morning, he decided to check if any new posters had been planted there. He pushed the button and waited for two women to limp out, avoiding the steel post of one's walker. He stepped inside and inspected the walls, spying his grim mug staring back. This time someone had superimposed his face on a hooded figure pushing an occupied wheelchair off a cliff. Other falling bodies cascaded down the cliff as well. The caption read: HE WILL DESTROY YOUR HOME AND FINISH YOU OFF!

*****

Back in his office Reginald had only approved three reqs and rejected two, when Dex Hanley's beefy body appeared in the doorway. "Can I speak with you, Chief?"

"Sure. What's up?"

He scratched his thick head of hair. "I've received several complaints that people have tripped over the torn rug in the entryway."

"So fix it."

"That's the problem. I put in a req to bring in a carpet repairman, but you turned it down."

"Use one of your current staff."

"No can do. Brian's out sick, Terry's on vacation, and you denied the personnel request to add a third person."

Reginald sighed. "Okay, bring in the outside service."

Dex whipped out a req from behind his back.

Reginald signed it and thrust it back into Dex's hot little hand.

"And Dex, I want you to have your security people keep an extra eye on my car. Since someone stole the hood ornament, I don't want anything else done to my Jaguar."

Dex scratched his head. "I still can't figure out why someone would do that to you."

"For the same reason as the insulting pictures of me in the elevators."

"I guess you really pissed off at least one person, Chief."

"It seems that way."

Reginald looked up to see Hector Lopez and Maurice Casotti waiting outside his office. Dex exited, and the office became filled with Maurice's large presence and Hector's thin but tall stature.

"We have a problem, Boss," Hector said.

"More than a problem," Maurice added.

Reginald put up a hand. "Okay, okay. One at a time. Hector?"

"I've had three complaints this morning of torn bed sheets."

"Well, replace them."

Hector twisted a rolled piece of paper in his hands. "We're out of replacement linen, and you didn't approve the requisition to add more."

"And I suppose you have a new req with you."

He grinned. "Yes, Boss." He held out the form to affix a Reginald Bentley.

"Maurice, what's your issue?"

"After the last two days I've had twice as many complaints as the previous two months combined. I followed your recommendation to decrease the size of portions and the residents seem really upset."

"I thought old fogies didn't eat that much."

"Are you kidding? Have you seen the appetites of some of these people?"

"Stay with the small portions, but let people have seconds if they want."

Maurice smiled. "Good idea. That should help."

They departed, and Reginald reached for his pen when six smoldering faces appeared in front of his desk.

"After you joined us at the Butterfly Pavilion yesterday, I thought you had just started acting like less of a prick, but now you do this." Jerry fumed, waving a sheet of paper.

Reginald scanned the accompanying glares from Henrietta, Karen, Belinda, Tom and Al.

Jerry slammed the paper down on the desk.

Reginald picked it up and read the notice he had told Vicki to post. "We have to add activity fees. Attributed to normal inflation."

Jerry banged his fist down on the desk, knocking several reqs off the pile. "This is outrageous. You charge more while services in this pigsty continue going in the crapper."

Henrietta aimed a sharp red fingernail. "Since you arrived, housekeeping spends only half the time cleaning as they used to."

"We found out that the trash will only be picked up on Tuesdays now instead of twice a week," Al protested. "Garbage will build up. It will stink around here."

"The salad served last night had brown lettuce," Belinda added, her arms jerking and trembling.

Tom bent over toward the floor for a moment and then straightened with a glint of steel in his eyes. "I received a surcharge on my medication."

"Everything's going wrong," Karen said, looking from side to side. "I can't remember just what, but it is."

Reginald held up his hands again. He was getting quite a workout warding off irate residents and visitors. "I understand your concerns, ladies and gentlemen. I have a business to run, and there will be some adjustments necessary."

"Adjustments . . . smadjustments." Jerry sputtered. "Consider this adjustment. If you don't fix things in a week, the six of us plan to move to another retirement home." Five gray heads nodded in unison.

With that they all turned like a marching band and strode out of his office, Al tottering at the rear.

Reginald sat there like someone had given him a sucker punch. He had a job to do, a turnaround to perform, a facility to save, but he had overreacted. True, he had to cut costs, but he needed to pursue this intelligently, as he had told his staff. He had to consider the flip side of cost containment—he needed to retain and add residents for his program to be successful. He had to find the appropriate balance between cost reduction and occupancy rate improvement. He couldn't afford to lose six residents.

And he had a desktop full of paperwork to complete. He began reviewing a requisition for toilet paper, when he sensed someone staring at him. He raised his eyes to see marketing manager Mimi Hendrix standing there.

"Yes?"

"I've been working on the marketing plan you requested, and I don't see any way to increase occupancy on the current budget. Do you want my resignation?"

He could see tears welling in the corners of her eyes. That caught his attention. "No, Mimi. I want you to stay. Let's do this. Continue to document what you can accomplish under the current budget. Then add a section on what you would like to add in spending and the expected results with such an increase. Let's review both parts when we meet on Friday."

She gave him a wan smile. "Thanks. I'll go work on it."

After she left, he signed for the next week's food purchases and had his pen poised to reject a request from Vicki Pearson for supplies for an upcoming picnic that seemed too expensive when the phone rang.

"Time's up, Edwards," that familiar voice said.

"This isn't Edwards!" he shouted to a dial tone.

His crazy world now consisted of old people and incompetent criminals. His sudden desire to put his head on his desk and take a nap as he had in kindergarten was interrupted by the appearance of business manager Alicia Renton.

"I suppose you don't have good news for me," Reginald said.

"That depends on how you look at it."

He let out a deep sigh. "Go ahead. Tell me."

"You turned down a requisition for additional printed forms."

"That's right. I checked and saw that we still have an ample supply."

"Yes, except that we order a quantity of each and receive a good discount for the volume. You overlooked one form that we've run out of. We have no more purchase requisitions."

Chapter 10

After Alicia left, Reginald sat in his office feeling the weight of the world on his shoulders. Balancing cost-containment with quality services wasn't going to be easy. He started to jot down some notes when he heard a click and a pop, followed by black smoke billowing up from under his desk. It smelled like rotten eggs. He charged out of his office as the fire alarm clanged.

Pandemonium reigned outside. Residents limped and pushed walkers toward the exit. A siren wailed in the distance and within minutes a fire engine raced up the Sunny Crest driveway. Shortly thereafter, two fire fighters dashed into the building.

"This way," Reginald said, leading them to his office.

One of the men donned a breathing apparatus and disappeared into the cloud of smoke. He emerged holding a smoking canister, carried it outside and doused it with water.

"What was that thing?" Reginald asked the other fire fighter.

"What you could affectionately call a stink bomb with a timer. Harmless, but I'd suggest opening all the windows to air out your office."

Reginald grimaced. "Who'd plant something like that?"

"You make any enemies recently?"

"Only two hundred residents, numerous family members, my staff and some guy who thinks I'm the previous retirement home director. I'll try to find out who the culprit is."

*****

Reginald made sure all the residents returned safely to the building. When he entered his aired-out office, he surveyed the damage. Some muddy footprints on the floor, more black smudges on the walls than left by

Edwards, and the requisitions in disarray. The whoopee cushion pad had been torn during the conflagration. He picked it up and pitched it into the trash can. Good riddance.

Next, he called Dex to join him. "Have your security people seen anyone sneaking around my office?"

"I'll check, but I haven't had any reports."

"I have my suspicions, but see if you can uncover any clues on who planted the stink bomb in my office."

"Yes, Chief. I'll look into it."

*****

Reginald found it difficult to concentrate on purchase requisitions. Giving up in frustration, he decided to take a walk to clear his head. A hawk circled the field next to Sunny Crest, ready to pounce on some unsuspecting mouse. Obviously, his staff and residents viewed him as a bird of prey, ready to rip them apart with his fiscal talons. His gaze turned to the mountains to see the August monsoon clouds building over the Continental Divide. He had been too wrapped up in his job to visit the high country. One of these days he'd have to head up there for a hike.

His stomach churned as he contemplated his actions of the first three days on the job. He had been decisive and made changes. Some of his actions had been necessary, but some had backfired. Then it struck him. He'd been arrogant to think that he could stuff cost-cutting changes down people's throats. He needed to change his approach. He'd taken on his staff and the residents with his pen, slashing expenses, but had overlooked the essential part of the equation.

A couple holding hands and laughing strolled along the bike path that skirted the field. That's what he had missed. Friendly cooperation.

He jogged back to Sunny Crest, entered the dining room and spotted Jerry with his two buddies at their table. Their lady friends were still eating at a nearby table. Reginald approached the men. "Are you gentlemen having a pleasant lunch?"

Jerry cocked an eye toward him. "We're sitting here reliving this morning's great evacuation. Most excitement we've had in weeks. Probably filled up a truckload of Depends. Fortunately, no heart attacks resulted. We've sure had a lot of commotion since you arrived on the scene, Reggie. You seem to bring out extreme reactions in people."

"You wouldn't have any idea who planted a stink bomb in my office, would you?"

Jerry gave a dismissive wave of his hand. "Probably just some kid pissed off because you cut his grandmother's rations. There may soon be an epidemic of people dying from malnutrition around here. You know, Reggie, they used to serve us a full sandwich in this joint."

"That's what I'd like to discuss. I want to invite you three gentlemen and your lady friends to join me for dinner at a restaurant this evening."

"You going to make us pay for the meal?" Al asked.

Reginald chuckled. "You have me pegged. No, I want to treat you. Do you have a favorite place?"

"I'm up for something Italian," Tom said.

"Let's try Carelli's," Jerry said.

"Good," Reginald replied. "I'll line up the van and meet you in front at six. You sure the ladies will join us?"

Jerry dropped his fork on the table. "They wouldn't miss this, Reggie. Methinks you're finally coming to your senses."

*****

That afternoon Maurice Casotti steered his large bulk into the director's office with a scowl on his face and his mustache aquiver. Reginald half expected him to pull out a butcher knife from under his chef's hat. Instead he waved a sheet of paper. "I think I've found our silverware thief."

"Have a seat and fill me in."

He sank into a chair. "A few minutes ago I had a chance to meet with Renee and review the visitors' log. Guess what we found?"

Reginald arched an eyebrow. "One visitor who came to lunch last Friday and this Monday and Wednesday."

Maurice's eyes opened wide. "How did you know?"

Reginald rolled his chair a few inches and leaned back. "Attribute it to my suspicious nature. Go on."

"Only one guest's name appeared on all of those days. Grayson Younger."

"Do you know who he visited?"

Maurice clenched the paper. "Mrs. Younger in room 702."

"Good work. I'll stop by to have a chat with Mrs. Younger. On another subject, how do we stand on the complaint level over food?"

Maurice ran his hand over his moustache. "Highest ever."

"I know. I made a mistake. Go back to full portions and purchase only high quality food products."

Maurice's eyes grew as large as Frisbees.

Reginald thought the chef might kiss him on both cheeks.

*****

Later Reginald took the elevator up to the seventh floor. To his relief, no offensive posters inside. Only a reminder for the family dinner on Saturday. He moseyed down the hallway and rang the doorbell to room 702.

A voice shouted, "Come in."

He entered through the kitchenette into a suite where a woman sat in a rocking chair, knitting. All around the room were mounted shelves containing miniature animals—on one, a collection of ceramic dogs; on another, cats; on a third, horses. Each piece of furniture had knit covers.

"Quite a collection, Mrs. Younger."

"Oh, yes. My two passions. Miniature animals and knitting. And you are?"

"I'm sorry I didn't introduce myself. I became caught up admiring your décor. I'm Reginald Bentley, the new director of Sunny Crest."

"Oh, yes. There used to be a different director, but I never saw much of him."

"He left last week, and I started on Monday."

She put her knitting on a table next to her. "What brings you up here, Mr. Bentley?"

"I understand you've had a visitor for lunch over the last week named Grayson Younger."

Her eyes twinkled. "Yes, that has been so exciting. My grandson starts attending the University of Colorado this year. He arrived in town from Colorado Springs and has found an apartment. He's been kind enough to come to see me for lunch before his school year starts. He has a part-time job on Tuesdays, Thursdays and on the weekend, but joined me for lunch beginning last Friday."

"I take it he lives in an unfurnished apartment."

She wrinkled her forehead. "Why, yes. Why would you say that?"

"Just a hunch. Tell me about Grayson."

"He's my son Robert's oldest boy. Grayson is an intense young man. I enjoy his visits, but he could use a lesson in manners."

"I imagine. What field of study has he chosen at CU?"
"Ethics."

*****

Reginald's dinner guests, the Jerry-atrics, immediately helped themselves to the toasty hot bread and began dipping pieces in olive oil. The table rested far enough from a central fireplace that the heat didn't disturb them on this August evening. Then everyone settled in to drink Chianti, munch on calamari hors d'oeuvres and order a wide variety of meats, fish, pasta and vegetables.

Henrietta curled a finger with its lethal red nail toward Reginald. "I understand you've been hitting on my daughter."

He almost spit pieces of squid all over the table. "I—I merely asked her to join me for the family dinner on Saturday."

She patted his arm. "I'm just teasing you. I think that's a wonderful idea. You two have a lot in common."

"Oh?"

"As Jerry says, you both tend to act like you have a corncob. . . I mean, you know, you're both wired kind of tight." She blushed.

Everyone snickered.

"I agree with Henrietta." Jerry picked up a piece of calamari, threw it into the air and caught it in his mouth. "You and Rebecca make quite a pair. She doesn't take crap from anyone, and you give it out all the time."

"Y'all, let's be polite to him," Karen said. "He's the one paying, isn't he?"

"That's right, dear," Belinda added. "We'll give him the benefit of the doubt until he proposes some new idiotic, cost-cutting scheme."

"Okay, Reggie," Jerry said, "you've plied us with wine and squid. What's on your mind?"

Reginald fiddled with a button on his Hawaiian shirt, adjusted his chair and leaned toward the table. "Let me level with all of you."

"It's about time," Henrietta said with a stern expression. Then her face lightened, and she winked at him.

Reginald took a deep breath. "As I told you, I came here to turn around the disastrous financial situation at Sunny Crest."

"Yeah, Reggie, we all know you're the hatchet man." Jerry popped a piece of olive oil soaked bread into his mouth.

"But it goes deeper than that. The CEO of Cenpolis Corporation, Armand Daimler, runs a very tight ship. He expects every property the company owns to make money. He told me to make Sunny Crest profitable or shut it down."

Karen blinked. "But I like living at Sunny Crest."

"Hush," Belinda said, putting a shaky hand on her friend's arm. "We want him to think we're prepared to leave if he doesn't fix things."

Reginald wiped the corner of his mouth with the white linen napkin and put it back in his lap. "I know all of you have been putting pressure on me to modify my recent cost-reduction decisions, and you're right. I took the wrong approach and now want to make amends."

Six pairs of eyes stared at him.

"I'm your typical corporate bureaucrat, trained to cut expenses and not pay attention to the human side of the equation. First, I want to apologize to all of you for my short-sighted thinking."

"Apology accepted, Reggie." Jerry held up his glass of wine.

"Second, I'd like to solicit your assistance in improving conditions at Sunny Crest and keeping it open."

Jerry scrutinized Reginald. "I'll consider it only if you're not asking us to con people."

"No, I want to enlist your help. Rather than me dictating inane cost-reductions as I've done so far, I'd like your recommendations on what we can do together to make Sunny Crest a top notch retirement community that people will be dying to get into."

"Bad choice of words, Reggie," Henrietta said. "We're not a funeral home."

He laughed. "Obviously, I need a lot of coaching from all of you. That's why I want to ask you this question. If you held my position, what would you change at Sunny Crest?"

"That's easy," Jerry said. "First thing you need to tackle—the quality of the food served in the dining room. We may be old, but what we eat is of utmost importance to us. You need to have variety, consistent good quality and none of the half-pint servings."

Reginald removed a small notepad from his hip pocket and began taking notes.

"Cookies are important," Karen said. "Y'all know I love freshly baked cookies after meals." She licked her lips. "Yum."

"Here's a thought. Would you be willing to meet with Maurice Casotti to spend time planning menus?"

"Damn right," Jerry said. "No one has asked us before."

"Okay," Reginald said. "I understand food is number one on your list. What else?"

"We all want a bright, cheerful and clean place to live in," Henrietta said. "Our building looks a little long in the tooth. Fresh paint, repairs kept up and good housekeeping. Those are all essential elements to make Sunny Crest a livable retirement community."

"And it has to be safe," Tom said. "We can't have any more scam guys traipsing through our halls and accosting our residents. If another one shows up without you doing something, I'll bring in some of my old army marksmen to take him out."

"You wouldn't have to resort to that," Al said. "Even with my stiff joints, I'd walk the halls to find him and bash him over the head."

Reginald held up his hands. "Whoa, gentlemen, let's forgo the violence. I don't think we'll have any more scam artists working the corridors. Other comments?"

"We're willing to pay a reasonable price for good service," Jerry said. "Just don't tack on all those piddly surcharges. That really pisses us off."

Reginald nodded. "Understood. One other item I'd like to mention to you. We still have to watch our expenses here and one idea discussed in my staff meeting entailed using volunteers in the business office instead of hiring another staff member. Would any of you be willing to volunteer to assist Alicia Renton?"

"I have my hands full with the tours for prospective residents," Henrietta said.

Belinda looked toward Karen. "I'd be willing to help out. Karen, do you want to work with me on it?"

"Oh, mercy, yes. What would we need to do?"

"Sit down with Alicia tomorrow morning," Reginald said. "She'll train you and have some specific assignments. Thanks for your willingness to pitch in. Now, what other suggestions do you have for improving Sunny Crest?"

By the end of the evening Reginald had twenty pages of notes and the agreement from all six to help him implement their suggestions.

Chapter 11

After dinner with the Jerry-atrics, Reginald returned to his office to work on plans to save Sunny Crest. Re-energized by pasta and the support of his new allies, he madly wrote notes and made calculations. This would not be an easy task, but ideas circled his head like the butterflies from the day before.

By ten p.m. he had a path in sight. If only he could increase the occupancy rate and escape any additional major expenses. He regarded his final numbers, satisfied that he could turn Sunny Crest around. He was collecting all his notes in a neat stack to wrap up for the day, when he heard the sound of a door squeaking open. He raised his gaze from his paperwork.

A man in a black ski mask rushed into the office and brandished a pistol. "Okay, Edwards, we're going for a little ride."

Reginald stared back, trying to maintain his composure. "You have the wrong person. I'm not Edwards."

The man chuckled. "Nice try. I've been hired to show you that your loan officer means business."

"It won't do you any good to kidnap me. Edwards resigned, and I'm the new guy taking his place. My name is Reginald Bentley."

The ski mask guy shook his gun. "That's a good one. No one would really have that stupid a name. Get up, Edwards."

Reginald stood. "Where are we going?"

"On a little one-way ride."

Reginald scanned the room. Although the walls still remained bare, he would miss his office if this guy planned to dump his body in a reservoir. *Think.* He had to delay any way he could. Only one thought came to mind. "You didn't set off a stink bomb in my office, did you?"

The guy snorted. "What the hell are you talking about? If I set off a bomb it would blow this place to smithereens. Now, you and I have some business to settle."

"Your boss will be mighty pissed off when he finds out you wasted all this time on the wrong person. Let me show you my identification." Reginald reached for his pocket.

The man pushed the pistol under Reginald's chin. "Keep your hands where they are. No sudden moves or I'll take care of you right here."

Reginald pulled his hands away from his pants. "I'm only trying to save you some trouble. You'd look pretty dumb taking the wrong person."

The man raised a fist. "Who you calling dumb?"

Reginald winced. "No one. But don't you think it would be better to check it out first?"

The man shrugged. "Nah. No skin off my back."

"Easy for you to say."

"Enough jabbering." He pointed toward the door. "Move."

Too bad Reginald's parents never sprang for any martial arts training. And even if the guy didn't have a gun, he held the advantage by a good fifty pounds and looked like he had been doing weight work rather than shuffling paperwork. This was a hell of a predicament for an accountant to be in.

Reginald should have been shaking with fear, but the situation seemed so bizarre that the implications hadn't really sunk in yet. Between the old fogies and the shenanigans around this place, he wondered if he should pinch himself to find if he'd sunk into some weirdo dream. Unfortunately, he remained wide awake.

The masked man marched him out of the office and to the outer door of the business area. Reginald reached for the handle trying to make as much noise as possible.

The masked man grabbed his shoulder. "Stand still." He peeked out the door and then motioned Reginald through it.

Reginald tried to veer toward the elevator, but the man clasped his arm and steered him in the direction of the stairwell. With a not too gentle shove they continued down the stairs. Reginald almost tripped but regained his balance. Would it be better to die on the staircase or at the hands of some hired psychopath?

On the first floor the kidnapper again checked before they exited the stairwell. He prodded Reginald toward the loading dock.

This guy meant to do him bodily harm. Reginald began to sweat. The realization struck him that this was no laughing matter. If he shouted none of the hearing-aid-assisted residents would notice. And if one of the old limping geezers showed up, what good would it serve? Probably end up with a whack on the head from the assailant. He couldn't risk hurting anyone else in the process. *Think.* What were his options?

No one around. Where was the damn security guard when needed?

Out on the loading dock they moved into the shadows away from the one small bulb, and down the stairs.

Behind them a voice rang out. "Drop the gun, scumbag!"

The captor's pistol bounced off onto the surface of the loading dock bay. "Down on the ground."

Suddenly the grip on Reginald's shoulder released, and he heard a body thumping down on the cement. He turned to see Jerry Rhine pressing the end of a broomstick against the back of the kidnapper, now spread-eagled face down on the dock bay floor. Reginald felt a surge of elation at the sight of this octogenarian holding a young thug in check.

"Grab the gun, Reggie."

He duly picked it up. It felt heavy and smelled of oil. He had never been a gun person. He didn't know how to fire the damn thing. If action were required, he'd probably shoot Jerry by mistake. He pointed it at the hit man, his hand shaking.

"What say we blow this guy away?" Jerry gave a wink. "Perfectly legal under the Colorado make-my-day law."

A moan emerged from the flattened figure.

"We don't need any further bloodshed on this dock," Reginald said. "Would you please explain to this thick-headed thug who I am? He thinks I'm the previous director named Edwards."

Jerry bent over the figure. "He's correct. This gentleman you've been harassing is none other than Reggie Bentley the Third. Not to be confused with the incompetent Edwards who left a week ago. You understand?"

The man mumbled, "Yes."

Jerry jabbed him in the back again with the broomstick. "Now you have three choices. We can blow you away right now. Maybe do it in pieces—a knee, the groin, the chest, the head. Second, we can call the police. Or third, we can let you hightail it out of here to inform your boss that Edwards has jumped ship."

"I'll take number three," came a faint response.

"You have chosen wisely. Get your butt out of here."

The man raised himself to all fours, stood, dashed into the darkness and disappeared out of sight.

Jerry chuckled. "I saved your tush, Reggie. For a moment I considered letting him take you away, but then figured since you've started acting human, it would make no sense to break in another retirement home director."

Reginald relaxed his tense shoulders. "Thanks, Jerry."

"You may want to wipe your fingerprints off that gun and throw it into the dumpster."

Not wanting to deal with the police about an issue that was now over, Reginald found an oily rag, wiped the gun, lifted the lid to the smelly dumpster and deposited the weapon inside.

They climbed the stairs to the dock level. "What brought you out here in the first place, Jerry?"

"I come out here to think and get away from all the old farts. I can only take so much of being around old people." He elbowed Reginald in the ribs.

"I know what you mean."

"And here I thought you were tottering on the brink of liking the older generation, Reggie."

"You're definitely different from my preconceptions."

Jerry slapped him on the back. "You're learning, Reggie." With that he gave the door to the building a tap, pulled it open and held it for Reginald to go inside first.

"I thought this door was locked. How'd you do that?"

"Just a little trick of the trade, Reggie. Good night."

Chapter 12

The next morning Reginald remembered to take the elevator down so that he could check for any more caricatures of himself. Inside the elevator, he found only the schedule of events for the week, the reminder about the Saturday family dinner and Alicia's notice requesting volunteers in the business office. Amazing how suddenly the derisive posters had disappeared.

At breakfast he expected everyone to make comments on how Jerry had rescued him. He steeled himself for the razzing and pointed remarks at his expense. Instead when he stopped by to see Jerry, Tom and Al at their table, no one mentioned a thing. After Tom and Al excused themselves, he whispered to Jerry, "I'm curious. Didn't you tell them what happened last night?"

"Nah. I thought it would be between you and me, Reggie. Our own little secret." He winked.

Reginald shook his head. "I'll never understand you, Jerry."

Jerry stood up and whacked him on the back. "Don't even try, Reggie."

*****

Back in his office to solve the day's bureaucratic challenges, Reginald had no more than dropped into his chair when Hector Lopez appeared, gasping for breath. "Boss. . . we have a problem."

He looked toward the ceiling for deliverance. "What now, Hector?"

"You know we have a regulation that residents can't keep pets."

On the corner of the desk Reginald tapped the pen he had once used to slash expenses. "Yes, one of my favorite rules since I don't like animals."

"Well, one of the housekeepers found dog poop in the hallway on the fifth floor."

"Has any visitor brought a dog here?"

Hector shook his head. "But I've had reports of someone hearing a dog barking on the fifth floor. I think we have an illegal pet on the premises."

"Have you searched all the rooms to ferret out the culprit?"

"We've checked but haven't found a dog yet."

"Have your people keep at it. Then we'll inform the violating resident to get rid of the defecating demon."

*****

Before Reginald had a chance to rid his thoughts of dog excrement, Maurice raced into the office. "I need some additional help washing dishes. It's impossible to keep up with cleaning everything between breakfast and dinnertime. Any chance of getting a personnel req approved?"

"No, but I have an idea for volunteer resources to assist you. I should have it worked out for you by the end of lunch time today."

Maurice scrunched up his nose. "We need something quick."

*****

After Reginald survived the rest of the morning without any additional crises or thugs appearing, he meandered down to have some lunch. He gobbled a quick salad and sandwich and then located Mrs. Younger and her grandson sitting at a table for two. Grayson wore tattered jeans and a bomber jacket even though the temperature topped eighty degrees. His face had a scruffy unshaved look that seemed popular among the teenage set, and he could have used a good haircut. As opposed to Grayson's appearance, Reginald had to admit that the oldsters in residence here dressed neatly and kept themselves well groomed.

Reginald watched as grandmother and grandson finished their meal. Finally, Mrs. Younger stood, kissed Grayson on the cheek and shuffled off.

Grayson waited until she had left and then scrutinized the room.

Reginald averted his eyes for a moment.

Grayson looked down at the table and in a swift motion grabbed something and stuck his hand inside his bomber jacket.

Bingo.

Grayson stood. Reginald jumped to his feet and dashed out of the dining room ahead of him.

When Grayson emerged in the entryway, Reginald grabbed his jacket and swung him against the wall. In one fluid motion he reached inside Grayson's jacket, extracted the silverware and waved the items in his face. "Grayson, you have an important decision to make."

Grayson gulped. "How do you know my name?"

"You've been stealing silverware from our dining room. I can report this to CU, which will get you kicked out of school before it even opens, to say nothing of how your grandmother will feel knowing that her grandson is a thief."

"I—I wouldn't want that."

"Or you can return all the silverware you took and repay your crime with a little community service here at Sunny Crest."

Grayson's shoulders sagged. "What do I need to do?"

"Monday morning you report to our chef Maurice Casotti with all the silverware. Apologize to him, and he'll have a work assignment for you for the next month."

"You won't tell my grandmother, will you?"

"Not unless you renege on our agreement. Monday morning."

*****

That afternoon Reginald called Maurice to let him know that his silverware would be returned on Monday and that he had a public service dishwasher three days a week for the next month. Then he met with Mimi Hendrix to review her marketing plan. She arrived, dressed in a dark blue skirt and white blouse, and coiffed in a perky flip. She marched into the office with a determined expression on her face, handed Reginald a presentation package and sat down facing him. He felt like he was back in Chicago dealing with top corporate issues once again.

"The executive summary appears on the first page. I want to cover the competitive landscape, what differentiates Sunny Crest from other retirement communities, what we need to do to maintain a sustainable competitive advantage, three specific recommendations and then a budget summary."

Reginald gave her a nod of acknowledgement. "Proceed."

"First, regarding competition. In the corridor from Denver to Longmont three newer facilities have been opened, but our building continues to be viewed as attractive, bright and accommodating, provided we invest in the maintenance and repainting that Dex has suggested." She studied him warily.

"I agree."

She sat up a little straighter. "Our pricing remains in line with the competition, assuming we don't go overboard on surcharges." She paused.

"Duly noted."

"The relationship with our two sister organizations provides a significant plus—having our independent living community associated with the Sunny Manor assisted-living facility in Louisville, Colorado, and the Sunny Home nursing home in Longmont—"

"Stop a moment there." Reginald held his hand up as if trying to wave down a speeding train. "I'm familiar with the names of both properties from reports I saw when at corporate headquarters in Chicago. What can you tell me about the two facilities?"

She shrugged. "Not too much. I've visited both. The Longmont building is older than ours, but the Louisville one is newer. Both provide solid services to residents who require more assistance than in an independent living facility such as ours."

"I'll have to stop by to speak with my counterparts one of these days. Do you know the directors at these facilities?"

"No. I haven't had a chance to speak to their administrative staff."

He waved her on. "Continue."

"The reason it's important that we're associated with an assisted-living and nursing home is that families and residents want a retirement package that can cover the spectrum of medical needs and our guarantee to deliver a space in the assisted-living and nursing homes, if required in the future, adds another competitive benefit. Also having them at distinctly separate locations provides a definite advantage in that the independent residents don't have to be constantly reminded of the assisted-living and nursing home life style."

"Yeah we wouldn't want to mix the Jerry-atrics with their oxygen-dependent, wheelchair-bound, drooling cousins."

Mimi glared at him. "I wouldn't describe the assisted-living and nursing homes that way, Mr. Bentley."

He ignored her comment and glanced at the next page of the presentation. "It makes sense to not wave health degradation in the faces of the independent-living folks. How do you rate the perceived quality of life here at Sunny Crest?"

She sighed. "We're okay but not great. We need to invest in more activities, rather than cutting back."

Reginald heard the cash register ping and imagined twenty-dollar bills flying away, but bit his tongue.

"Our food service has received a good evaluation, although not this week." She wrinkled her brow.

Reginald tapped the presentation package as he recalled the comments from the Jerry-atrics at the restaurant. "That's been fixed."

"Good. Medical service remains solid and housekeeping continues to be competitive. Now to other advantages we have. Our location near the greenbelt provides an exceptional view. We need to promote our location, our solid services and continue to deliver on those services."

"And the punch line?"

"I would recommend three specific programs. First, advertise in the *AARP Magazine*, the *Boulder Daily Camera* and the *Denver Post*. Second, hold regular open houses and third, sponsor a Sunny Crest senior triathlon."

He skimmed ahead to the budget page and realized that these proposals would empty the till. He could just picture Daimler bouncing off the ceiling of his spacious Chicago office and leaving a permanent dent in the acoustic panel. "I understand everything except the senior triathlon."

Mimi's eyes shone. "I've come up with this great idea. I figured we need something to publicize that our independent living residents remain robust, active and interesting people."

"You only have to put Jerry Rhine and his friends on display."

She giggled. "That's right. Nothing's ever boring with the Jerry-atrics."

"Don't I know it. Now what's this senior triathlon?"

"Oh, yes. Here's the essence of my idea—we sponsor a mini-version of a triathlon. The city of Boulder hosts all kinds of bike events, walkathons and running races to serve our outdoor-oriented community. What better way to highlight our active seniors than an event for people sixty-five and older? The senior triathlon would involve a swim of one hundred yards, a bike ride of five miles and a walk of one mile."

Reginald pictured a herd of geezers and geezerettes limping toward a finish line. "Something that wouldn't kill them."

"That's right. We want to show them active, not having heart attacks."

"And you think this might be a good publicity stunt?"

Mimi pursed her lips. "I think of it as an event, not a stunt."

"Right."

"In fact I've already enlisted the Jerry-atrics. They love the idea and are all starting to get in shape for it."

Reginald thought of the people in the group. "I can see three of them doing it, but would such an event put a strain on Tom's heart?"

"He's supposed to exercise anyway, and this would be perfect for him."

"But Belinda with her Parkinson's. I can't imagine her participating."

"She also needs to exercise regularly. Doctor's orders."

Reginald tapped a finger on his desk. "All right. But you can't convince me that arthritic Al Thiebodaux will be competing. Do you think he could even complete the course?"

"Sure. He's very interested. He swims and uses a stationary bike for therapy. He may be a slower walker than the others, but he could use walking poles. Think of it." She spread her arms wide. "The first annual Boulder Senior Triathlon. Sponsored by Sunny Crest Retirement Community, home of robust senior citizens."

"You've made your point." Drops of sweat formed on Reginald's brow at the thought of presenting Mimi's concept to his boss. He'd be out on his butt in two seconds. Directly approaching Daimler with these plans would be like thrusting his hand into a buzz saw. He'd have to strategize on how to increase the marketing activity, but saw no way of implementing all of Mimi's recommendations in the near future. He'd have to be selective. "Thanks for an excellent presentation. I want to evaluate each of the points in light of our financial objectives, and we'll discuss them again next week."

At that moment, Hector Lopez burst into the office. "We found the dog."

Mimi's jaw dropped. "Dog?"

Hector punched his right fist into his left hand. "Yes, we caught Mrs. Seneca in room 525 with a dog. What do you want me to do next, Boss?"

"I'll go speak with her right now."

"Okay if I tag along?" Mimi asked.

Reginald stood. "Sure."

"I'll let you two cover it." Hector trotted away.

After an interminable wait for the elevator followed by an equally slow ascent, they arrived on the fifth floor, and knocked on Mrs. Seneca's door.

"Come in."

They entered the well-lit suite to find a woman in a bright flowered dress sitting in a lounge chair with what looked like a rag mop nestled in her lap.

He strode right up to her. "Mrs. Seneca, I'm Reginald Bentley, director of Sunny Crest. We have a rule of no pets here."

She placed the rag mop on the floor, and it shook its fur. "I know, but Sophie is such a good companion. She never causes any problems."

"We've had reports of your dog barking as well as leaving a mess in the hallway." Reginald pointed to the white, black and brown mass of hair. "What kind of creature is that?"

"Sophie is a Shih Tzu."

Sophie waddled over toward him, sniffed his shoe and bit his ankle.

"Ouch!" Reginald jumped back.

"Sophie, what's gotten into you?" Mrs. Seneca turned toward Reginald. "She's always friendly unless someone threatens her. She knows you don't like her."

"That's right. I don't like dogs. But irrespective of that, we have explicit regulations—no pets."

Both the beast and Mrs. Seneca looked at him with wide, pleading eyes. "Some retirement homes actually encourage pets. Animals are very therapeutic and help with depression. I've seen one facility where cats and dogs roam the halls. You should change the policy here, Mr. Bentley."

"Well, we're not that kind of retirement home. You're going to have to get rid of Sophie."

Mrs. Seneca rose from her chair and confronted him with all of her five-foot-two of height. "I will not give up Sophie. I'll leave Sunny Crest instead if I have to." She crossed her arms.

"Mr. Bentley, may I speak with you outside?" Mimi asked.

"I suppose. Mrs. Seneca, if you'll excuse us for a moment?"

"I'm calling my grandson while you're out there." She reached for her phone as Mimi and Reginald stepped into the hallway.

He looked down to make sure there wasn't any dog poop to step in. "Yes?"

Mimi shuffled her foot for a moment. "You know we're struggling to hold and increase our occupancy rate."

"That's correct."

"Well, we can't afford to lose any residents right now. I think we should consider a creative solution to keep Mrs. Seneca here."

"And you have a suggestion?" Reginald looked down the hallway, imagining a pack of wild dogs prowling the corridor at night.

"Why yes. We have a visitor's suite on the first floor, that isn't used very often. It has a small enclosed patio. We could offer that to Mrs. Seneca and her dog. It would eliminate the problem of a dog in the main building and allow her to stay. It would also open up one more paying room."

Mimi knew exactly how to reach the cold heart of an accountant. She had him at the words "paying room." Still, he couldn't give in too easily. "I like your thinking in terms of increasing revenue. But wouldn't permitting this dog in residence set a bad precedent?"

"I don't think anyone will object. We could try offering her the alternative and see if she's amenable."

"Why not? It's not crazier than anything else around here."

They re-entered Mrs. Seneca's room. She stood there with her arms crossed, daring Reginald to throw her out on her ear or other part of the anatomy.

"Ms. Hendrix has an idea that may solve this problem, Mrs. Seneca. You can keep your dog if you move into a suite on the first floor."

Mrs. Seneca's face brightened. "Oh, anything so that Sophie can stay here. And I really like Sunny Crest, so I'd prefer not to have to leave."

"Good. I'll have Dex Hanley work out the moving arrangements with you."

Sophie ambled over to Reginald.

He drew back, preparing to be attacked.

But instead of biting him, she licked his left sock.

*****

Back in his office, Reginald sat in his chair, wondering if he had gone nuts allowing this dog to stay in the facility. He seemed to be violating all his principles. If he didn't watch himself, he'd even start liking old people. Before going farther off the deep end, he called Dex and explained the moving arrangements for Mrs. Seneca to be scheduled for Monday.

He didn't have a chance to catch his breath after hanging up before the phone rang. His worst nightmare had invaded his cozy domain—Armand Daimler on the line.

"What's this I hear that a murder occurred at Sunny Crest?"

Reginald gulped. "It's only considered a suspicious death at this time, not necessarily a murder."

"Dead is dead."

Reginald sighed. "It's a good-news, bad-news situation."

"I can't imagine any good news."

"Actually it did solve one problem. We had this scam artist taking advantage of our residents. The scammer won't be causing problems here anymore—he's the dead man."

"Still doesn't look good for a retirement community to have a suspicious death publicized. You've been there one week now. This isn't the way to fix things."

"I know, but I'm implementing other tactical plans. I'm extremely optimistic that we'll have a very profitable future at Sunny Crest."

"Well, I don't share that optimism. It's time to fry it."

Reginald took a deep breath. "I can turn this place around. We have a solid facility and can boost the occupancy rate significantly."

"That's good real estate out there, Reginald. The lost opportunity cost of our investment sitting fallow doesn't please me."

"You originally gave me six months to fix it, Mr. Daimler."

"No longer applies. You now have two weeks."

Reginald's stomach did a queasy somersault. "Two weeks?"

"Or we can fry it today."

"I'll take the two weeks."

Chapter 13

Reginald slumped over his desk with his head in his hands, wondering if he should resort to Advil or Tylenol. He couldn't believe it. Daimler had just shortened the fuse. In their next conversation, Daimler was apt to say fix it or fry it in one day. His boss had no appreciation for what it took to turn around a facility like Sunny Crest.

Reginald thought back to all the times he had been the one putting pressure on some poor SOB running one of the Cenpolis properties, casually stopping by to inform the unfortunate sap to fix things or close the doors. Now for the first time, he knew what it felt like to be on the receiving end. He gulped in a deep breath. Still, he wouldn't wallow in his predicament. He had to get his butt in gear and use all of his business acumen to pull off a miracle.

At that moment, Dex rushed into the office, waving a requisition. "All worked out, Chief. I convinced the security system contractor to reduce the price, not a mere ten percent, but twelve percent. We're ready to roll. If you sign this today, they can start Monday and be done by the middle of next week."

Reginald reviewed the req, while Dex stood alternately on one foot and then the other as if he needed to use the restroom. He picked up his pen, pushed aside the pain surging through his head, signed the requisition with a flourish and handed it back to Dex. "Well done. On another subject, any leads on the stink bomb?"

Dex shook his head. "No reports of anyone entering your office other than you and your regular visitors."

"Obviously someone snuck in."

"Do you lock your door?"

"No."

Dex held his large hands open. "It would be easy for someone to just walk in, leave a stink bomb under your desk and disappear."

"But who would be capable of making something like that? It would be the kind a prank a kid would pull, not some geriatric."

Dex shrugged.

"You'd think old people would have better things to do than set off a stink bomb," Reginald said.

"I'll keep after it, Chief."

After Dex left, Reginald twiddled a pencil and looked out his window at the open space, remembering how his office had been engulfed in foul-smelling smoke. Not the best reception for a new retirement home director, but he had deserved it. He had started on the wrong foot by trying too hard to cut expenses. That had been short-sighted. Now he knew he needed to balance cost-reduction with good service to keep and attract new residents. He peered out the window again at an isolated pine tree shaking in the breeze, wishing he could hike off into the wilderness, rather than worry about turning this place around. It would be so easy to walk out of Sunny Crest and keep going. Kind of like what his predecessor, Edwards, had done. His pounding headache had become a dull background roar.

Focusing his attention back to the sheet on the desk, he reviewed the occupancy numbers. If he could keep from losing any residents in the next two weeks, and if he could find some way to fill fifteen rooms, he'd be close to breakeven, and at sixteen rooms he'd show a small profit.

Reginald had the creepy feeling that someone was watching him. He jerked his head to see Rebecca standing there. His heart started racing. "How—how long have you been standing there?"

She stepped forward and tapped a bright red fingernail on the corner of the desk. "A minute or so. You're very intense when you work, Reggie."

Reginald only gave a small twitch at the misuse of his name. "Yeah, I'm trying to figure out how to keep this place open." *Oops.*

Her eyes narrowed as she stared intently at him. "What?"

"Well, the cat's out of the bag. If you have a minute, take a seat and I'll tell you what's happening."

Rebecca sat down with feline grace, and the only thing that shook was in Reginald's chest. She leaned toward him and opened her succulent red lips. "Okay, Reggie, spill the beans."

He was lost in her sky blue eyes. He took a deep breath. "I came to Sunny Crest to turn this place around financially."

"Everyone knows you arrived bearing a sharp hatchet."

He pushed the image of the first elevator poster from his mind. "Today my boss gave me an ultimatum: make the place profitable in two weeks or shut it down."

She placed her hands on the desk and leaned toward him. "What? Two weeks? You'd have to be a magician to do that in two weeks."

A creative solution struck him like a lightning bolt. "Rebecca, you're a genius!" Before he knew better and she could move, he bent over the desk, grabbed her cheeks in his hands and planted a juicy kiss on those attractive lips. "You've given me the perfect idea."

Rebecca froze. Then she raised a hand to one blushing cheek. "I—I stopped by to get an update on my mother."

He couldn't believe what he had done. Heat rose up his neck. Still, she hadn't slapped him or raked him with her claws. A good sign. He looked at his watch. "Hey, it's getting late. Do you want to grab a bite to eat, and we can discuss your mother over a good meal?"

"I guess so. Give me a minute to freshen up."

She stood and scampered out of the room.

He admired the retreating figure and noticed one other thing. His headache had disappeared.

*****

Reginald opened the door to his car for Rebecca to climb in. Then he scrambled around to his side and jumped in behind the wheel, grasping the thin black rim.

Rebecca patted the black leather seat. "Quite a car, Reggie."

"Feel the wood over the glove box."

She ran her hand over the varnished brown deep-gloss panel. "Nice. Smooth as a baby's bottom."

"Smoother. I keep the passenger compartment in mint condition. You won't find anything like this outside a showroom. "

He inserted the key in the ignition like a lover giving a French kiss. The 3.8 liter I6 Jaguar XK engine came alive with a smooth purr. Like an orchestra conductor, he tilted his ear to the side to listen for any dissonance. All in perfect harmony. He shifted into reverse and carefully backed out, making sure to avoid any curbs or other obstacles.

Rebecca pointed toward the hood. "I thought Jaguars had those doohickey ornaments on the front?"

His stomach tightened at the reminder of the desecration. "Yes, my car used to have a Jaguar leaping cat on the hood."

"What happened to it?"

He clenched the steering wheel as if strangling a snake. "It's a long story."

"Given your car's wonderful condition, I'm surprised you haven't replaced it."

"I've been too busy to search for a new one. Maybe in a week or so I can break free." He snuck a glance at Rebecca. She was as beautiful as his car. No, even more beautiful. "You know this town better than I do. Where'd you like to eat?"

"Somewhere down on the Pearl Street Mall. Let's try the Black Cat."

She gave him directions, and he shot off like a flying furry mammal out of the underworld. He hadn't gone more than three blocks when a siren pierced the air accompanied by flashing red and blue lights. *Oops.* He pulled over to the curb.

"You going too fast?" Rebecca asked.

"I guess I was a little distracted."

The police officer approached the side of the Jaguar. "Driver's license, registration and proof of insurance, please."

Reginald reached in his wallet and then leaned across Rebecca to retrieve the registration and insurance form from the glove compartment.

The police officer took the documents and returned to his vehicle.

"You get tickets often, Reggie?"

"No. As a matter of fact, I've never received a traffic citation before."

She gawked, disbelief showing in her eyes. "That's surprising. The way you zoomed out of Sunny Crest, I thought this might be a regular occurrence for you."

"I guess I wasn't paying attention."

The officer returned and handed over a speeding ticket. Reginald had violated section 7-4-58 by going fifteen miles over the speed limit. *Double oops.*

Reginald waited until the police officer returned to his car and then started up, careful to stay within the speed limit for the rest of the drive.

"You'll have to pay a fine, and that will add points to your record," Rebecca said. "Don't continue to do stupid things or you could lose your license."

"Great. That's all I need."

Within minutes, they reached their destination with no further attention from the Boulder Police Department. The sun had disappeared behind the

Flatirons, the rock formations overlooking the west side of town. An early evening crowd of teenagers, tourists and families surged along the outdoor mall's walkway.

As they strolled toward the restaurant, Rebecca grabbed his arm. "Now tell me about this big revelation you had back in your office."

"You triggered an idea with the word 'magician.' Jerry Rhine does magic tricks. I thought we could put on an entertaining show for prospective residents, something to catch their interest, intrigue them and appeal to their sense of humor. Do you think Jerry would be willing to perform?"

She came to an abrupt halt and faced him. "Are you kidding? That's what he lives for. You'll never be able to get him to stop once you turn him on. Just be careful what you wish for."

Reginald regarded Rebecca's red lips, realizing what he really wished for but willed himself to stay focused. With Daimler breathing down his neck, this was no time to lose his concentration. "Good. I'll have to discuss it with Jerry."

A light breeze rustled the leaves of the trees lining the path. Spaced at intervals of approximately ten yards, planters displayed colorful arrays of posies. Near one street corner, a performer walked on a tight rope two feet above the ground, and in the next block several musicians played soulful tunes, with their violin cases open for donations. A summer crowd wandered by, people in their cutoffs, T-shirts and Crocs.

They reached the Black Cat and were seated at a table with a crisp white tablecloth.

After their bottle of Bordeaux arrived, Reginald raised his glass to Rebecca. "Thank you for joining me. I've been so wrapped up in work this week, that I appreciate breaking away and having the opportunity to enjoy your company."

Rebecca's eyes sparkled. "You surprise me, Reggie. I thought you were too uptight, but you seem to be loosening up."

He laughed. "You'd be surprised. Your mother says we're a lot alike."

"I don't know whether that's good or bad." She took a sip of wine.

"I think it's good. Definitely good. Tell me more about yourself, Rebecca."

She shrugged. "Nothing special. I grew up in Denver, went to CU, worked in high tech marketing until this year, when I decided to change careers."

"Oh?"

"Yeah. I'm taking sociology classes back at CU. Working on a Master's."

"And your family? Your dad?"

Rebecca twirled the wine in her glass, a faraway look in her eyes. "He died six years ago. Mom fell in a funk for a year, then moved to Sunny Crest. She met Jerry Rhine and has rebounded to her old feisty self again."

"If I'm not prying, I heard that you had been married."

She clicked her tongue. "The major disaster of my life. Peter was a frat boy who caught my interest. We married after graduation, and it lasted only two years. I caught him playing around with an exotic dancer and walked out. Simple as that."

"You're not a woman to be messed with."

Her eyes flared, and she pointed a sharp red nail at him. "And you better remember that."

He held up his palms. "Oh, I will."

She took another sip of wine and put the glass back on the table. "Your turn. What's your story, Reggie?"

"Pretty straightforward. East Coast upbringing. Syracuse undergraduate in finance, then an MBA at Wharton, passed my CPA. Worked for several small firms and then Cenpolis Corporation hired me into the finance department as an accountant. I moved up the ranks to corporate controller, and then Armand Daimler, the CEO, selected me to come here to turn around Sunny Crest."

"Never married?"

"No, my work kept getting in the way. That and never meeting the right woman."

She looked at him thoughtfully. "You don't happen to be gay or a virgin, do you, Reggie?"

He gave a nervous laugh. "Pretty blunt, aren't you, Rebecca? But the answers are no and no."

Her face brightened. "That's a relief."

They both ordered the duo of Colorado Beef, hers medium and his medium rare.

"Now I know you're not a vegetarian," Rebecca said.

"I've cut down on red meat," he said, patting his taut stomach, "but enjoy an occasional steak. Can't eat fish, chicken or veggies all the time."

Her probing eyes regarded him. "You seem pretty fit."

"I try to exercise regularly. Mainly walking. And you, Rebecca, appear to be in fantastic shape."

"Are you hitting on me, Reggie?"

"I'm merely admiring a beautiful woman." He held up his wine glass again.

She clinked it and winked.

The dinner and conversation flew by. It seemed like they had been there for a matter of minutes, but when Rebecca excused herself to go to the powder room, Reginald checked his watch and discovered that they'd been talking nonstop for three hours.

He paid the bill, and they sauntered along the mall. He found her hand in his and tingled at the warmth and pressure of her fingers. Looking in shop windows, watching the local characters and eating ice cream cones passed in what seemed like moments, but when he glanced at his watch again upon returning to his car, over another hour had passed.

Back at Sunny Crest, she pointed out her white BMW in the parking lot.

Reginald pulled in next to it, jumped out, jogged around to the passenger's side of his car, opened the door for her and gave a sweeping gesture with his arm.

She swung her legs out, baring her knees and lower thighs.

He gawked.

"Are you ogling me, Reggie?"

"I'll say."

"Good." She stood and placed her arms around his neck, leaned against him and delivered a passionate kiss.

Reginald felt like he'd stuck a finger in a light socket as his body erupted in electricity. He held her close and returned the kiss until both of them came up for air.

"Thanks for a wonderful evening," Rebecca said in a throaty whisper.

He stepped back, held her hands and admired her face, radiant in the moonlight. "The pleasure was all mine."

They kissed again, and then she grabbed the keys from her purse, opened the door to her car, hopped in, started the engine and backed out. She stopped and rolled down the window. "See you tomorrow at the family dinner." She waved and then drove off into the night.

Reginald stood there wondering what had hit him.

Chapter 14

Reginald awoke Saturday morning, glad for the first time to be in Colorado. He stretched and felt a warm glow permeate his body. Sure, he had a few minor problems: dealing with a possible murder, keeping members of his staff from attacking each other, nearly falling victim to a hired hit man and figuring out how to save Sunny Crest in two weeks. But he had met Rebecca.

Although, in theory, his workweek was done, he had a mission to accomplish, and today he needed to make some progress. Then a pleasant thought popped into his mind. This evening he'd see Rebecca again. Images of ruby red lips filled his brain. He'd fallen for the Dragon Lady.

In the dining room, Reginald grabbed a sweet roll, downed a cup of coffee, which no longer smelled of smoldering socks, and trotted over to Jerry Rhine's table. The three men were all waving their arms around in animated discussion.

"Are all of you Italian?" Reginald asked.

Tom glared at him. "What's that supposed to mean?"

Reginald moved his hands around in circles. "You were all talking with your arms."

"Oh, that," Jerry said. "We like debating politics. None of us agrees on anything. That's why we're such good friends. Tom here is to the right of Attila the Hun, and Al would have been called in front of McCarthy in the '50s if the Committee on Un-American Activities had been able to catch him."

"What about your politics, Jerry?" Reginald asked.

"Oh, I have all the correct answers, not like my two friends."

They thrust their arms airborne, and the Italian debate renewed.

Finally, Reginald leaned toward the table. "Jerry, there's something I'd like to discuss with you."

Jerry put his hand to his ear. "You'll have to speak up, Reggie."

"You and I need to talk, Jerry."

"You're not going to give me more crap about sleeping arrangements, are you?" His eyes narrowed with suspicion. "Particularly since you were seen in the company of Henrietta's daughter last night."

Reginald's cheeks grew warm. "No, this is something completely different. I want to ask you for a favor."

Jerry's eyes glinted. "Good. Then you'll owe me another one."

Reginald nodded at the reference to being rescued from the thug. "That's right. I'll be even more in your debt."

"As long as it doesn't involve anything too illegal."

"No. It's quite legitimate. Given that you do magic tricks, I wonder if you'd be willing to entertain our prospective residents when they visit."

Jerry's eyes grew as large as two DVDs. "You want me to perform magic?"

Tom chuckled, "That's like asking a junkie if he's ready for a fix."

"Or asking Karen if she'd like to go buy shoes," Al said. "That woman may not remember yesterday from yogurt, but she sure recollects that she likes shoes."

Jerry eyed him thoughtfully. "What do you have in mind, Reggie?"

"A simple, informal program to entertain Sunny Crest prospects—something with humor. Mimi Hendrix tells me that when people visit, they often feel uncertain about taking the step of moving into a retirement home. I think a little levity and seeing an active old fart like you doing something silly would do some good. What do you think?"

"Since you put it like that, how can I refuse? Damn, I'll put together a whole routine." Jerry cupped his hands around his mouth and turned toward the women's table. "Hey, Henrietta. Reggie and I have a great addition to your introductory tour."

Reginald slapped Jerry on the back. "Thanks for your enthusiasm. I'll go discuss it with Henrietta."

"I have just the program, and it's available on a moment's notice. I can't wait to get started. I'll wow 'em, Reggie."

"I'm sure you will, Jerry."

Tom dropped his fork onto his plate. "You know this will make him impossible to live with, don't you?"

"We may have to hide his hearing aids if he gets too obnoxious," Al added.

Leaving Jerry gesticulating and telling his buddies which tricks he'd perform, Reginald sauntered over to see the ladies. He bowed and was greeted by three sets of questioning eyes.

"Reggie, what caused Jerry's outburst?" Henrietta asked.

"I proposed that he help out by performing some magic tricks to entertain prospective residents."

"Oh, my God." Belinda slapped her hand to her forehead. "Do you realize what you're saying? Will that attract people or scare them away?"

Karen looked puzzled. "Jerry does magic tricks?"

"Yes, dear." Henrietta patted Karen's hand. "Unfortunately, he does."

"Ladies, where's your enthusiasm? I think this will be a light and humorous way to show prospective residents that this is a fun place to live. We can demonstrate that Sunny Crest exudes life and vitality with the example of you Jerry-atrics."

Henrietta put her right index finger to her cheek. "You know Reggie, you have a point. When I lead tours, it's always the kids trying to sell their parents on the place, and the parents themselves that need the convincing. It's a tough decision, coming to a retirement home. People our age are afraid of losing their independence. It's a slippery slope from here to giving up the car keys and wearing Depends. So I can see how something light and entertaining would be useful... but Jerry?"

"Jerry is enthusiastic, and I would appreciate your support, Henrietta."

"We'll give it a try. But while you're here, Reggie, I heard a rumor that you smooched my daughter in the parking lot last night."

"Actually she smooched me as much as I smooched her." He enjoyed the surprised expression on Henrietta's face, and then the corners of her mouth turned into a pleased grin.

He bowed again. "Have a good day, ladies."

*****

Later that morning Reginald decided to take a stroll around the facility to admire the workings within the great white behemoth. Outside the dining area, he spotted Henrietta leading a group of approximately a dozen visitors. He sidled up to listen to her spiel.

"And next, I'd like to show you our expansive and accommodating dining room. You'll notice the large windows that overlook the open space. We often see deer grazing outside."

A woman in the group sighed.

Reginald half expected to see Jerry Rhine dashing past the window holding antlers over his head and a feather duster behind his butt.

"What kind of food do you serve here?" an old man in a spotted suit asked.

"That's the best part. We have an outstanding chef who keeps us well fed. Our menu has recently been expanded, so you'll find variety and good-sized portions." She gave a purposeful nod in Reginald's direction. "You have three choices of entrees for dinner every night, a regular salad bar and tasty desserts. Main courses include steak, lamb, halibut, salmon, chicken Marsala and lasagna. For breakfast our award-winning chef offers the choice of omelets, pancakes, waffles, French toast and the usual pastry, bagels, cereal, fruit and juices. Lunch includes options of sandwiches or main courses with delicious freshly-baked cookies piled high on a plate in the center of the table."

"Do you have low sugar and low salt diets available?" a woman clutching a small black purse asked.

"Good question. Our chef always has selections available for people on restricted diets and accommodates special requests. Now if you'll step inside, I have a treat for you."

The group went through the sliding door, and Reginald tailgated at the back of the crowd, feeling like a kid sneaking in under a circus tent.

"Please take a seat," Henrietta said, pointing to chairs set up facing a table covered with a black cloth.

Reginald quickly sat in the back row. An undercurrent of whispered voices passed through the crowd as people settled into the chairs. Everyone waited to see what would happen next.

Henrietta moved forward and stood in front of the group. "Now I'd like to introduce the Jerry-atrics." She gestured toward the kitchen door.

Jerry burst through and jogged up to the table, waving to the crowd. He wore a tuxedo and top hat. Behind him followed Karen strutting in a gold sequin outfit and Tom pushing a box on a dolly.

Jerry bowed, took off his hat and showed it to the audience. "As you can see my hat is empty. This is how I felt when I lived alone in my cramped condo. Lonesome and by myself. Then I came to Sunny Crest." He turned his hat away and reached inside, pulling out a bouquet of yellow daisies. He handed them to a matronly woman in the front row. "Now my days are full of sunshine and good friends. Speaking of friends, do you know how many friends I had when I lived in the condo?" He held out a deck of cards to a man in the front row. "Here point to a card, any card."

The man ruffled through the deck and selected a card.

Jerry slid it out and held it up for the audience to see. It was blank. "Now do you know how many friends I have at Sunny Crest?" He presented the deck to a woman wearing a flowered hat who touched a card. Jerry deftly removed the designated card from the deck and held it up to show the number fifty surrounded by many little hearts.

The people tittered and chuckled.

Jerry bowed and received a rousing round of applause.

"Now I'd like to show you how I used to feel when I slept in my condo." He turned the box on the dolly toward the audience and opened the door. Karen climbed in and folded herself into an uncomfortable-looking pretzel position. He closed the door again and unfurled a black cloth that he held in front of the box. "When I moved to Sunny Crest, this is how I slept." He took away the cloth.

Everyone gasped.

Karen floated above the box with her hands on her stomach and her eyes closed, as peaceful as an angel.

Jerry and Tom placed their hands under Karen and lowered her feet to the ground. She stretched, yawned and smiled at the audience.

Everyone applauded.

Henrietta stepped to the front again. "Jerry has resided at Sunny Crest for five years and has the opportunity here to pursue his life-long passion of performing magic tricks. Whatever you enjoy doing, you'll have the chance to follow your dream at Sunny Crest. Now if you'll come with me, I'll show you our fitness center and aquatic area."

Reginald had a sudden desire to be thirty years older and living here. Wait a minute, he did live here.

He remained seated until the group had departed and watched Jerry organize props. Then Reginald jumped up to grab Jerry's hand. "Just what we needed. Quite a show."

"Reggie, you ain't seen nothin' yet. That's what I put together with two hour's notice. Wait until my next performance. I'll dazzle 'em."

*****

That afternoon, Reginald returned to his office to find Mimi Hendrix pacing

105

back and forth.

"What brings you here on a Saturday?" he asked.

"I wanted to work some more on my marketing plan. Do you know what just happened?"

Reginald's heart started racing at the thought of yet another problem. "I hope nothing too terrible."

She gave him a conspiratorial smile. "No, it's good news."

"That I can use."

"We booked four rooms for folks from the group that Henrietta took around on the tour earlier. That's never happened before."

He blinked. "That's great. How many terminations have we had this week?"

"We had two on Tuesday and three on Wednesday, but by Friday they all had changed their minds and decided to stay. No one else gave notice the rest of the week. And two new signups yesterday."

Reginald started calculating. "If we can fill ten more rooms . . ."

"I have groups coming in twice a day, every day next week. If we're even half as successful as today's tour, we should be able to achieve that. Can I start my advertising campaign?"

He waved his hands as if trying to protect himself from an attack by killer bees. "Not yet. I still need to review the justification and work out a few financial details."

"Just remember, we have some momentum now and this is the time to capitalize on our recent successes."

He liked her persistence. "I'll keep that in mind."

After Mimi left, Reginald started recalculating his budget estimates. His fingers danced over the keys of the calculator on the desk. With the increase in food services, the new security system and part of Mimi's promotional plan, he would need to fill twelve rather than ten additional rooms to break even. He looked out his window wishing he could turn prairie grass into paying customers. Could he achieve the necessary number of new residents? Would it be enough to convince Daimler to keep Sunny Crest open?

Chapter 15

In the late afternoon, Reginald took a break from his paperwork. The image of the loading dock area and the dead Willie Pettigrew surged through his brain. Nothing he could do about that today. He decided to explore more of the facility. He hadn't had a chance to visit the aquatic area, so he headed down to the pool located on the first floor of the east wing. In an exercise room, one elderly woman in emerald stretch pants was riding an exercise bike, and a geezer was sweating on a slow-moving treadmill. The pool area consisted of a twenty-five yard pool and a Jacuzzi. Several gray-haired women shuffled around in the shallow end of the pool. Another woman was in the deep end pushing a kickboard in front of her as periodic jets of water shot up from her feet breaking the surface.

"Grab your swimming togs and come join us, Reggie," Jerry bellowed from the hot tub. "The water's just the right temperature."

He approached the six Jerry-atrics soaking there. "Not today, but I'll have to try it out one of these days. I heard from Mimi Hendrix that we'll have some new residents from today's group of visitors."

"Henrietta leads a mean tour," Jerry said. "She flirts with all the old codgers, and they immediately sign up to move in here."

Henrietta elbowed him. "To say nothing of the entertainment."

"We all needed to relax after the activity today," Tom said. "Jerry made me lug that heavy box from his room down to the dining room and back."

"The exercise is good for you, Tom." Jerry splashed some water in his face.

This led to a retaliatory squirt from Tom's fist held at water level.

"Gentlemen, please behave yourselves," Henrietta wiped some drops off her face. "We don't need this rowdy behavior after the show."

"Show, y'all?" Karen gave a blank stare. "What show?"

"When you wore the sequined costume, dear," Henrietta said.

"Oh, yes."

"I appreciate all of your efforts," Reginald said. "This will really help keep Sunny Crest solvent."

"We aim to please," Jerry replied. "Now, I'm loosened up enough to make a practice pass at the senior triathlon."

"You mean for the event that Mimi is proposing?" Reginald asked.

"Exactly. She doesn't have it scheduled yet." He curled an eyebrow in Reginald's direction. "Something about funds needing to be approved. Do you know what tightwad is keeping that from happening, Reggie?"

"Well. . . uh. . . yeah. . . uh, it's still under evaluation."

Jerry lifted himself out of the Jacuzzi, grabbed a towel and flicked it at Reginald. "After all we've done for you, Reggie, I'd expect you'd be jumping all over this activity. Keeps us fit and makes Sunny Crest look good. A win-win all around."

"I'll give it due consideration."

"Okay, Reggie, at least come watch my practice session." Jerry sauntered over to the pool. "First the swimming." He dove in and swam freestyle with smooth, fluid strokes. After four laps, he climbed out of the shallow end of the pool and toweled off.

"You swim very well, Jerry."

"Used to compete as a kid. Something you never forget. Now onto the bike. Follow me." He padded out of the aquatic area and headed to the exercise room and climbed on a stationary bike, put his feet in the straps and started pedaling like crazy.

"You're obviously in good shape, Jerry, but can all your companions keep up with you?"

"Sure. I'll whoop 'em in the actual event, but they'll all complete the race."

"Even Al?"

"Especially Al. He'll have to warm up in the Jacuzzi ahead of time to loosen his joints, but once he gets going, he'll do fine. You'll have to give this a try as well, Reggie."

"I haven't ridden a bike in twenty years."

"No time like the present to start again. A young kid like you should have no trouble with this triathlon."

Reginald didn't want to participate in something where an eighty-year-old would beat him. "When Mimi schedules the triathlon, I'll officiate."

Jerry chuckled. "Good. You sound more certain this will happen. I figure we should hold it in approximately a month. I'll be in peak condition then."

"I'll pass your request on to Mimi. I've always wondered why triathlons start with swimming and then bike riding."

Jerry's feet kept pedaling, and he gave no indication of being winded. "It's simple, Reggie. Get the swimming out of the way when the athletes are fresh so no one drowns. You wouldn't want any floaters in your event, would you? Then ride the bikes to dry off and make sure the legs can keep the pedals moving and people don't wobble into each other. The running part is the least risky and so it goes last."

"Makes sense." Reginald couldn't believe all the things he was learning from these old farts.

Next, Jerry hopped off the bike, set the speed on the treadmill and stepped aboard. His arms began swinging as he strode at a good clip.

"Is there anything you can't do, Jerry?"

"I'm not much at corncobs, Reggie, and I'm glad to see that you've given up yours. I think Rebecca is having a good influence on you."

Pleasant memories surged through Reginald's brain. "Yeah, she's quite a gal."

"Takes after her mother." Jerry turned off the machine and grabbed a towel to wipe sweat off his forehead. "I think I'll head back to the Jacuzzi to keep my muscles loose. I understand we'll be seeing you tonight, Reggie."

"Wouldn't miss it."

*****

That evening Reginald rummaged through his closet, trying to decide what to wear. He instinctively reached for his dark suit but stopped himself in mid-flight. No, he wouldn't wear a suit and tie. Instead, he selected a pair of Dockers and a Brooks Brothers long-sleeved shirt. He admired himself in the mirror—a good casual outfit for an evening with the Dragon Lady and the Jerry-atrics.

He paced the foyer waiting for Rebecca to arrive. He looked at a large vase of fresh flowers decorating the lobby and immediately thought of how much they cost. Then he caught himself. They made the place look cheerful and appealing. He had to retrain himself. He was seeking more residents not just cutting costs. He resumed pacing.

Jerry sauntered up. "You look a little nervous, Reggie."

"Merely waiting for my guest."

"Hot date tonight, I hear."

As a diversionary tactic, Reginald gave Jerry the accountant's stare and changed the subject. "Are you going to be performing as part of the program this evening?"

"Nah. Nothing formal. I did my main entertaining for the visitors today." He flexed his arms, reached up his sleeve and pulled out a single red rose. "Here's something for your date."

Reginald took the flower. "And what an effective show. I want to thank you again for helping with our efforts to attract new residents."

"Hey, happy to be of service. Now maybe you'll keep Henrietta on with her unpaid job as official greeter and tour guide."

"You two are quite a duo."

"Yeah. Not bad for a pair of oldsters. Now don't get all hot and bothered waiting for Rebecca. See you inside, Reggie." Jerry slapped Reginald on the back and headed off toward the dining room.

Reginald kept his eyes peeled and finally spotted a white BMW pulling into a parking space. He waited a moment, took a deep breath and then strolled outside as if he had arrived at that moment himself.

Rebecca sashayed toward him in a slinky red dress.

"You're gorgeous." He handed her the rose. "Something of beauty to complement a beautiful woman."

She parted her red lips, revealing pearly white teeth. "You look quite dapper yourself, Reggie. No suit tonight?"

"No, I've reformed."

She grabbed his hand, leaned toward him and planted a juicy kiss on his cheek. "Let's go find my mom."

They entered the dining room and made their way to a table for eight where Jerry, Henrietta, Al, Karen, Tom and Belinda sat.

"I thought this was a family dinner," Reginald said to the group. "Aren't other relatives of yours coming to sit with us?"

"This is our whole crowd," Jerry replied. "Rebecca happens to be the one attending for the Jerry-atrics tonight, and, Reggie, you're an honorary member."

"I couldn't imagine a better family to be a part of."

Jerry pointed his fork at him. "You remember that. We want everyone to keep living here. Don't shut this place down, Reggie."

Reginald gave him a friendly salute. "Don't you have any other family members attend these dinners?"

Tom placed his hands on the table and leaned toward Reginald, who had a momentary fear that the table would collapse. "Sometimes Jerry's mom joins us."

Reginald's jaw dropped. "His mom? She'd have to be over a hundred years old."

Jerry gave a satisfied nod. "Yup. A hundred and one to be exact. Still going strong."

"She puts the rest of us to shame," Al added. "Even plays golf. She has arthritis like me but still moves around using a cane."

"Why isn't she here tonight?" Henrietta tapped Jerry's arm.

Jerry unfurled his napkin and dropped it in his lap. "She had a hot date."

"Well, she could have brought her beau," Belinda said.

"I told her that." Jerry straightened his silverware as if he were getting ready for inspection. "She said she didn't want to bring him here with all the kids around. Thought it would cramp her style." Jerry looked up. "Close your mouth, Reggie."

Reginald snapped his jaw shut, realizing that he had been gaping. He had enough trouble accepting the romantic urges of octogenarians. Now Jerry's mother at over a hundred?

"You'll get a chance to meet Maude one of these days, Reggie. My mom is quite a gal. You'll get a kick out of her." He chuckled.

"Like the time she booted the previous director in the butt because he wouldn't give Jerry a discount on his room and board?" Tom asked.

"Yeah," Jerry replied. "She's not much on taking no for an answer."

"Must run in the family," Reginald said.

Maurice Casotti had come through with an outstanding menu, and they feasted on shrimp cocktail, lobster bisque, grilled halibut and crème brulee. Reginald closed his eyes as each dish arrived, sniffing the culinary delights. After dinner, the activities director, Vicki Pearson, approached their table, leaned over and whispered, "Mr. Bentley, we'd like you to make a few comments. You can stand and address folks from here."

Reginald raised himself from the chair, and Jerry picked up his fork and began tapping his water glass like a xylophone player. In moments the room had hushed.

Reginald took a sip of water and scanned the crowd of expectant faces. "My name is Reginald Bentley, but if you're like the people at my table you can call me Reggie."

Jerry clapped his hands, and Henrietta elbowed him in the ribs.

"I'm the new executive director of Sunny Crest and want to thank all of you who have joined us tonight. Sunny Crest is an outstanding residence because of the people here."

"Just a minute, Reggie," Jerry said, standing up next to him. "There seems to be something on the back of your head." He reached over and a white dove flew up to the ceiling.

Everyone laughed.

"Where else could you have a wonderful meal, followed by the enchanting magic of our own Jerry Rhine?" Reginald gestured toward Jerry who bowed to a round of applause.

"Sunny Crest isn't merely a building with rooms," Reginald continued. "It's a vital community consisting of staff members dedicated to providing outstanding services, and of residents living the lifestyle they choose. I welcome all of you and your family guests here tonight and look forward to many more occasions such as this evening." He sat down to another round of applause.

"Short and sweet," Jerry commented.

"After the dove showed up, I couldn't add a thing. By the way, I notice it's perched right above your head, Jerry. I hope it's housebroken."

Jerry looked up and then placed a white linen napkin on top of his head.

Rebecca leaned close and whispered in his ear, "You have a way with words, Reggie."

He shrugged. "I've had to give my fair share of corporate talks."

She squeezed his arm. "But you sounded genuine."

Reginald thought for a moment. Yes, this place now meant a great deal to him. To say nothing of the attractive woman breathing on his neck.

"How do you plan to retrieve that dove?" Al asked.

"I'll wait until everyone leaves and put some birdseed on the floor." Jerry removed the napkin from his head. "There's some birdseed stored right here in Reggie's ear." He reached over and extracted a handful of seeds. "You been growing something in there, Reggie?"

"Lots of new ideas sprouting." He winked at Jerry and turned toward Rebecca. "Your mother and friends put on quite a program today for a group of visitors. And Jerry's next gig may be in Las Vegas."

"Nah," Jerry said, dusting the seeds into an empty dish. "Sunny Crest provides the right venue for me. I gave up my public ambitions when the

Ed Sullivan Show went off the air."

After dinner the older generation headed off to the Rec Room to watch a DVD of *Casablanca*.

"Would you like to see the movie or take a walk?" Reginald asked Rebecca.

"Let's go outside."

Stars began to twinkle in the dusk as they strolled close together along the pathway. He put his arm around Rebecca's waist, and she leaned toward him. They came to a bench and sat down to watch the last faint pink in a cloud over the Continental Divide. Rebecca snuggled against him, and he held her tight.

"You think you'll be at Sunny Crest long, Reggie?"

"If I'm successful at turning it around, I would expect to stay here at least two years. But that's assuming a lot. The financial picture isn't very pretty, and my boss has given me a very short fuse."

"What if you're not able to turn it around?"

"Then I'll probably have an opportunity to look for a new job."

Rebecca winced. "Your boss can't be that ruthless."

"Oh, he can, and he is. Armand Daimler only cares for bottom-line results, not people."

"That's the way you appeared when I first met you, Reggie. But now I think you do care about people."

"Particularly you, Rebecca."

They found themselves locked in an embrace, and their lips met, sending sparks through his whole body.

They both gave a start at the sound of rustling in the bushes, but it was only a rabbit scampering off, apparently disrupted by their loud smooching. It bounded across the lawn and disappeared into the tall grass of the open space.

"What do you want to be when you grow up, Reggie?"

"First, I don't think I want to grow up, and if I did, I'd want to be with you, Rebecca."

She leaned close against him and rested her head on his shoulder. "It's too bad we didn't meet when we were younger."

"We'll just have to make up for it." He took her chin in his hand and gave her a long, deep kiss.

"You're not bad at that, Reggie."

He smiled. "I haven't had much practice lately, but you definitely inspire me."

They watched a cloud move out from in front of a silver half-moon, providing enough light for them to see each other's glowing cheeks.

"I'd like to stay with you tonight, Reggie."

His body jolted as a shot of adrenaline spiked through his system. "My bachelor pad isn't much, but I can't think of anything I'd rather do than be with you."

They stood and held hands as they headed back toward the building. Inside, not wanting to wait for the slow elevator, they dashed up the four flights of stairs, Rebecca giggling like a schoolgirl. When they reached Reginald's apartment, he opened the door and checked both directions to make sure no one saw them. Then he leaned over and raised Rebecca's svelte, sexy body and carried her across the threshold.

She kissed him as he held her in his arms. "This didn't even happen on my wedding night."

"Then it's the perfect time." He set her down, thankful that they both had stayed in good shape.

She looked around the bare walls of the living room. "You definitely need some decorating, Reggie."

"I haven't had time to do anything yet."

"Maybe I can help you, but not right now." She kissed him again, and he led her into the bedroom.

"This room looks just as bare as your living room. We may have to make it barer." She reached out and unbuckled his belt.

They began grabbing at each other, and soon an untidy shambles of clothes covered the carpet. Rebecca pulled down the covers and hopped into bed, patting the mattress for him to follow. He admired her full breasts above a slim waist and rounded hips. A part of his anatomy that had been on vacation while he worked too much came to attention. Their bodies met as their mouths, chests, stomachs, hips pressed together.

Every cell of his body felt like exploding. Then they merged into one, and the mattress began to shake. For a guy out of practice he held his own, and they both gasped as his hips thrust forward and Rebecca shuddered.

They lay there breathing heavily and then kissed deeply again. When he later rolled off her, Rebecca pulled the covers up, turned on her side and fell asleep.

Reginald lay there half awake, his eyes shut but seeing a kaleidoscope of colors whirling inside his eyelids. Flashes of red, green, orange and blue shot through his Rebecca-drugged mind as if he had plunked down in the middle of a fireworks display. Then he drifted off into a blissful sleep.

*****

The next thing Reginald knew the lights flashed on, and a man's voice shouted, "Oh my God. Whose parents am I going to have to notify first?"

Chapter 16

Reginald blinked and rubbed his eyes as he sat up in bed, finding Jerry Rhine in the bedroom doorway with his arms crossed.

Rebecca ducked under the covers.

"What are you doing here?" Reginald demanded.

"The door was unlocked. In the heat of the moment, I guess you forgot to lock it." Jerry chuckled.

"You might have knocked first," Reginald huffed.

"Hell, people never knock on my door before they burst in." He pointed to the floor. "Kind of messy place you keep here. Look at all these scattered duds."

"Why are you in my apartment in the middle of the night, Jerry?"

"Henrietta saw Rebecca's car still here and got worried."

"So you came here to check on her?"

"Right. Don't want Henrietta being upset all night. She's much more passionate when she's relaxed."

"Too much information," came a muffled response from under the covers.

"Hey, Reggie. You have a talking bed. That's something I could use for one of my magic shows."

Reginald held his chin high, trying to look as dignified as possible, which was impossible. "Well, you can assure Henrietta that things are very much under control."

"I'd say that things are under the blanket."

"Jerry, do you always wander around in the middle of the night?"

"Yeah. I don't need much sleep anymore. I often roam the halls. Don't usually come to the high rent district though." He laughed. "Or come across such a compromising scene. But I'm glad everything is copacetic."

"Well, thanks for your concern." Reginald pointed toward the door. "We'd like our privacy now."

"Okay. Good seeing you too, Rebecca."

A few fingers peeked out of the blanket and waved.

The light went out, and the door closed.

"That certainly was an unexpected visit," Reginald said.

"Since we're awake anyway, we might as well make the most of it," Rebecca said, climbing on top of him.

*****

The next morning they slept late, and after each dashed to the bathroom, they made love again.

Afterwards Reginald said, "You're very addictive. I don't think I ever want to go back to work again."

Rebecca twirled a hair on his chest. "I can't see you lying here in our cozy nest until the bulldozers come to demolish the building."

*****

They finally surfaced again around noon.

Rebecca leaped out of bed and began collecting her strewn clothes. "I have a cat that will destroy my apartment if I don't head home."

Reginald admired the view for a moment and then slung his legs out of bed. "I'm not letting you get away that easily. What if I come with you and then we go up in the high country to enjoy this summer afternoon? I still haven't seen the mountains up close and could use a tour guide. I'll drive and you can leave your car here."

She shook her head. "No way. My mom will go nuts if she sees my car still here this afternoon. We'll drive separately. You can follow me."

He put on his hiking clothes and Rebecca her sexy red dress. Then they snuck down the stairwell and out to their cars. As they headed down the driveway, Jerry Rhine stood alongside the road waving.

Reginald followed Rebecca's car and had to push the pedal to the metal to keep up with her. The Dragon Lady liked to move quickly. As their cars approached the intersection of Twenty-eighth and Arapahoe, the light changed to yellow. Rebecca shot through. Not wanting to lose her, he followed as the light turned red. He saw a flash like a strobe light go off but refocused on her white BMW to reduce the space between them.

*****

Reginald parked on a street in downtown Boulder and followed Rebecca up to a loft much more impressive than his place. It resembled a modern art museum with colorful abstract paintings dotting the wall, metal sculptures in the corners and a collection of pottery lining the shelves.

He shook his head. "You're definitely going to have to help me decorate my monk's cell."

"I think you've given up your monk status after last night."

"You're the best thing that's ever happened to me, Rebecca."

Right at that moment a streak of white shot past. He recoiled. "What's that?"

"That's Princess. Come here, kitty." She clicked her tongue and a white Persian cat scampered over and rubbed against Rebecca's leg.

The cat regarded Reginald with a wary eye.

"Is that thing dangerous?" he asked.

"Princess?" She laughed. "Not unless you're afraid of your leg being rubbed to death when she does one of her fuzz-bys."

He pulled Rebecca toward him in an embrace and planted a deep kiss on her lips.

She gasped and pushed him away. "I need to change. I'm not going to let you seduce me again. We have a date to go up in the mountains." She pointed to Princess. "You two can entertain each other while I get ready."

He sat down on a reddish brown couch to wait. Before he knew it, Princess jumped up on the couch and maneuvered onto his lap. She turned around three times, kneaded his legs with her front paws, plopped down and curled into a ball.

He sat there in dismay. He hadn't touched a cat since one scratched his hand when he tried to pick it up as a kid. He gingerly risked putting a hand on the cat's fur. It felt soft and silky. He ran his hand along Princess's back. Suddenly, a noise emerged from the cat like a combination of sawing and humming. The damn cat purred and rubbed its head against his arm. He chucked it under the chin and the sound increased.

Suddenly he experienced a feeling of guilt. He was playing hooky. He wondered if Detective Aranello took days off in the middle of a murder investigation. Reginald hoped the detective would soon find out what happened to Willie Pettigrew so the suspicious death wouldn't be looming over the future of Sunny Crest. He pushed aside those thoughts as Rebecca emerged from the bedroom wearing brown hiking shorts, a long-sleeved tan shirt and a baseball cap.

"Well, look at you two," she said.

Reginald admired her succulent thighs and whistled. "You're as sexy in a bush outfit as in that red dress."

"Why thank you. Now quit trying to distract me. I'll feed the cat, pack a picnic lunch, and then we'll get going. Speaking of the cat, you must really rate. Usually Princess runs away from strangers, and here she is in your lap."

"I'm not a stranger."

"No, Princess liking you is a very solid endorsement. I guess you've been accepted as part of the family." Rebecca whisked into the kitchen, attracting both his interest and that of Princess. Princess arched her back, stretched, gave Reginald a contented gaze, hopped off his lap without scratching him and strutted into the kitchen to consume her meal.

He stuck his head into the kitchen to see Princess gobbling some gray slimy stuff that looked like liver pâté in extra grease. Then Rebecca emerged, holding a picnic basket in her slender hand.

*****

Reginald agreed to drive, and after they headed downstairs to get in his car, he noticed an envelope under the driver-side wiper. "Damn, a parking violation."

"Please, my delicate ears." Then Rebecca pointed to the curb. "You're part way into a red zone, Reggie. You always this careless?"

"I guess I'm completely distracted by the beautiful woman with me."

Rebecca directed him to drive up Boulder Canyon where they passed sheer cliffs with young people climbing and hanging from precarious rock formations. Boulder Creek gushed over rocks and submerged branches, and Reginald gushed over Rebecca. "I can't get over how lucky I am. You're an incredible woman."

"I guess it's better to be the incredible woman than the Dragon Lady."

After they arrived at the Hessie trailhead, past the town of Eldora, they crossed Boulder Creek, climbed a hillside covered with yellow, purple, white and pink displays of golden banner, lupine, wallflowers and wild rose, and then re-crossed the creek.

"There's a waterfall a hundred yards ahead," Rebecca said.

Finding a spot on a rock overlooking the surging whitewater, Rebecca spread out a blanket, unpacked sandwiches and drinks for their first meal of the day.

"I thought I'd pass out from lack of nutrition after the hike and all you did to me earlier," Reginald said.

"I don't want to be around any wimps. I'm only testing you."

"I hope I passed." He took a bite of sandwich as the turkey and American cheese tingled his tongue.

"Yes. With flying colors."

After finishing their food, they continued up to Lost Lake and then explored some of the abandoned mine sites nearby. They clambered over a pile of yellow tailings and peeked inside an old wooden shack. While inspecting a large rusted boiler with an embossed manufacture date of 1910, Reginald said, "Can you image bringing this up that hillside?"

"Or living up here during a long, cold winter?"

He grabbed her hand. "I wouldn't mind being trapped up here with you, Rebecca."

"You're sweet, but I think you'd go stir crazy in eight feet of snow and having to chew on the heels of your shoes for nourishment."

"I noticed we passed some grass-covered ski slopes on the way up. Do you ski?"

Rebecca's face brightened. "I try to get out a dozen or so times a season. I'm an adequate intermediate skier."

"We'll have to go up together. I've skied in Vermont but never in the Rockies."

"You'll enjoy it. Powder and hard pack, not the ice of the East Coast."

"Speaking of ice, will you be able to join me for drinks and dinner tonight?"

Rebecca frowned. "Not tonight. I have a dinner with two of my friends—women friends, that is."

"Just as long as it's not with any men friends. Would you be available tomorrow night?"

She placed a finger to her cheek and gazed off in the distance above the pine forest. "Let me think if I can make it." Then she put her arms around his neck and gave him a passionate kiss before stepping back at arm's length to look at him. She ran her tongue over her teeth. "Yes, I think I can schedule it."

As they hiked back, he felt in his pocket and realized that in all the excitement, he had left his cell phone back at his apartment. Oh, well, it was Sunday. He figured no one would need to reach him anyway.

*****

Resisting the urge to get to know Rebecca even better, Reginald dropped her off at her apartment and drove back to Sunny Crest. The car seemed to drive itself, skimming over the streets of Boulder. As he floated up the walkway, Hector Lopez burst through the front door. "Boss, we have a major emergency."

Chapter 17

Reginald stared at health services director Hector Lopez, wondering if the emergency was of the Jerry-and-Henrietta carnal variety or the dead-body-on-the-loading-dock type. Hector impatiently tapped the toe of his shoe as the white façade of Sunny Crest loomed over him.

"I've been trying to reach you on your cell phone all afternoon, Boss. I kept getting your voicemail."

"I'm sorry. It's Sunday and I didn't have it with me."

"Emergencies happen any time." Hector scowled. "I had planned to go on a picnic with my family today, but I had to cover this problem."

"I'm sorry you couldn't reach me. What happened?"

"Mrs. Rasputin in 804 broke her hip."

Reginald headed into the building with Hector next to him. "And where is she now?"

"An ambulance took her to Boulder Community Hospital. She's scheduled for surgery. But that's not all of it."

Reginald raised an eyebrow. "Go on."

"One of her relatives is all up in arms over her injury. Her lawyer grandson says he's going to sue Sunny Crest and you personally for a bunch of money."

Reginald came to a screeching halt in front of the reception desk. "Me?"

"That's right. He heard that you had instigated cost-cutting programs and blames her accident on you because your expense-reduction measures caused unsafe conditions at Sunny Crest."

"That's absurd. How did she break her hip?"

Hector lowered his eyes as if he needed to check the carpet for unwanted crawling members of the Formicidae family. "She fell down in the bathtub."

"How can that be my fault?"

Hector continued to inspect the rug. "There was no safety railing in her tub."

Reginald headed over to the elevator and punched the button. "I thought we had safety railings in all the bathrooms."

Hector followed him. "We do, but the one in Mrs. Rasputin's apartment had been removed. Nolan Rasputin claims that your financial direction led to the lack of timely repair of the safety railing in her tub, and, therefore, you're responsible for her injury."

"That's ridiculous."

"Maybe so, but he's going to file a lawsuit, and we may have trouble with our insurance covering Sunny Crest and you."

"Why is that?" Reginald pounded on the button again, but the elevator from slow-as-molasses hell didn't appear.

"Alicia added a negligence clause to the contract this week as a step to reduce our insurance premium per your directive to cut expenses. If we're negligent, then we're not covered by the insurance. And this lawyer grandson is making a major issue that you and Sunny Crest are negligent."

"Why would the safety railing have been taken out and not replaced in her tub?"

"I don't know, but I have a call in to Dex Hanley. He'll have to check with his maintenance crew tomorrow."

The elevator doors opened, and a hunched-over old woman emerged. She whacked Reginald on the shin with her cane and pushed past him. He grimaced in pain and pictured a lawyer going through his pockets, while he hung upside down from a rafter.

*****

Sunday night found Reginald staring blankly at the wall in his apartment. It was as if someone had scooped out the inside of his chest. He couldn't ever remember that feeling before. And he knew it wasn't indigestion or a heart attack. He wanted to be with Rebecca every possible chance. He would do everything he could for this relationship to work. Had he finally found his woman?

He paced around his deserted apartment thinking over all that had happened to him in the last week—the sudden move to Colorado, his initial attempts to cut expenses, the quirky characters he'd met. Then he flinched and balled his fists. And the suspicious death. He made a mental note to follow up with Detective Aranello in the morning.

He had difficulty falling asleep as he tossed and turned with visions of lawyers sailing down Boulder Creek in bathtubs and shooting arrows at him that looked like safety railings but turned into rolled up legal documents.

*****

After a hasty breakfast Monday morning, Reginald pulled his staff together for a meeting. They looked as happy to see him as he was to face the lawyer grandson.

"First thing, I want to know why Mrs. Rasputin's tub didn't have the safety railing installed." He stared at Dex Hanley.

"I've looked into it, Chief." He scratched his head. "Very strange. I can't figure out what the deal is. The safety railing used to be in her tub, but someone removed it. I've checked, and none of my staff did it. No one knows what happened."

"I've seen your people do some pretty weird things," Hector said.

Dex glared at Hector. "You stay out of this."

"All right, you two. No more of this infighting." Reginald turned his attention back to Dex. "So in addition to all the other things going on around here, do we have someone stealing safety railings from our residents' bathrooms?"

Dex shook his head. "No. It's not missing. Benny found it stashed in the corner of her bathroom."

Reginald pushed both palms onto the table and leaned toward him. "And no one noticed before that it wasn't installed?"

Dex flinched as though he'd been attacked. "I guess not." He swiveled toward Hector and gave him the evil eye. "Maybe housekeeping should have said something to alert us to the missing railing."

"My people aren't responsible for fixing your mistakes," Hector sputtered, shaking his fist at Dex.

"Enough already." Reginald collapsed back into his chair. "Very odd. Anything new on Mrs. Rasputin's condition?"

"So far, so good," Hector said. "She'll be in the hospital for three to five days."

"And I understand our insurance may not cover this." Reginald looked at Alicia Renton.

"That's right. Remember, you told me to reduce the insurance premiums.

The revision with the liability rider appeared to be the only opportunity to do that. Your cost-cutting directive led to us assuming more risk."

Reginald sighed. "Okay. Go back to the original policy, and we'll have to work around this situation."

"It would have been a lot easier never to have changed it in the first place," Alicia mumbled under her breath.

"I heard that," Reginald said. "And you're right."

Alicia looked surprised.

"On another subject, Belinda Davenport and Karen Landry indicated an interest in helping out in the business office. Did they contact you, Alicia?"

"Yes. They both showed up last Friday. I put them to work immediately. Karen said she had been a legal secretary and volunteered to help with filing. Belinda agreed to assist with typing."

Reginald tried to give an encouraging smile, but he sensed it only appeared like he was gritting his teeth. "Does that make up for the staff person you wanted to add?"

Alicia hesitated. "Not. . . exactly."

"Something isn't working?"

Alicia let out a sigh strong enough to blow out all the candles on an octogenarian's birthday cake. "Belinda is fine, but Karen's lack of short-term memory causes problems. She files things and then can't remember where. I'm spending more time searching for documents she files than was saved by having her file them. I hate to consider it, but I may have to dismiss Karen from her volunteer job."

"Maybe you could switch Belinda and Karen's roles," Reginald said. "Karen should still have excellent typing skills. You could train Belinda to do the filing, and she'd remember."

Alicia regarded him thoughtfully. "Belinda plans to be out of town for a while, but I'll give it a try when she gets back and see if that works any better. In the meantime I'll restrict Karen to typing."

Reginald looked around the table at the other members of his staff. "Dex, why don't you give an update on the new security system?"

Dex's face lit up with a huge grin. "Today, we begin setting up our new security and surveillance system. You'll see workmen here in an hour installing cameras and new mechanisms on all the outside doors. This will really improve our security."

"It's about time," Hector said. "Your security people should have caught that scam artist ages ago. We don't want any more criminals sneaking in."

Reginald rapped on the table. "Dex, go ahead."

"We'll be alerted if someone tries that," Dex said. "We'll also have to notify all the residents that the emergency door alarms will now be armed at night. We don't want anyone accidently setting off the new alarm."

"How long will this take to be implemented?" Alicia asked.

Dex looked as proud as a new father snapping pictures through the hospital nursery window. "Everything will be completed on Wednesday."

"Thanks, Dex. Now, Mimi. Give us a report on occupancy rate."

"We lost no residents last week and are approaching ninety percent occupancy with new clients scheduled from the flurry of activity on Saturday. The Jerry-atrics made quite a hit with our new prospects. In addition to the signups, I received numerous positive comments from visitors on the tour regarding the new program."

"Yes," Reginald said. "Let's keep that show running."

"Jerry approached me afterwards," Mimi said, "and asked for us to give him ten percent of all new sales for his contribution."

Reginald almost spit out his mouthful of coffee. "What?"

Mimi's eyes crinkled mirthfully. "I had the same reaction you did, but he pulled a bouquet of flowers out of my hair, handed it to me and said he was kidding."

*****

After the meeting when Reginald returned to his office, Jerry sauntered in, resplendent in a bright orange Hawaiian shirt.

"Hey, Reggie. We need to talk."

"Come on in."

He plopped down in a chair facing the desk. "Reggie, I notice you have some scratch marks."

Reginald automatically put his hand to the back of his neck, remembering exactly how he had received those in the heat of passion.

Jerry chuckled. "I hope you used some kind of protection the other night during your little romp with Henrietta's daughter. We don't need any little Reggies wandering around this place in nine months."

Reginald suddenly had an interest in the ceiling tiles.

"That's the advantage of being old, Reggie. Henrietta and I don't need to worry our heads over that sort of thing. If something happened, we'd make a million bucks and have an entry in the Guinness Book of World Records."

Reginald regarded him warily. "Does this visit have a purpose?"

Jerry winked at him. "We're all dying of curiosity. What are your intentions regarding Rebecca?"

"You sound like her father."

"Well, yeah. Since her real father died a number of years ago, I'm the surrogate. Shall I get my shotgun?"

A smug smile appeared on Reginald's face. "I'm sure my intentions are as honorable as yours with Henrietta."

Jerry nodded. "Good. The mother of the Dragon Lady and I might be getting hitched sometime. I'll tell Henrietta there may be a double wedding in the works."

Reginald thrust his hands out, knocking over his pen holder-award he'd received as a commendation for reducing the corporate overhead rate by two percent three years ago. "Whoa. Don't jump the gun. Rebecca and I haven't progressed that far yet."

Jerry picked up the pen, which had sailed out of the holder and landed in his lap. He set it back on the desk. "I thought of hiring Al Thiebodaux to snap some pictures of you the other night. That might be good blackmail if you start cutting costs again, but I didn't want to compromise the Dragon Lady."

"You're all heart, Jerry."

"But I have my eye on you." Jerry pointed forked fingers in his best Robert De Niro impersonation.

In spite of himself, Reginald laughed. "As long as you're here, I have a favor to ask."

Jerry looked at him askance. "You're going to end up even deeper in my debt. What could your cost-cutting, conniving mind be up to now?"

"It's nothing like that. It's a personnel issue. I've inherited a good staff, but I have one problem. Dex Hanley and Hector Lopez get along as well as two bucks during mating season. I've tried everything but can't get them to work together cooperatively. Neither threats nor encouragement have kept them from squabbling."

"Yup. I've seen how those two act. Like two little kids drawing a line in the dirt and daring the other to cross over. You think I can help?"

"Don't you have some magic pixie dust or something you can throw on them to make them act like normal human beings?"

Jerry gave an eye roll. "I could make them disappear, but I can't make them get along."

127

Reginald shuffled an unsigned requisition around on his desk. "Since you know a lot that goes on around here, I thought you might have some ideas."

"Let me noodle on it a little, Reggie, and see what I can come up with. There's always itching powder that could be applied every time they start bickering."

Reginald batted his hand as if hitting a tennis backhand, careful to not knock anything over this time. "Get out of here. I have work to do."

"By the way, keep this place open, Reggie. You wouldn't want all of us old farts turning into homeless bums."

Jerry left the office only to be replaced by Alicia, who stomped in and thrust a document onto the desk. "Mrs. Rasputin's grandson has sued us."

Reginald picked it up and read how Sunny Crest and Reginald Bentley III had perpetrated gross negligence and, consequently, were facing a lawsuit for two point three million dollars for medical expenses, mental anguish and punitive damages."

He shook his head. "Do we have a lawyer we use?"

"Yes. Larry Samuelson. But I don't have any money in my budget to cover legal expenses. We haven't had any problems until. . ."

"I know. Until I came here. See if you can reach him and have him come over this afternoon."

"Okay, but that will shoot my budget."

"I understand. I won't hold this against you."

Alicia spun on her heels and stalked out of the office. Before he could look down to read the lawsuit in more detail, Hector Lopez charged into the office.

"Boss, we have another problem."

Chapter 18

Reginald thought of renaming Sunny Crest, Problems-Are-Us, as he stared at his health services and housekeeping manager. "What now?"

Hector looked around the office as if checking for hidden recording devices, twiddled his thin moustache and said in a soft voice, "I'm following up on a report of stolen jewels. Karen Landry can't find her diamond necklace."

"She has short-term memory loss. She probably misplaced it."

"No, Boss. I spent time up there with one of the housekeeping maids, and we went through every inch of her apartment. No necklace."

"And you're sure she really has this necklace, and it isn't a figment of her imagination or poor memory?"

"Yeah, Boss. I've seen her wear it before."

Reginald had an image of another criminal creeping into the building and raiding the jewelry boxes of all the little old ladies. "Has Karen called the police?"

"Not yet."

"Ask your staff to check the entire facility. Have you had any problems with any of your employees taking things?"

Hector looked aghast. "Never. The people we hire are honest."

"There's always a first time."

"I'd trust any of my folks with my wallet, and there'd never be a dollar missing."

Reginald scowled. "I hope you're right. Please get back to me this afternoon, and then if the necklace hasn't turned up, we'll talk to Karen to determine if she wants to call the police."

"Did I hear someone mention calling the police?" Detective Aranello stuck his head in the office.

Damn. Reginald didn't want Aranello overhearing this discussion, but it couldn't be avoided now.

Hector looked from side to side, then leaned forward and in a too-loud whisper said, "The stolen necklace?"

"What stolen necklace?" Aranello asked.

Reginald cleared his throat. "We're not sure if a necklace has been stolen or lost. If it appears to be stolen, that wouldn't be in your jurisdiction, would it?"

"No, that would be the responsibility of the general crime detectives." Aranello stared at him. "If that's the case, it would give Sunny Crest a clean sweep—involving all three of our detective departments with the scam, suspicious death and theft. I didn't know a retirement home could be such a hotbed of crime."

"It didn't used to be that way before. . ." Hector caught himself in mid-sentence and twitched.

"I know. Before I came here. Look, Detective, I've asked Hector to check this out, and we'll call your department this afternoon if the necklace doesn't turn up. I think it's too early to report a theft."

"Have it your way," Aranello said with a shrug. "Now I need to speak with you regarding the suspicious death."

"I'm out of here." Hector scurried away.

"Okay, Detective, I want to talk to you as well. What's on your mind?"

Aranello dropped into a visitor's chair. "Best indication is that the death took place between one and four in the morning. We've finished checking out your staff and residents again. Same as before. No one saw or heard anything. I would have thought that someone would have been wandering around at that time."

"I guess these people sleep pretty soundly. Either that or they're too decrepit to be out exploring in the middle of the night."

"You sound like you don't care much for old people."

Reginald let out a sigh. "I definitely used to feel that way. Some of these codgers have started to grow on me. Kind of like a skin rash."

Aranello frowned. "I've alerted your staff to keep their eyes open for any evidence such as a possible murder weapon that may have been hidden in a resident's room."

"You haven't searched the rooms?"

"No, I'd never be able to obtain a search warrant without probable cause. But I want to leave the same message with you. Let me know if you find anything suspicious. We'll keep working on it, but we have no leads at this time."

"What about Harold Sykes and the possible link to our employee, Danny Jenson?"

"We've issued a nationwide alert. Nothing has turned up so far."

Reginald drummed his fingers on the desk. "If you locate Danny Jenson, how will you be able to determine if he's Harold Sykes?"

"We have Sykes's fingerprints from a previous government employer who required them for a background check."

"And no fingerprints on file for Danny Jenson."

"That's correct, Mr. Bentley."

"And do you have any findings yet from the coroner on whether it was a murder or accident?"

"Still nothing conclusive, so it will remain classified as a suspicious death for the time being."

*****

After Aranello left his office, Reginald called Dex Hanley and asked him to stop over. Within two minutes, Dex stuck his head through the doorway.

"The police still haven't been able to locate Danny Jenson," Reginald said.

"And no word here. You'd think he would have told someone if he was going away for a while. He's always been dependable, but now he just up and disappears."

"Hard to tell about some people. On another subject, who was on duty the night of the scam artist's death?"

Dex shuffled his feet as he stood near the desk. "Only two people. Bea Hilliard on the reception desk and Seth Kenyon on guard detail. That's it."

"I remember Seth from the loading dock. I assume you've interviewed them both extensively?"

"Oh, yeah, Chief. Both me and the cops."

Reginald twirled a pen in his fingers. "Detective Aranello told me that the police have no clues as of this time. And nothing definitive to determine if it was an accident or a murder."

"And the detective asked me to speak to all my people and have them report anything unusual. I've put out the word."

"I received the same lecture." Reginald tapped his pen on the desktop.

"I'd like to speak with Bea and Seth as well."

Dex shrugged. "Sure. They'll be on duty tonight from eleven until eight. You'll be able to stop by the front desk to see Bea and catch Seth on his rounds."

"One other thing. I've had enough complaints. Go back to having the trash picked up twice a week."

"Good idea, Chief. They're already scheduled for the Tuesday pickup tomorrow, but I'll change it after that to our previous Monday and Thursday dates."

After Dex scrambled out of the office, Reginald tried to push all the problems away for a moment. An image of Rebecca blowing him a kiss popped into his mind. He missed seeing her. For the first time in his life, the thought of little Reggies wandering around, as Jerry so aptly put it, intrigued him. What was happening to him?

But he couldn't daydream. He had a facility to save. Then an idea occurred to him. He remembered that Jerry often wandered around at night. Could the crazy magician have heard or seen anything? He looked at his watch. Close to lunch time. He'd had enough fun for one morning, so he decided to stop in the kitchen before grabbing a bite in the dining room and then speak with Jerry.

Entering Maurice Casotti's domain, Reginald sauntered up to the stove where the chef stood, mixing a large vat of soup.

"Did Grayson Younger return all the silverware?"

Maurice adjusted his toque. "Yes. And I have him on duty at the sink."

Reginald spotted the young man scrubbing pots and pans. His long locks were bunched up in a hairnet. "Is he cooperating?"

"Kind of a sullen fellow, but he did what I asked." Maurice shouted to one of his assistants to get some more salad from the refrigerator.

Reginald watched Mrs. Younger's grandson for a moment and strolled over to the sink. "Grayson, I'm glad you turned up to rectify your mistake."

"Yeah, yeah." He continued to scrub a large pot with caked crud lining the inside.

"Have you ever worked in a kitchen before?"

"No. It isn't exactly my career plan."

"What is your career plan?"

Grayson stopped, opened his mouth and shut it again. "I don't know."

"In that case consider this an educational experience and not just a punishment. Maurice happens to be an excellent chef. You might learn a few things from him, so pay careful attention."

Grayson glared at Reginald, thought better of it and returned to his work.

"You should be off duty soon and be able to join your grandmother for lunch. Remember our bargain. You do your part, and she doesn't need to know that you've been stealing silverware."

Grayson let out a sigh. "I understand."

"Good."

Reginald headed into the dining area, and after a fruit salad, yogurt and cup of coffee, stopped by Jerry's table. "I hope you gentleman are enjoying a good lunch today."

Jerry gave him a long, searching glance. "You checking up on our eating habits, Reggie, or making sure we don't walk off with the silverware?"

Reginald cringed at the mention of silverware. "Actually, we have lost some silverware, but it's all been returned."

"That's good." Tom dropped his fork onto his plate. "I'd hate to have to resort to eating with my fingers."

"I wouldn't mind eating with my fingers," Al said. "I sometimes have trouble holding the silverware."

Jerry reached out, touched Reginald's pants and a spoon appeared in his hand. "Looky here. You've been packing."

"Save that for one of your command performances. May I join you for a moment?"

"Sure. There's an extra chair, and we'll only charge you a buck to use it."

"I'd hold out for two dollars," Tom added.

"Do I hear a bid of three?" Al chortled and then broke into a coughing fit. Tom whacked him on the back.

Reginald sat down. "Put it on my account."

Jerry pointed his fork. "I've been thinking about the two guys we discussed earlier today."

"You mean Dex Hanley and Hector Lopez?" Reginald asked.

"Yeah, the two miscreants," Jerry replied.

"What do you have in mind?"

Jerry's lips curled upward. "It will be a little surprise, but I have something that may solve your problem."

"I hope it's a good surprise."

"I think you'll appreciate the results."

"Jerry, I have another question for you."

Jerry regarded Reginald. "Sounds like a setup to me."

"You told me that you sometimes wander around at night. Last Monday night into Tuesday morning did you hear or see anything unusual?"

"I didn't hear anything." He tapped his hearing aid. "Not my strong suit."

"But you have good eyes."

"Let me see." Jerry fluffed out his napkin. "That must have been the night the scam artist met his maker."

"Correct."

"Nah." Jerry poked his fork into his chocolate cake. "That night I slept like a baby as a result of a little female companionship."

Tom chuckled. "That's why you weren't in your apartment when I went to get you for breakfast the next morning."

"Yeah," Jerry said. "Henrietta invited me for a sleepover."

Reginald looked toward the ladies' table and saw only Henrietta and Karen. "I see one of your lady friends hasn't shown up for lunch."

"Belinda has gone on a trip for several days to visit her son in San Francisco," Tom said. "Lucky broad. She escaped this place for a while."

"I thought you liked it here, Tom," Reginald said.

"It's okay, but the trash sure has started to stink."

Reginald eyed Tom warily. "But it doesn't smell as bad as my office did from that stink bomb."

Tom averted his eyes.

"Besides, the garbage gets picked up tomorrow, and you've all convinced me to have it collected twice a week again. I've already told Dex to change back to the previous schedule starting next week."

"Will wonders never cease." Jerry nodded and then lifted the last bite of his chocolate cake in a salute before popping it into his mouth.

*****

The afternoon began no better than the morning had for Reginald. He opened his mail and found a past due notice from the medical clinic he used in Chicago. Xbest Medical Service had again refused to pay for the eye pressure examination he had called about last week. He grabbed the phone and went through the same routine to reach a rapid resolution representative. This time a woman named Elise said she would help him. "And I spoke with Jennifer just last week about this matter. And while you're looking at my account, Elise, you should find an indicator record highlighting this problem. A year ago another representative named Lindy said she'd put a reminder there, not that it has done any good."

"I'm looking at your record, Mr. Bentley."

After thirty seconds during which he could hear frantic keystrokes, Elise said, "I don't see any indicator in your records."

"Typical. May I speak to your supervisor, please?"

"I'm sorry, we can't transfer you to anyone else."

"So no one who is in a position of authority can help me?"

"I'm responsible for resolving your problem, Mr. Bentley."

Then he remembered something from one of his earlier encounters with Xbest. He thumbed through his file of notes. "Try this. There was a Nancy Fierson in your Phoenix Center who said if I ever had this problem to have the rapid resolution representative speak with her."

"One moment please. Let me check."

He listened to another Xbest Medical Service advertisement about how they could handle his every need. If only they could solve this one little problem.

Finally, Elise came back on the line. "I'm sorry, Nancy Fierson no longer works for us."

Reginald smacked his forehead with the heel of his palm. "This could all be resolved in five seconds if I could speak to someone who understands the doctor's charge codes. It's a reoccurring problem that comes up every time my doctor submits my bill. It would save your company and me a lot of time and trouble if I could speak to someone who understands the codes."

"That's not possible, Mr. Bentley."

"My God. Your company's poor service hasn't changed one iota over the last six months. I guess I might have a heart attack from the surprise of someone actually solving my problem."

"Mr. Bentley, I'm the person who can help you."

He groaned. "Okay, Elise. You'll look into it, and it won't be fixed. I'll call again and spend half an hour listening to a recording of how responsive Xbest Medical Service is before jumping through the hoops to speak with some other rapid resolution representative who won't fix the problem again. On the fourth try, it might get fixed. By then it will be time for my next doctor's appointment so we can start the process all over again."

"I'll see what I can do, Mr. Bentley."

He thumbed through his Day-Timer on previous calls he had made to Xbest Medical Service. "And, Elise, please say hello to Lindy, Georgianne, Ralph, Helene, Betty, Raoul, Cindy, Carl, Bernice, Andrea, Craig, Barbara, Carmen, Inga, Mandy, Hal and Jennifer for me."

After hanging up, things did not improve. He had barely touched the stack of purchase requisitions when Hector Lopez burst into the office.

He held up the index fingers of both of his hands and alternately wiggled them back and forth. "Boss, I have some good news and bad news for you."

Reginald looked up. "Start with the good news. I could use some."

He gasped, trying to catch his breath. "One of the maids found Karen Landry's missing necklace."

"That's progress. And the bad news?"

"It showed up in the linen closet of Henrietta Marlow's apartment."

"Who discovered it?"

"Arleen who handles the sixth floor was returning some laundered sheets and happened to feel something lumpy in the stack of pillow cases in Mrs. Marlow's closet. She reached underneath and discovered the necklace."

"How did it end up in Mrs. Marlow's closet?"

Hector shrugged. "No one knows."

"Have you spoken to Mrs. Marlow yet?"

A bead of sweat formed on Hector's forehead. "Er. . . ah. . . not yet. I thought you might want to. . . uh. . . do that."

"Set up a meeting in my office for later this afternoon with Karen Landry and Henrietta Marlow."

He let out a sigh of relief. "Okay, Boss."

Hector departed, and the phone rang. The receptionist informed Reginald that Larry Samuelson had arrived to see him.

Larry strode into the office like he owned the place, which he probably would after the money he'd earn defending Sunny Crest and Reginald from Nolan Rasputin's lawsuit over Mrs. Rasputin's broken hip. He had slicked-back black hair and dark beady eyes that resembled bullet holes.

After introductions, Reginald handed him the document, which he perused for fifteen minutes. "So what happened to the safety railing in Mrs. Rasputin's tub?"

"That's what we can't figure out. The maintenance people claim they never removed it. No one can explain why it wasn't still attached."

Larry tapped the document. "That will be the key issue here. If your people removed it and didn't replace it expediently, we will probably lose. If it can be shown that the resident tampered with the railing, then it's a different story."

"What do you think of the damages they're after?"

Larry gave a dismissive wave. "Pure bull pucky. He threw out a large number to scare you. Worst case, they probably wouldn't win more than a million dollars each from you and Sunny Crest."

Reginald almost choked on his saliva. "That would put Sunny Crest out of business, to say nothing of forcing me into personal bankruptcy."

"Not to worry. As I said, that's worst case. I'll need to speak with your maintenance people."

"You can begin with Dex Hanley. He can set up whatever you need."

Larry rubbed his hands together. "I'll get started immediately."

Reginald called Dex and told him he'd have a visitor in a few minutes.

Larry picked up the document. "I'll give you a call tomorrow with my assessment of the situation, Mr. Bentley."

"You do that."

Larry Samuelson slithered out of the office.

Reginald closed his eyes and imagined hundred dollar bills flying out the window and being sucked into the pockets of two slimy lawyers.

Then he heard the sound of someone clearing his throat. His eyes popped open to see a stranger in a rumpled suit standing in his doorway. He wondered if he needed to start closing his office door.

"Mr. Bentley?"

"Yes."

The man strode in and held out a paw. "I'm Frank Ralston, the real estate agent who Armand Daimler contacted to sell this property."

Chapter 19

Reginald blinked like he had awakened in the middle of a bad dream. "Sell this property? What do you mean?"

"Didn't Mr. Daimler inform you?"

Reginald regarded Frank Ralston closely. "No, he didn't."

Frank plastered on an affable smile and shoved a document onto the desk. "Here's an offer I received this morning. I think it's quite fair. Mr. Daimler wants you to read through it and sign it." He offered a gold pen.

Reginald stared at it as if it was something from the evil-smelling dumpster. He wondered if this was the same kind of pen the President used to sign declarations of war. "Hold your horses, Ralston. Your involvement is way too premature. Odds are we won't be selling at all. Daimler hasn't made a decision on the property."

"Seems to me he already has. He told me to start on this last week, and as I said, I'm pleased to report that great progress has been made. Not many agents would have an offer for you this soon. And without an inspection tour, no less. Quite a deal. I'd suggest you snap it up."

Reginald squinted at Ralston and thought of a snapping turtle. "In that case, I'd say we're leaving money on the table. That is, if we plan to sell, which we're not."

"You won't get a better offer than this one." Ralston tapped the document again. "I happen to know a developer who has had his eye on this property for years. He gave us a pre-emptive bid, but we need to respond within a week."

Reginald gave a resigned sigh. "Okay. Leave the document with me. I'll speak with Mr. Daimler."

"You've been given an excellent opportunity to make a great return. Here's my card. Call me right away once you've decided to accept it."

Reginald took the card, stood and shook hands.

Ralston grabbed his gold pen and trotted out of the office.

Reginald peered down, half-expecting a trench to be furrowed in his carpet from all the visitors. Dropping back in his chair, he picked up the document and, after thumbing through the typical legalese, realized the offer appeared reasonable. Now he was really screwed.

He called Armand Daimler whose admin said Daimler had left town, but she'd get a message to him to call back the next day.

After hanging up, Reginald heard a commotion in the hallway, and four people pushed their way into the office: Jerry, Henrietta, Karen and Tom.

Jerry, Henrietta and Tom had their arms crossed. Karen looked confused.

Reginald didn't think they were here to give him kudos on what he had done at Sunny Crest.

Jerry stepped forward. "I understand you want to speak with Henrietta and Karen."

"That's right. What brings you and Tom here as well?"

"If there's a problem with any of the Jerry-atrics, we all show up. Belinda would be here except she's out of town and didn't leave a number, and Al's having his physical therapy right now. What did you want with Henrietta and Karen?"

Reginald held up his hands. "Calm down. We have a situation here and need to see if we can get to the bottom of it."

"What situation?" Jerry asked.

"Let's start with Karen. I understand you were missing a necklace. Is that right?"

She wrinkled her forehead as if trying to figure out which planet she was on at the moment and then brightened. "Oh, yes, y'all. I couldn't find my diamond necklace."

Reginald gave her his best corporate smile. "And you thought it might have been stolen."

"Someone must have taken it. That nice Madeline and Mr. Hanley helped me look all over my apartment. The necklace had vanished into thin air."

"And you weren't sure where it went?" Reginald asked.

She shook her head. "No. It disappeared. We looked and looked but couldn't find it anywhere in my apartment."

Then Reginald turned toward Henrietta. "This afternoon the necklace appeared in your linen closet."

Henrietta gaped. "What? Why would it be there?"

"That's what I want to discuss with you. Henrietta, can you give me any explanation of why the necklace would be in your closet?"

"No. I didn't know it was there." Henrietta's gaze bored into him. "You're implying that you think I stole it. If so, you're wrong."

Reginald held up his hands again. "I'm not accusing anyone of anything. The facts remain that the necklace went missing and then appeared in your closet."

At that moment Rebecca marched through the office door. "Are you accusing my mother of stealing?" Her eyes flashed. The Dragon Lady had resurfaced.

"Everyone please stay calm," Reginald said. "I'm only trying to see if we can piece together what happened."

"Well, don't go accusing any of the Jerry-atrics of theft," Jerry said. "Come on, gang."

With that, the four Jerry-atrics marched out of Reginald's office like aging storm troopers, leaving him to face the Dragon Lady.

"Are we still on for dinner tonight, Rebecca?"

She stomped up to his desk as if she intended to push it over. "Don't even think that I want to see you after accusing my mother of stealing!" She looked down and picked up the real estate offer. "What's this?" She scanned it and gasped. "You're selling Sunny Crest! Of all the gall." She reached out and swept her arm across his desk, knocking the pens, pencils, calculator, notes and purchase requisitions onto the floor. She swiveled and stalked out of the office.

Reginald sank deep into his chair, reeling. He put his hand to his cheek to see if the Dragon Lady's fire had singed him. His head swirled. He had this necklace snafu to resolve, a lawsuit over Mrs. Rasputin's broken hip, infighting within his staff, a silverware-stealing grandson to reform, a resident with an ankle-biting dog, a suspicious death, plus he faced having to shut down Sunny Crest and being out of a job to say nothing of losing Rebecca who had been the best thing that ever happened to him. A week ago he sat here with a new job, and now everything had crumbled around him like a building being demolished. His forehead became clammy. He clenched his fists.

He stared out the window, considering the urge to walk off into the open space and never return. He could become Reginald, the mountain man, living on roots and berries in the wilderness of Colorado, wearing a raccoon hat and deerskin moccasins. Let everyone else deal with all the problems and work it out without Reginald Bentley the Third to kick around.

No! He sat up straight in his chair. He'd never been a quitter. He had succeeded in business by stepping up to problems, not running away from them. He would tackle each issue systematically and deal with them. He'd talk to Daimler regarding the real estate deal when he called back. The necklace situation would need some time to cool down. He knew in his heart that Rebecca and he belonged together, but he had no clue how to start winning her back.

That would take some real creative thinking to resolve. However, he could take a first step on the suspicious death later tonight by speaking with the night receptionist and guard. And right now he could also do something concerning the lawsuit. He'd go visit Mrs. Rasputin in the hospital.

As he drove to Boulder Community Hospital, he tried to put all the turbulent events since his arrival at Sunny Crest into perspective. A little exercise he often employed in situations like this: imagine the worst thing that could happen. That was easy. He'd be out of a job, be sued, lose all his savings, be penniless, declare bankruptcy and have to start his career all over again. He could live with those problems. But he also had people counting on him to keep Sunny Crest open. Worst case they would all be out looking for new homes and jobs. It wasn't fair to two hundred residents, fifty staff members and their families to have to go through the trauma. And there was still the suspicious death hanging over everything. It might have only been an accident, but his gut feeling was that the police would eventually find evidence that pointed to murder. Not that anyone seemed too torn up over the demise of the slime-bag scammer Willie Pettigrew. And one of his employees might have been involved.

But Rebecca. She was a different story. He had often despaired of ever finding a woman to love. He didn't know if this was love, but it certainly was the first time he really cared for a woman. And now he'd ended up on her hate list. Even if he could convince her that he hadn't been accusing her mother of stealing or trying to sell off Sunny Crest, would she ever be interested in him if he became a penniless bum? And the worst that could happen? Never seeing Rebecca again.

He swerved from the right lane into the left lane and heard a horn honk and the screech of brakes. *Damn.* He hadn't been paying attention and cut off a car. He waved an apology but moments later heard a siren and saw flashing red and blue lights behind him in the rearview mirror. The police officer pointed toward the curb, so Reginald carefully changed back into the right lane and pulled over.

The policeman asked for his driver's license, registration and proof of insurance.

Reginald received a citation for violating section 7-4-36 of the city ordinance by making an improper lane change. Just what he needed.

On this happy note, he parked, careful not to dent the neighboring cars, entered the door of the hospital and received directions from the receptionist on where to find Mrs. Rasputin. As he approached her room, he heard voices inside. He peeked in and saw an old woman in bed and a young man in a nearby chair speaking to her.

"Grandma, I'm suing the bastards who did this to you." The man stomped his foot like an angry child.

"Don't trouble yourself, Nolan. We don't need any lawsuit. I'm a tough old bird, and I'll recover in no time."

"It isn't that simple. We can't let them get away with this."

"I appreciate your concern, but I don't cotton to this lawyering."

"They'll pay, Grandma. They'll pay."

Reginald decided to find the cafeteria and grab a snack. No sense speaking to Mrs. Rasputin with F. Lee Bailey in attendance.

After eating a pre-wrapped sandwich that made him appreciate the Sunny Crest cuisine, he slunk back to Mrs. Rasputin's room and peered inside. This time she had no company.

He knocked on the door.

"Come in," a wispy voice said.

"Mrs. Rasputin, I hate to bother you. I'm Reginald Bentley from Sunny Crest and want to say how sorry I am that you injured your hip."

"Thank you." Her eyes lit up. "You're the new young man who spoke at dinner the other night."

"Yes. I've been at Sunny Crest a week." He pulled up a chair to her bedside. "We're all confounded that the railing had been removed from your bathtub."

She chuckled. "Has anyone told you my story?"

Chapter 20

"You listen carefully, young man." Mrs. Rasputin jabbed a withered but solid finger into Reginald's arm. "My husband was a very good plumber. I took an interest in his profession and learned everything that he did. He died young, not quite thirty, but we had three boys by that time. I was a housewife who suddenly had to do something to support my children. I became one of the first female plumbers in Colorado. Supported my family right well, I did."

"Good for you. A lot of women wouldn't have had the gumption to jump into a new business."

"That's right." She sighed. "I was full of piss and vinegar. And I know a thing or two about bathroom fixtures. Now, the railing in my bathroom at Sunny Crest." She paused and took a sip of water from the glass by her bed. "I hated that nuisance. Got in the way every time I used the tub. I still have my tools, so I removed the damn thing."

Reginald did a double take. "You removed the safety railing from the tub?"

"Yes, siree. My own damn fault that I slipped."

"Did you know your grandson has filed a lawsuit against Sunny Crest and me because of your accident?"

She took another sip of water. "Nolan's a very intense young man. He means well but goes overboard."

"His going overboard could cause Sunny Crest to be shut down."

Her eyes widened. "I don't want that to happen. I like the place. I'll talk some sense into the whelp."

"I'd appreciate that very much. Let him know you removed the safety railing and we're not to blame. We're doing everything we can to make Sunny Crest a top retirement home, but a lawsuit will ruin us."

She patted his hand. "Don't worry over it, young man."

When he left, he hoped that Mrs. Rasputin had a better memory than Karen Landry.

*****

Back in his office, Reginald sat ruminating on all the things he needed to fix. One remained at the top of his list. He punched in Rebecca's phone number, and she answered on the fourth ring.

"Rebecca, I'd like to explain what happened this afternoon—"

The phone disconnected.

He peered at the phone wondering if smoke and flames would shoot out of the earpiece. He called again and listened to her sultry recorded voice. He took a deep breath. "I know you don't want to talk to me, but please let me explain. I was only trying to understand what happened to Karen Landry's necklace, not accuse your mother. And the real estate deal for Sunny Crest. My boss Armand Daimler set that in motion, not me. I know you're mad at me, but I would like to speak with you and see you again."

He hung up wondering if she would even listen to what he said. He pictured a dragon shooting flames at the offending message machine, turning it into charcoal.

*****

At a little after five, Reginald put down his expense-slashing pen and considered taking a short break to stretch his legs when Hector pushed a man into the office.

"Look who just showed up, Boss."

Reginald gave a slow, appraising glance at a man in his late thirties with scraggly blond hair and several days of blond fuzz on his chin. "I don't recognize him, Hector."

"This is the missing Danny Jenson."

"Well, well. Sit down, Danny, so we can have a chat. Have you notified the authorities, Hector?"

"Yes, Boss. Detective Aranello is on his way over."

Hector shoved Danny into a chair and stood behind him as if on guard to make sure he didn't make a run for it.

Reginald gave Danny his most menacing stare. "Is your name really Harold Sykes?"

Danny blinked with surprise. "Harold Sykes? Who's that?"

Reginald watched him carefully. He either wasn't Sykes, or he was a good actor. "Where have you been, Danny?"

Danny's eyes darted back and forth. "I already told Mr. Lopez. My brother got real sick, and I went to help him in Phoenix."

"Why didn't you tell anyone?"

Danny turned his head back toward Hector. "I left a note in the laundry. I said I'd be gone for a week."

"No one found a note," Hector said.

"I left it right on the counter."

Hector frowned. "Uh-oh. Dirty clothes are thrown on the counter. The note might have been covered up. Now that I think about it, Agnes found a clump of wet paper in a load of clothes last Wednesday."

At that moment Aranello arrived.

"Danny Jenson is here, Detective."

"I'd like to speak to him alone," Aranello said. "And, Mr. Jenson, I want you to give me a set of fingerprints."

Danny looked confused again. "Why do I need to do that?"

"We either do it here or I can take you to police headquarters."

Danny winced. "No need to go there. I'll do what you want."

"You can use my office, Detective." Reginald stood, tapped Hector on the shoulder and led him outside.

"What do you make of all that?" Reginald asked Hector as they went to grab cups of coffee.

Hector scratched his head. "Danny hasn't been a problem before. I don't know."

"If he was Sykes, I would have thought he'd have averted his eyes or acted in a more suspicious fashion. I wasn't able to rattle him as I tried to do."

"And he might have left a note as he said."

They moseyed back, and in a few minutes Aranello stuck his head out and motioned them inside the office. "Danny Jenson's fingerprints don't match Sykes's."

"You can tell already?" Reginald asked.

"Yeah. I brought copies of Sykes's prints with me. Mr. Jenson, you're free to go."

"I'm not going to lose my job, am I?" Danny glanced at Hector and then at Reginald.

"No," Reginald replied, "but when you have a family emergency directly speak with Mr. Lopez and call in to report your whereabouts."

After Danny disappeared around the corner, Aranello said, "That clears up one question, but I'm still trying to track down Harold Sykes."

"No real link to him at Sunny Crest at this time, right, Detective?"

"Other than the one hint of him being in Boulder, nothing definitive. I'll keep working on it."

*****

Reginald grabbed a quick dinner in the dining room, deciding to eat by himself. A sense of relief passed through his tired body. With Danny Jenson turning out not to be Harold Sykes, he didn't have to worry about a murder suspect working at Sunny Crest. But now they were back to square one on the mysterious death of Willie Pettigrew, scam artist. And Harold Sykes still had not been located. Had he somehow tracked Pettigrew to Sunny Crest and whacked him over the head? Reginald's gut told him that was a low probability. So many questions still unanswered.

As he finished dessert, he noticed the Jerry-atrics weren't at their usual tables. Probably somewhere up to no good and planning his demise.

After dinner, he returned to his office to review the day's misadventures. Before he had reached a decision on whether to slit his wrist or run off into the Amazon jungles, Vicki Pearson barged in, panting as if she had just run a marathon. "I was. . . *gasp*. . . hoping. . . *gasp*. . . you were still here."

"And here I am."

She looked like she had lost her best friend. "I have a problem."

He waved her toward a chair. "I'm going to put a sign on my door— 'Reginald's Problem Solving Agency.' What's up?"

She panted, "I'm. . . I'm taking a group of residents to the Boulder Dinner Theater in half an hour—"

"I thought theaters were dark on Monday nights."

She took a deep breath and regained her composure. "They usually are, but this is a special performance for all the retirement communities in Boulder County. We and the other establishments are bringing vans of people to see *Chicago*."

"I assume the Jerry-atrics signed up. That would explain why I didn't see them in the dining room."

"Yes, the Jerry-atrics are coming, as well as a dozen other residents. I'm supposed to go with them, but I ran into a personal problem." She paused.

Reginald felt as if he were trying to pry thick putty out of a jar with a toothpick. "Which is?"

"I'm a single mom with a son. My babysitter just canceled, and I can't find a replacement at the last minute. Would you be able to either take my place on the trip or watch my son?" Her eyes pleaded with him.

He faced a devil's dilemma. Since he disliked being around both old people and kids, what would he rather do? He considered an evening with Jerry and his old gang as well as a dinner theater full of other old geezers. He'd been dealing with old people and their problems all day. "Why not take your son to the show with you?"

She lowered her eyes. "All the seats are sold out and besides, he needs to be in bed by nine for school tomorrow."

Reginald sighed. "I've already eaten dinner so going to the dinner theater isn't that appealing. I suppose I could spend the evening with your son." Then he remembered the incident his first week at Sunny Crest when the little terror kid named Tyler attacked him. "How old is he?"

She gave a relieved sigh. "Mason's ten, and he's a darling. He won't give you any trouble. Come here, Mason."

A towhead wearing glasses appeared from around the corner. "Mr. Bentley, meet Mason. Mason, say hello to Mr. Bentley."

Reginald stood up, cautiously approached the lad and held out a hand, ready to jump back at any time if the kid attempted to kick.

Mason gave a firm handshake. "How do you do, sir?"

Reginald let out a breath he had been holding. Mason hadn't kicked or punched him. Maybe this wouldn't be so bad after all.

Vicki looked at her watch. "We have just enough time for us to go to my apartment and for me to get back here to catch the van to the dinner theater."

"I'm about done here, so we can go any time," Reginald replied.

"I have a blue Honda Accord. We'll meet you in the parking lot, and you can follow us."

Once in the Jaguar, he spotted her and followed, thankful they were avoiding a repeat of the wild ride behind Rebecca's car the day before. They pulled into the parking area of a condo complex near Boulder Creek off 28th Street.

Vicki rushed Mason up the stairs with Reginald trailing behind. She shot a glance over her shoulder, "I don't know how to thank you."

"You can show your appreciation by keeping the Jerry-atrics under control tonight. We don't need any headlines in the paper tomorrow reporting that Sunny Crest residents burned the stage, trashed the dinner theater or caused a riot."

Inside the apartment, she pointed to the refrigerator. "Lots of snacks there."

Reginald suddenly realized he had no clue what to do with a ten-year-old boy. "Um, what does Mason like to do?"

Vicki had her hand on the doorknob by this time. "He likes video games, Harry Potter and magic tricks. Bed by nine. I'll be back around eleven. Bye." The door slammed.

Great. Mason should be spending time with Jerry Rhine.

Reginald surveyed the living room, noticing a large television with video game equipment attached, a mountain scene painting on the wall, a bookcase with misaligned books and a pile of magazines on the floor. "You want to give me a tour of the place, Mason?"

"Yes, sir. I have my collection of Wii video games over there." He pointed to a stack of boxes near the TV." He marched into the hallway as Reginald followed. "Here's my room."

Reginald stuck his head inside expecting to see spiders and scorpions. Instead he found a neatly made bed, an uncluttered desk with several books and notebooks, a dresser with a Spiderman action figure on top and the room wallpapered in a silver pattern with black images of old cars. "Any homework to do, Mason?"

He shook his head. "No, I finished it all this afternoon at school. I usually get done before Mom picks me up."

"You hungry?"

His eyes lit up. "Yeah. I can make a big sandwich." He spread his arms wide. "I'll create a Mason special. You want one too?"

"No, I've already eaten. I'll watch you prepare it."

Mason dashed into the kitchen, and Reginald followed. Within minutes, the kid had bread, mayonnaise, mustard, pickles, tomatoes, lettuce, pieces of sliced ham, turkey, roast beef and three kinds of cheese out on the counter. He began slathering and assembling until he had a sandwich two inches thick.

"That's what I call a sandwich," Mason announced with pride.

"You going to eat that whole thing?"

"Sure."

Mason poured a glass of milk and began chomping away on the sandwich. That tyke could sure put away the food. After he ate every scrap and crumb, he cleaned up and returned all the makings to the refrigerator.

Reginald had always thought of little crumb-gobblers as messy. This kid took care of things better than he did.

"Want to play a video game?" Mason asked.

"I guess I can give it a try, although I haven't played one since PAC-MAN."

"What's that?"

"A video game from the Dark Ages I played when I was your age."

Mason nodded as if trying to comprehend something from an alien culture. "Come on, I'll show you one of my cool games."

Mason handed him a handheld control with buttons on it and told him to slide the strap over his wrist.

Reginald duly followed directions as Mason pushed some buttons on a similar device he held. Then a war scene appeared on the television screen. "You need to shoot all the bad guys in the black uniforms."

"How do I do that?"

"Move your hand to aim and then push the button on the top to shoot."

"If you say so."

Black figures came jumping out of buildings, running up streets, throwing grenades and shooting semi-automatic rifles. Reginald tried to move the device to aim at one of them. The screen went red and faded to black.

"You took too long, and they killed you."

"Took too long? I hadn't even pushed the button yet."

"You have to be quick. Here let me show you." Mason reset the game with his device. The black figures appeared again, and he began rotating his hand and jamming the button down like a berserk arm wrestler.

In moments, the black figures on the screen gave off screams and fell to the pavement. A sign flashed on the television screen, "Threat eliminated."

"See, nothing to it," Mason said, giving a thumbs up. "Give it another try."

Reginald flexed his fingers and prepared for the next assault. The television screen flashed and the black figures reappeared. He began jamming his hand from side-to-side and pushing the button like crazy, and saw one black figure crash to the ground, giving off an ear-piercing screech. He continued poking the button, but nothing seemed to happen until the screen flashed, "You lose, painful death with only one threat eliminated."

"Why didn't any more of them disappear?" Reginald asked.

Mason frowned. "You kept missing them. You're not very good at video games are you?"

"No, I guess not. I'm thirty years out of practice."

"Let's try some of my sports games. They're pretty easy."

They proceeded to play tennis, golf, bowling and baseball. Mason clobbered him at each one. Finally, Reginald slipped the strap off his wrist and surreptitiously regarded his watch. Not Mason's bedtime yet.

Mason squinted at him through his thick glasses. "Let's do something else. You want to see a magic trick?"

"Sure, why not?"

Mason disappeared into his room and returned momentarily with a deck of cards. "Here take a card, any card."

Reginald ruffled through the deck and extracted one from the middle.

"Look at it, but don't tell me what it is."

Reginald peered at the six of hearts.

"Now slide it anywhere into the deck."

Reginald did as directed.

Mason banged the deck onto the table to even out the cards, shuffled the deck three times and then spread the deck out, face down on the table. "Okay, point to a card."

Reginald picked one, part way in on the left.

Mason slid it out and turned if over. The six of hearts. "This is your card."

"Yes, but I bet the whole deck consists of six of hearts."

"Turn them over and check."

Reginald did so to discover a normal deck. "How did you do that?"

Mason tapped his forehead. "Magic and skill. A magician never divulges his secrets."

Reginald shook his head in amazement. "I'll have to get you together with a resident at Sunny Crest named Jerry Rhine. I'd call him up and invite him over right now except he's at the theater with your mom. He was a professional magician."

"Cool. I always like meeting other magicians. Does he know the Siamese chamber of death trick?"

"I have no clue. I don't know much about magic."

Mason gave Reginald a slow, appraising look. "You should learn some tricks. Maybe people would like you better then."

Reginald winced. "Do you put on shows?"

Mason shrugged. "Only for Mom and my friends. But I'm adding new tricks all the time. I got a neat book of magic tricks last Christmas. I've been practicing a bunch of them. Want to see another?"

"Okay, you can amaze and astound me again."

He shuffled the cards, asked Reginald to cut them and proceeded to make four aces show up on the top of the deck.

"Not bad for a little kid."

"I'm not so little. I'm ten."

"I consider anyone little who doesn't have their driver's license yet." Reginald looked at his watch again. "Your mom said you needed to be in bed by nine. Time to get ready."

"Aw, please can I do one more trick?"

"No. Get marching."

Mason let out a resigned sigh and loped into his room to change into his pajamas before brushing his teeth. When he finished, he appeared holding a large book. "Mom always reads to me before I go to sleep." He handed Reginald one of the Harry Potter books, jumped into bed, pulled the sheet and blanket up to his chin and wiggled once. "Okay, I'm ready. You can start."

Reginald opened it to the bookmark and started reading to him the adventures of Muggles, Quidditch and Hogwarts. That school sounded like a good place to send the Jerry-atrics. They would fit right in. He wondered if he could change the name of Sunny Crest to Hogwarts Senior Residence.

After two pages, Mason threw off his covers. He sat up and shouted, "Stop! You're not reading it right."

"What?"

Mason whacked the mattress with his hand. "You sound like you're reading something boring, like a school report. You need to make your voice more exciting."

Reginald's mouth fell open. This kid wanted to manipulate him like a marionette on strings. What did Mason think he was? He'd spent his career as an accountant, not an entertainer.

Mason adjusted his covers. "Try again, Mr. Bentley. You can do better. With feeling."

With feeling. Reginald took a deep breath and belched forth, shouting out parts, lowering his voice in the scary parts, slowing for the suspense and then racing forward for the action. Beads of sweat ran down his forehead. He concentrated so hard he didn't realize how tired he was until he came to

151

a chapter break. Then as his voice ran out of steam and he croaked out the last sentence, his arms collapsed, dropping the book onto the bed covers. "All right, young man. Time for you to go to sleep."

Mason gave a smug grin. "See how much better you read after our little talk? That was more like it."

"Yeah, maybe so, but I feel pretty drained now." Reginald pulled the blanket back up to the kid's chin and patted him on the head. "Good night, Mason."

"Good night, Mr. Bentley. You're not such a jerk as my mom said."

On that positive note, Reginald turned out the light and adjourned to the living room. He had survived an evening of babysitting without any more damage than a dent to his ego from his ineptitude at video games, and a worn-out voice.

While waiting, he picked up a woman's magazine lying on an end table in the living room. He scanned the table of contents to see if it had anything about taming dragons, but the closest thing he could find was an article on successful relationships. It didn't cover retirement home romances, misunderstandings with mothers harboring missing necklaces or real estate sale fiascos. The only relevant advice related to building a relationship upon trust and mutual respect. Hard to do when the other party wouldn't even speak to you.

Vicki dashed in a few minutes after eleven. "How can I ever thank you, Mr. Bentley?"

"Keep doing the good job you're doing at work."

"How did things go with Mason?"

"We had a fine time together. He taught me how to shoot at terrorists in video games, make a gigantic sandwich, do magic tricks and read Harry Potter with gusto. Did you keep the Jerry-atrics under control?"

"Not exactly. Before the show the cast performed a little skit and asked for volunteers from the audience. Jerry jumped up and hopped on stage. He proceeded to disrupt their whole routine by performing his own magic tricks."

"Sounds like he and Mason would make an interesting pair."

*****

Back at dear old Sunny Crest, Reginald congratulated himself for surviving the world of ten-year-olds and checked his watch. At eleven-thirty he introduced himself at the front desk to Bea Hilliard. "I understand you were on duty last week when the suspicious death took place out on the loading dock."

Bea lowered her eyes. "Yes. I worked here that night."

"Did you see anyone wandering around after midnight?"

She shook her head. "I only saw one person the whole night—the security guard, Seth Kenyon. He stopped by my desk every hour or so to check in."

"Is that his regular routine?"

She pushed a dog-eared paperback novel to the side. "Oh, yes. I stay here, and he makes the rounds."

"Where can I find him?"

Bea tapped a schedule sheet on her desk. "He'll be working his way down from the top floor. You should be able to catch him by the elevators on any of the floors."

Reginald thanked her and took the elevator up to the fifth floor. In a few minutes a man in a brown guard's uniform stepped out of the stairwell.

"Seth, I'd like a few words with you."

He looked surprised. "I haven't ever seen the executive director on my rounds."

"Times they are a-changin'. Let's sit down over there." Reginald pointed to two chairs in the commons area.

Seth glanced at his watch. "I suppose. I can't spend too much time. I need to keep my schedule."

"This won't take very long. I have a few questions regarding the night before you found the dead body."

Seth frowned. "I've covered all that with the police."

"I know, and I appreciate that you stayed late last Tuesday morning to help out after a full shift on duty. I'm trying to understand a few things. Did you see anyone wandering around that night?"

He shook his head. "No one. Sometimes I run into Jerry Rhine. He's often walking the halls." Seth chuckled. "Jerry even shows me magic tricks. Usually has a deck of cards with him. And he makes coins appear and disappear like that." He snapped his fingers.

"And did you see Jerry that night?"

"Nope. As I said, I didn't run into anyone. I saw Bea when I went by the front desk but no one else."

"Any sounds or anything unusual?"

Seth thought for a moment. "Pretty quiet night. I did hear what sounded like footsteps once, but never saw anyone."

"Could you tell where the sound originated?"

"I had just entered the east wing of the sixth floor. The faint noise sounded like it came from the west corridor."

"What time did you hear that?"

"Maybe three a.m."

"Do you ever look in the residents' rooms?"

"No, sir. I'm only supposed to check all the halls and make sure all the offices and outside doors remain locked."

Reginald had run into a dead end. "Thanks for speaking with me, Seth. I'll let you return to your duties."

*****

Reginald awoke Tuesday morning with a start. Something nagged at the back of his mind. He had dreamed of a mysterious figure flinging something into the dumpster. Then it struck him. Trash pickup would occur this morning. His subconscious had broken through to tell him something. The police had searched the dumpster, finding nothing. But that was a week ago. If Pettigrew had been murdered rather than accidentally fallen, someone could have bashed him over the head with some weapon and then disposed of it later in the dumpster, much like he had deposited the thug's revolver there.

Reginald imagined being the person who had come upon Pettigrew and whacked him over the head with a stick or club. What would he have done next? If he had to get rid of a murder weapon, he'd wait until after the police had searched the dumpster and then dispose of it right before the trash service picked it up. That would avoid detection and eliminate the evidence.

Reginald changed into his grubby jeans and headed down to the first floor. He found a rock to leave the outer door to the loading dock propped open and went outside. Opening the lid on the dumpster, he almost fell over, reeling from the stench. He found an old chair on the dock and carried it down and placed it in front of the dumpster. Then he stood on the chair and began rummaging through the trash. He pushed aside plastic bags and paper sacks, lifted a large black trash container that had garbage from the kitchen. More bags of foul-smelling crud. He gasped at the offensive odor

154

of over a week's worth of garbage before reaching farther down into the dumpster to move bags around.

Then he spotted a wooden handle sticking out of a paper bag. Carefully removing the bag from the dumpster, he grabbed a rag and pulled out a souvenir Rockies mini-bat. He stared at it, noticing a crack right at the meat of the bat. A few black hairs stuck in the crack.

Chapter 21

The mini-bat almost slipped out of Reginald's grasp. He juggled it to prevent it from falling back into the morass of garbage, managing to retain his grip on the rag and the bat. Stepping down from the chair, he placed the sack, mini-bat and rag on the ground and closed the lid of the dumpster, somewhat alleviating the stench of dead fish. Then he opened the paper bag and spied a sheet of paper inside. Using the rag again, he extracted the crumpled sheet. Straightening it out on top of the dumpster, he saw that it was a life insurance policy application. The name of the policyholder remained blank, but the beneficiary had already been filled in—Willie Pettigrew with an address of a Post Office Box in Longmont.

He heard the grinding sound of the garbage truck approaching. Time to get out of here. He carefully put the bat and insurance form back inside the paper bag and stuck it under his arm, brushing a banana peel off his shoulder in the process. Entering the building with his discoveries, he had almost reached the stairwell, when Reginald felt a tap on his shoulder.

Reginald spun around.

Tom sniffed. "You been dumpster diving, Reggie?"

Reginald hid the bag behind his back. "Yeah. I'm practicing for my new profession when they kick me out of here."

Tom scowled. "You certainly won't last much longer if you go around accusing Henrietta of stealing necklaces. That's completely unacceptable."

"I didn't accuse her of anything. I wanted to see if we could figure out what had happened."

Tom shook his head in disgust as if spotting a new army recruit who hadn't polished his boots correctly. "And I hear you really pissed off the Dragon Lady."

Reginald's shoulders sagged. "Yeah. I think I blew it with Rebecca."

"Cheer up. She probably won't do more than punch you out the next time she sees you. In any case, Karen has her necklace back. None of us could understand how or why it ended up in Henrietta's linen closet."

"Me neither."

Tom poked a thick finger into Reginald's ribs. "I have some advice for you—let Rebecca cool off a little. Then maybe you can wear out your knees with some begging and apologizing." He punched Reginald in the shoulder good-naturedly and headed down the corridor.

Reginald rubbed the bruise, wondering what hurt most—being on Tom's bad side or his good side.

He took the paper bag with its contents up to his room and stashed it in a cupboard before taking a long, hot shower and using up most of a cake of soap. As he toweled dry, a warmth spread through his chest. He had located a potential murder weapon. Then dread surged through his damp body. What to do next? That little bat appeared innocuous, but it could have been a deadly weapon, having all the appearance of the blunt instrument that had killed scam artist Willie Pettigrew.

And his suspicion of who had used that little bat rested on the Jerry-atrics who had recently collected such bats at a Rockies game. He considered the list of suspects. Karen appeared too weak and scatterbrained to use a weapon to whack Pettigrew. She certainly didn't appear to be the mean or violent type anyway.

Belinda always acted jolly, and, besides, she shook too much from her Parkinson's disease to be able to clobber someone over the head. Al had a wiry build but couldn't do much with his hands because of his arthritis—he probably wouldn't be able to even clamp his fingers around the bat, much less wield a blow to someone's head.

Tom had the military training and strength, although it would have put a strain on his heart. He wouldn't have had any qualms about taking out someone who was a threat. But Tom wouldn't resort to some picayune bat. He'd prefer to run the guy over with a tank.

Henrietta had the determination to whack someone if she had to. Much like her daughter decimating his desk, Reginald could imagine Henrietta taking whatever action she deemed necessary to protect herself or someone important to her.

And then there was the illustrious Jerry Rhine to consider as a suspect. That crazy magician appeared in good enough shape to take out a bad guy, but he seemed to be the type who would trick someone rather than bash a person over the head.

Should he call Detective Aranello? Reginald hesitated, his hand hovering above the phone. A part of him wanted to resolve this whole suspicious death matter, and a part of him remained reluctant to put the Jerry-atric six under police scrutiny. But he had to do what he considered right, so he picked up the phone and punched in the number from the detective's card.

"Detective Aranello's line."

"May I speak to him, please?"

"He's out of town until Friday. Do you want to speak with one of the other detectives?"

Reginald thought for a moment. He didn't want some rookie covering old ground in his establishment. That wouldn't be the least bit productive. "No, tell him to call Reginald Bentley at Sunny Crest Retirement Community when he returns."

After he hung up, he paced the room, ruminating on his options. He'd turn the bat over when Aranello got back in town, but in the meantime he'd do a little investigating on his own. He pulled out the directory and jotted down the room numbers of each of the Jerry-atrics on a sheet of paper. He could easily check on things in Belinda Davenport's apartment since she had gone on a trip out of town and he possessed a master key.

Taking the elevator to the fifth floor, Reginald made sure that no one saw him, quickly turned the key in the lock and entered her room. Once inside with the door closed, he considered for a moment if he should be doing this. It wouldn't look good if someone spotted the retirement home director snooping in a resident's room. Still, what would be the harm? He didn't intend to disturb anything inside—only check to verify if she possessed a Rockies mini-bat or not. He scanned the foyer and saw a clean kitchenette with nothing more on the sink than a dry dishrag and a bottle of dishwashing soap.

Belinda had a one-bedroom apartment with the living room decorated in blue: blue Persian rug, light blue flowered couch and blue curtains. Reginald expected bluebirds to be perched on the chandelier. At least the ceiling wasn't painted sky blue.

He strolled around the room noticing a collection of vases, a bookshelf with romance novels and a few colorful still life paintings (blue backgrounds in each). On an end table rested several framed photos of middle-aged people and kids in their teens and twenties—probably her children and grandchildren. He picked up one picture and looked closely at a younger Belinda, not quite as plump with a radiant look on her face as she stood surrounded by her offspring. He heard a whooshing sound and fumbled the picture. It slipped out of his hand and struck the end table. The glass in the photo frame shattered.

"Damn," he muttered. He paused to listen and determined that the noise was nothing more than a toilet flushing next door. He looked down at the glass shards covering the rug. That couldn't be left unattended. He strode over to the cabinet under the sink in the kitchenette and opened the door hoping to find a plastic bag of some sort. Nothing. He looked through several drawers and finally found a Baggie. He returned to the living room and proceeded to pick up all the pieces of broken glass, being careful not to cut his fingers and leave tell-tale blood on the rug. He could imagine the news article: Retirement home director sacked for sneaking into a resident's apartment, breaking picture glass and leaving blood on the rug. The crime discovered through DNA analysis of the bloodstain. Reginald Bentley the third now held in chains and irons before a sentence of drawing and quartering.

He removed the remaining splinters of glass from the frame and set the picture back where he had found it, no worse for wear except minus the glass cover. Hopefully, Belinda wouldn't notice.

Now to the task at hand. As long as he had gone this far, he sure as heck had better determine if Belinda possessed a Rockies mini-bat.

He walked around the perimeter of the living room, careful not to touch anything else. No Rockies mini-bat visible here. He made another quick scan through the immaculate kitchenette, then into the short hallway that led to the bathroom and bedroom. He took a deep breath before proceeding into the bedroom, feeling like a prowler invading private territory. A white and blue quilt covered Belinda's neatly made bed.

Reginald wondered if Belinda and Tom tumbled around like Jerry and Henrietta did. He still had trouble accepting old people making love. Images of sweating, wrinkled masses, panting and having heart attacks, coursed through his brain. He squeezed his palms against his forehead. *Focus.*

Surveying the room, he spotted it—a Colorado Rockies mini-bat resting on the dresser. He inspected it without daring to pick it up. Identical to the one he had found in the dumpster, minus the crack—solid wood with a Colorado Rockies logo and the words "Coors Field."

His cell phone rang, and he jumped, almost knocking over the mini-bat. He answered, and the receptionist said she had tried his office. He had a visitor named Nolan Rasputin demanding to see him.

"I'll be right there."

He stashed his phone, grabbed the Baggie full of glass shards, took one last look around the living room to make sure he had picked up everything and opened the front door, peeking out to verify that no one stood nearby in the hallway. Then like a thief in the night, he tiptoed away and deposited the Baggie in a trash bin by the elevators. Letting out a sigh of relief, he descended to the lobby to meet the ambulance-chasing grandson of Mrs. Rasputin.

Reginald recognized the man he had seen in the hospital room. Face-to-face, the guy looked even angrier than he had sounded before.

Nolan wore a dark suit and carried a black briefcase. His downward scowl matched the two thick arches of eyebrows. Reginald held out a hand, which the lawyer refused to shake.

"Would you like to come to my office or do you want to litigate in the lobby?" Reginald asked, giving his most sincere smile.

Nolan glared. "Your office."

"Follow me. But be careful that no walkers impale your wing tips."

In his office, Reginald offered Nolan coffee, which the lawyer refused. Instead he shook a fist at Reginald. "You run an unsafe establishment and have endangered the life and safety of my grandmother. You're going to pay for that."

Reginald gave him his actuarial stare. "No, Mr. Rasputin, we run a safe establishment and provide safety railings in all bathrooms to assist our older residents when they bathe."

"My grandmother's tub had no safety railing, and you are financially liable for her injury and resulting mental turmoil."

"I could agree if we had been negligent. But a railing had been installed in your grandmother's apartment as in all residents' bathrooms at Sunny Crest. We provide a safe living place that meets all required standards."

Nolan crossed his arms and stared defiantly. "There was no railing in her tub."

Now Reginald moved in for the kill. "Did you bother to ask your grandmother why the safety railing wasn't there?"

"No. It's obvious you and your organization provide sloppy and negligent maintenance." He gave a self-satisfied nod.

"I suggest you speak with the client you claim to represent."

Nolan stared at Reginald. "What are you implying?"

"I'm not implying anything. The simple facts are that we properly installed the safety railing, it remained in good working order, but your grandmother chose to remove it. She knows that her action of taking out the safety railing caused the problem. She has no issues with Sunny Crest or me. Before you go off half-cocked next time, gather the facts." Reginald handed him a piece of paper. "This has the phone number of my lawyer, Larry Samuelson. You can contact him to withdraw your unsubstantiated claim. Now if you'll please leave my office, I have some work to do." Reginald stared at Nolan until he stood up, grabbed his briefcase and beat a retreat.

For the time being, one of Reginald's problems seemed to have been eliminated.

His next challenge of the morning came when he received a call from his boss Armand Daimler.

"You wanted to speak with me, Reginald, but first I have an assignment for you."

Reginald looked up toward the ceiling hoping it might spring open and provide an escape hatch. The word "assignment" might mean anything from closing down a facility to packing his bags and heading to a new life within a day. Reginald gritted his teeth. "What do you have in mind?"

"Pretty simple. I want you to immediately stop by and check on our Sunny Manor assisted living facility in Louisville, Colorado. Headed by a guy named Fred Dickinson. I thought you two should exchange ideas on the future for your two properties."

Reginald gave a sigh of relief. That sounded pretty risk free. "Yes, sir, be happy to. I'll give him a call and set up an appointment. Now here's why I want to talk to you. This guy named Frank Ralston showed up yesterday claiming you had charged him with selling the Sunny Crest real estate."

Daimler cleared his throat. "I'd been meaning to speak with you on just that subject, Reginald."

"You and I had an agreement for me to turn this place around. As you always tell me, fix it or fry it. Well, we're not ready to fry it, Mr. Daimler. I'm fixing it, and I plan to demonstrate how I can deliver an excellent return on investment for Cenpolis Corporation by retaining Sunny Crest."

"You're speaking with some passion, son."

"Yes, sir." Reginald took a deep breath. "I will demonstrate to you a sustainable return on investment for Sunny Crest. Real estate prices continue to rise well above the rate of inflation in this area, and I think it's prudent to retain this valuable property, use it as a retirement community for the foreseeable future and allow the property to increase in value, rather than selling out today. Besides, you gave me two weeks to provide you with a plan."

"No longer possible. We need to make a decision this week."

Reginald smacked his hand against his forehead. "This week? Do you realize the hoops I'm jumping through to complete it in two weeks?"

"If you believe you're right, show me this Friday. Give me a call in the afternoon. I'll be looking forward to it."

The line went dead.

Reginald slammed the phone down. He couldn't believe what Daimler had done to him. Then he remembered their conversation last week. Yes, every time he spoke with Daimler, the fuse got shorter. Daimler continued to play him like a brook trout on a line. The original dictate had been to turn the place around. Now, the latest marching orders made that next to impossible. Daimler seemed intent on quickly selling the place.

But Reginald couldn't let that happen. He'd be damned if he would be manipulated and thrown out on his behind. He would fight to the finish to justify and demonstrate how this turnaround would be beneficial to Cenpolis Corporation. Then Daimler would have to listen.

But how did he get himself in this situation? He hammered his fist on his desk and shouted, "Damn. Damn. Damn."

A head poked into the office followed by the body of Jerry Rhine. "Having a bad hair day today are we, Reggie?"

"I'll say." Reginald only wished he could use some of Jerry's magic to make Daimler disappear. "My boss wants me to show him this Friday why we should keep this place open. Before I thought I had another week."

"Hey, we'll help you out. We'll sell off all our dentures and prosthetic limbs to help fund your boss's bonus plan. How's that?"

Reginald couldn't hold back a laugh. "Just keep working your magic with the prospective clients. I need to show an increase in the occupancy rate and that we can sustain it."

"No problemo, Reggie. Henrietta has whole crowds coming through the rest of the week. She'll sit them down in chairs, and I'll continue to wow the old fogies with my magic. We'll sign 'em up, so this place will be packed to the brim. You'll have more people clamoring to move in here than Carter has little liver pills."

"That's exactly what I need."

"And another idea for a fund raiser. I could run a poker tournament for you. We could raise a lot of money that way. Think of it. The first annual Sunny Crest Texas Hold 'em poker fest." He waved his hands in the air. "Think of all the cash we could rake in."

"No thanks." Reginald could picture the cops raiding Sunny Crest for illegal gambling. "Besides, Daimler doesn't believe in gambling. He wants sure things."

As his visitor retreated from the office, Reginald tried to imagine if Jerry could swing an eighteen inch bat hard enough to bash someone's skull. If so, maybe Jerry could be contracted to go after Armand Daimler.

Chapter 22

After grabbing a cup of coffee from the dining hall and checking out the elevator to make sure no new pictures of him had appeared, Reginald called Fred Dickinson at the Sunny Manor assisted living facility. He had never met nor even spoken to Fred, who answered the phone like they were old buddies. "Reginald, I've heard so much about you. When can we get together?"

"That's the reason for my call, Fred. Armand Daimler suggested I stop by to see you."

"Sure. Sure. I'll give you the grand tour of my facility. We can exchange ideas on how to keep these places running smoothly. I'll tell you my secrets if you tell me yours." He chuckled like Santa Claus had overdosed on Christmas cookies.

"Okay, Fred. When's a convenient time for me to visit you?"

"Any time this afternoon. I'll be here figuring out ways to keep the inmates happy."

*****

Later that morning, Reginald received a call from his lawyer, Larry Samuelson, who said, "I understand you had a visit from Nolan Rasputin this morning."

"Word gets around fast."

"I spoke to him moments ago. Quite a piece of work, isn't he?"

"Yeah." Reginald thought how he wouldn't mind siccing the hoodlum who had tried to kidnap him on Nolan. "And has he withdrawn the lawsuit?"

There was a pause on the line. Reginald wondered if Samuelson was delaying so he could account for fifteen minutes to bill for this call. "Not exactly. He's modifying it."

Reginald groaned. "What?"

"Yeah, he's withdrawn the claim of your negligence in removing and not replacing the safety railing in the tub. Now he's suing you and Sunny Crest for allowing his grandmother to have dangerous tools on the premises and not supervising her use of the tools. He claims that through your negligence Sunny Crest failed to properly care for his grandmother and this led to her injury."

"But we have an independent living facility here." Reginald kicked the leg of his desk. "She chose to do this herself. Sunny Crest and yours truly are not responsible for her removing the safety railing."

"Calm down. We'll work something out. Nolan doesn't have a leg to stand on. "

That set off an image in Reginald's mind. Maybe the thug could be convinced to kneecap the little twerp. "Do this, Larry. You go speak with Mrs. Rasputin at Boulder Community Hospital. She doesn't support the litigation her grandson has undertaken. You'll get a straight read from her."

"Good idea. I'll head over there right now and interview her."

As Samuelson hung up, Reginald could have sworn he heard "ka-ching" rather than a dial tone.

*****

Reginald thought briefly about how to increase occupancy at Sunny Crest. Leaving that problem in the capable hands of Jerry and Henrietta, he instead decided to do a little investigative work and pay Karen Landry a visit. He looked up her room number on his secret sheet, stuffed it into his pocket and took the elevator to the seventh floor. He knocked on the door.

"Come in," rang out a sing-song voice.

He entered and found Karen sitting in a rocking chair, knitting. She wore the diamond necklace.

Her face brightened. "The leaky faucet for you to fix is in the bathroom."

"I'm not the plumber. I'm Reginald Bentley, the executive director of Sunny Crest."

"Oh that's right." She looked at him over the top of her reading glasses. "You're the young man causing all the problems around here."

Reginald drew back as if she had slapped his face. "No, but I'm trying to solve all the problems."

She tilted her head to the side. "But that doesn't include my sink?"

"You got me there. I'll make sure someone comes right away to fix your faucet."

"That would be nice."

"I see you're wearing your diamond necklace. I'm glad it turned up."

She looked puzzled and put her hand to her neck. "Oh, yes, that's right. It disappeared, but someone found it. For the life of me I can't figure out what happened." She scratched her nose and stared at him. "And why are you here?"

He figured he could use a direct approach with Karen since she probably wouldn't remember it later anyway. "I understand you and your friends recently attended a Colorado Rockies baseball game."

She wrinkled her brow. "We went somewhere that had scrumptious hot dogs. Nice and warm with plenty of mustard. Was that the baseball game?"

"Probably so."

"Yes. And I had popcorn as well. I like it with just a smidgen of butter. Not all greasy but enough to give it the flavor needed."

"Yes, they serve all kinds of food at baseball games. Do you remember receiving a small souvenir bat?"

She put her knitting down on an end table and regarded him suspiciously. "I don't remember visiting a cave. I don't like bats."

"I mean a small baseball bat made of wood."

"Oh. That's possible. Let me show you my souvenirs." She stood and ambled over to a bookshelf in the corner. "Here's a clay lion my son, Benjamin, made for me in kindergarten. Quite the potter. And a potholder my daughter, Judith, gave me on Mother's Day in 1963."

"You remember things fine from the past."

"Oh, yes. Ask me anything you want from when I raised my little ones." She frowned. "It's lately that things have become kind of fuzzy. I wonder why that is."

He needed to make sure Karen stayed focused. "Keep looking to see if you can find a small baseball bat."

"Oh, yes. Maybe back here."

Karen reached behind a row of pictures. "No. Nothing there."

"There's that long red box on the bottom shelf." He pointed to it.

"Now what do I keep in there? Let's look." She lifted the box off the shelf and removed the lid. "Oh yes. I kept the medals my children won for swimming and track in here. And there's a cute little baseball bat. I don't know where that came from."

She handed Reginald a Rockies mini-bat like the two he had seen earlier today. Success.

"That's the one you received when you went to the baseball game with your friends."

"Gracious, I guess I put it with the other sports souvenirs. Let me show you pictures of people I once worked with." She pointed to a row of photographs of men in suits and several women in austere skirts. "I used to be a legal secretary."

He squinted at one of the pictures. "Not many women in the picture."

She shook her head. "Back then it was a man's profession. But they couldn't have succeeded without our secretarial support. We kept the firm going."

"Where did you work?"

"At Higgins, Clarke and Bain in downtown Denver. For twenty years." She sighed. "I took the job after my children entered high school. Kept me busy and entertained."

"I have a few difficulties with attorneys myself. How did you handle lawyers?"

Her eyes danced. "They like to think they're smarter than everyone else. You just have to put things in terms of their financial best interest. Money is everything to them."

"Sounds like you know your lawyers."

"I did. More recently things haven't been as clear."

Before he left her apartment, Reginald used her phone to call Dex and arranged to have a plumber come fix the leaky faucet as soon as possible. Since he seemed to be on a roll, he decided to try another of the Jerry-atrics and, after checking his sheet, went to Tom Balboa's apartment on the fourth floor.

When he knocked, a booming voice invited him in, and he found Tom reading a *Sports Illustrated* magazine.

"You must be a sports fan," Reginald commented.

"Damn right. Broncos, Nuggets, Rockies and Avalanche. All the home teams." Tom sniffed. "You smell better than this morning. No more dumpster diving?"

"I've given up the rotten fish aftershave."

Tom raised an eyebrow. "I've never had a visit from the retirement home director before. What gives?"

"I want to thank you for helping out with Jerry's magic show for the prospective residents. That seems to be very useful in convincing people to come to Sunny Crest, and I'm appreciative of your efforts."

His eyes widened. "You don't seem like the type to hand out atta-boys."

Reginald shrugged. "I guess we all can change. I did have a question for you. The night of the murder, did you see or hear anything suspicious?"

"No, but I have to admit, I was a little preoccupied that night." He winked at Reginald. "Belinda and I spent most of the night together in her apartment."

"You sly devil."

"Can I offer you a beer?"

Reginald's initial inclination was to say no, being on duty, but he decided what the hell. "I'll take one before I head back to the land of bureaucracy."

Tom pulled himself up and lumbered into the kitchenette, opened the refrigerator and handed Reginald a silver Coors can.

"I see you support local beer as well as the sports teams."

"Yup. I'm Rocky Mountains through and through."

They sat down. "How long have you lived at Sunny Crest, Tom?"

"Going on four years. After my wife died, I decided to give up the large house and came here."

The room looked typically male—sports magazines stacked on shelves and a print of a fox hunt hung on the wall. Not a doily or knit blanket in sight.

"You seem to have a good group of friends."

Tom's eyes shone. "That's the best thing at Sunny Crest. You can't beat the likes of Jerry and Al." Then a large grin crossed his face. "And of course Belinda."

"I'm curious, if you don't mind me prying. With you couples, why don't any of you get married?"

Tom let out a sigh. "Belinda and I have discussed it, but it's too complicated. We don't want the hassle of the kids being upset over who's going to inherit what. It's much simpler to keep our affairs separate, except for our affair." He winked at Reginald again. "I had a long and happy marriage to my wife. She died of cancer. Belinda and I are content to leave things as they are for now."

"Do you miss your days in the army?"

"Yes and no. I had a good career, did my duty for my country and met some fine people. But there's a point to move on. Besides, now I have all the time I want to watch sports." He tapped his remote.

Reginald pointed toward his bookcase. "I see some army souvenirs there."

Tom clambered up again from his chair. "Come here. Let me show you what I have."

Reginald emptied the last bit of beer, stood up and followed him.

"Here's a picture of me receiving a commendation from General MacArthur. What a leader."

"Controversial."

Tom wrinkled his nose. "You're not one of those pinkos who was soft on Communism?"

Reginald stepped back. "No, but MacArthur seemed too eager to use nuclear weapons on the Chinese."

"If you had been there, you would have understood, but you're too young. Did you serve in the military?"

"Only ROTC in college. I grew up after Vietnam and before Desert Storm."

Tom eyed Reginald suspiciously. "You missed something by not serving." Then he turned back to the shelf. "Now here's a beauty." He handed over a grenade.

Reginald shuddered as if he had been given a live grenade, which it just might have been. "I hope this isn't armed."

"I could pull the pin and we could find out." A glint shown in Tom's eyes.

"No thanks." Reginald handed it back as he noticed a box on the floor. It contained what could have been a small detonator. Not wanting to be distracted from his main mission, he asked, "Do you have any sports memorabilia?"

"Do I? Come into my bedroom."

Tom led the way into the adjoining room with a bed made as taut as a drum. The wall held various Bronco and Rockies pennants. From a bookshelf he picked up a framed picture. "Here's a photograph of the Bronco team after their first Super Bowl victory. Autograph of John Elway."

"That should be valuable."

"Damn straight. And this." Tom picked up a baseball. "Signed by Todd Helton of the Rockies."

"Speaking of the Rockies, I understand you went to a game recently."

"Yeah. Great game. Rockies pulled it out in the bottom of the ninth. We all took home souvenirs." Tom grabbed a mini-bat from behind another picture and held it up.

With his mission accomplished, Reginald looked at his watch. "I better head back. I'm still a working guy."

"Yeah, you're too young to have earned the right to laze around all day."

⚘ ⚘ ⚘ ⚘ ⚘

Back in his office Reginald confirmed that Karen Landry's faucet had been repaired and then shuffled paper until lunch time. He gritted his teeth and tried Rebecca again. Each ring of her phone sent a pulse through his aching chest. When she answered, he blurted out, "Please don't hang up—"

With the dial tone ringing in his ear, he replaced the receiver and pondered how to reach the Dragon Lady.

Moments later, Mimi Hendrix bounded into the office, holding up a handful of papers. "Four more residents added today! That's another two percent boost to our occupancy rate."

"Good work."

"It's because of the Jerry-atrics. Their little show seems to really do the trick." She flushed. "So to speak."

"Keep it going. I need to see the tally on Friday so I can report back to Armand Daimler on end-of-week results."

She nodded. "I'll have it to you early afternoon on Friday."

Mimi pivoted, her dress swishing around her, and dashed out of the office. It was good to see Mimi's enthusiasm compared to the day she had shown up in tears and offered her resignation. Nothing like some positive results to perk up a marketing type.

Reginald sat back strategizing on how to present to Daimler on Friday. He needed facts, figures and the right hook to land him. He'd have to give the sales pitch of his life to keep this place open.

*****

After lunch Alicia raced into Reginald's office. "There's some sort of altercation in the parking lot."

He followed her out of his office, down the stairs and outside. A small crowd had gathered around two tottering old men facing each other in the parking lot. Both appeared skinny and frail but had their hands up in fighting position. One took a wild swing and missed the other by two feet. The other man jabbed ineffectively in response.

170

"Break it up," Reginald shouted.

The two men dropped their hands to their sides and stood there breathing hard as if each waited for the other to drop from a heart attack.

Reginald approached Jerry in the crowd. "What's going on?"

"Pete and Henry were duking it out. Pete's the skinny one, and Henry's the skinnier one."

"Aren't they a little old for this?"

Jerry kicked a pebble across the asphalt. "Nah, it's a good way for them to keep their circulation going."

"But they might hurt each other."

"No way. They both have such bad eyesight that they couldn't hit a barn door. And if one of them accidently connected, there's no power behind the punch. It would be like being hit with a marshmallow."

The crowd had now dissipated except for Reginald, Jerry, Alicia, an old woman and the two pugilists who still stood in the same place, gasping for breath.

"Jerry, what led to the fight?" Reginald asked.

"They both are courting Mrs. Fenton. They happened to call on her at the same time and decided to settle matters out in the parking lot."

"And has anything been resolved?"

Jerry scratched his head. "I don't know. The winner may be the one who doesn't pass out first."

Reginald approached the two panting men. "Gentlemen, can't you find a better way to settle your disagreement?"

"He's trying to steal my woman." Pete waved a scrawny hand toward Henry.

"She's my girl. You're interfering." Henry tried to slap Pete and missed by a foot, almost falling over in the process.

"Well, what does Mrs. Fenton think of this?" Reginald asked.

The old woman stepped forward and placed her hands on her hips. "They're both idiots. I don't take a fancy to either one of them."

The two men looked perplexed.

"I'd suggest you two make up and pursue some other alternatives," Reginald said. "This place is jammed full of eligible woman. You should each be able to find one who's more interested in you than Mrs. Fenton is."

"You don't like me?" Pete asked Mrs. Fenton, a quaver in his voice.

She scrunched up her nose as if the dumpster had just been opened. "Not in the least."

"But you do take a shine to me," Henry interjected.

"Nope. You both can get lost." She turned on her heels and stomped up the stairway.

Pete and Henry looked at each other.

"You up for a game of shuffleboard?" Pete asked.

"Sure," Henry replied. "Soon as I catch my breath."

Chapter 23

Next on Reginald's agenda was the trip to Sunny Manor in Louisville to meet with Fred Dickinson. As he drove at exactly the speed limit onto US-36, he checked his rearview mirror to make sure no highway patrol cars loomed in the distance ready to pounce on him for any infraction. He wondered how Fred's facility compared to Sunny Crest. Probably more debilitated residents than in an independent living facility. Reginald's folks had all the symptoms but probably not the extremes. The Jerry-atrics represented almost the full spectrum of ailments with Jerry's hearing deficit, Henrietta's macular degeneration, Al's arthritis, Karen's memory problems, Tom's heart disease and Belinda's Parkinson's. Take each of their problems another level, and they'd end up at Sunny Manor.

He considered what Mimi had told him. Cenpolis did have an advantage here in Boulder County with the three types of care within a thirty-mile radius. If a resident at Sunny Crest declined in physical or mental acuity, Sunny Manor was right up the freeway. And from Fred's facility, if a resident really dropped into la-la land, Sunny Home provided nursing care around-the-clock.

Then his thoughts returned to the dead scam artist. Reginald clenched his teeth. He still had three rooms to check for Colorado Rockies mini-bats. He should be doing that at this very minute, but instead he was off to visit an assisted living facility. He let out a loud sigh. It was best to follow his boss's orders. He had to stay on Daimler's good side and see if he could convince him to keep Sunny Crest open.

He exited the freeway, drove up a hill and over the crest where he had a view out toward Denver. The Brown Cloud, as residents affectionately called the smog, was visible in the distance, snaking its way north from Denver. He took a deep breath. Hopefully more clean air from the mountains circulated here than in the pollution spewing from the cars commuting back and forth between Denver and the myriad suburbs.

Compared to his white monster of a building, Sunny Manor was a one-story facility spread over a larger lot. He parked his Jag and sauntered up to the door. Locked. He pressed a keypad and was buzzed inside. That was one way to prevent scam artists. Keep the place locked. But it made more sense for an assisted living facility than for an independent living community like Sunny Crest.

He went through another set of doors and came to a receptionist who directed him to Fred's office. His footsteps echoed as he strode down the linoleum hallway. Watercolors with the resident's name and age in neat script lined the corridor. One painting showed a realistic mountain lake with snow covered peaks in the background. He half expected a moose to step up to lap the water.

When Reginald reached his destination, Fred leaped up from his chair, sending it spinning back toward a bookcase. "Reginald! At last you've come to visit." He shook hands as vigorously as if Stanley had found him in the jungles of Africa.

Fred had frizzy brown hair that tried, but failed, to hide a growing bald spot on top of his head. A little overweight and probably ten years Reginald's senior, he had rosy cheeks, a small pointy nose and eyes that darted from side to side as if taking in a ping-pong game.

Reginald wondered if he'd look like this after another decade in the retirement facility business.

Fred waved toward a chair. "Take a seat. Then we can compare notes on how to stay financially solvent." He plopped down in his own chair behind his desk.

Reginald dropped into the one indicated. "Yes, I'm glad we have a chance to get together. As I mentioned to you, Armand Daimler wanted to make sure we met."

Fred's sunny demeanor turned cloudy. "Yes. . . ah. . . I'm sure you've had conversations with headquarters as well. They're on a cost reduction tear. I get missives almost daily asking what I'm doing to save the corporation money. I've cut to the bone but can't sacrifice services by reducing expenses further."

Reginald nodded. "Daimler runs a no-frills organization and expects all of us to do the same."

Fred took a sip from a water bottle on his desk and set it down. "I've never met him in person. Is he the tyrant he seems over the phone?"

"Worse. He's a short pudgy man who bullies everyone working for him. He loves to stand inches from someone's face, poke a stubby finger in the miscreant's chest and threaten to have him chopped into goose liver."

Fred's eyes widened. "He can't be that bad."

"Nah. I'm only kidding. About the goose liver part, that is. The rest is accurate."

Compared to Reginald's anemic office decorations, Fred's walls were lined with photographs of him shaking hands with dignitaries, several bowling and golf trophies, and the requisite picture of a wife with smiling brood. A window offered a view out toward a courtyard where two old ladies sat in the sun on a wooden bench. One of them handed something to the other one. Reginald cocked an eye to see if it was knitting, a book or a picture of a grandkid. Nope. It was a card deck. "I see two of your residents out in the courtyard."

Fred turned toward the window. "Oh, yes. Mabel and Bernice go out there every afternoon when it's sunny."

"They playing cribbage or trumps?"

"Nope. Texas Hold 'em. I have to watch those two. They're both card sharks. They like to suck in unsuspecting people for money." He leaned forward and whispered. "I lost twenty bucks to Mable last week. If they invite you for a game of poker, don't be suckered in."

"But this is an assisted living facility. I didn't think the residents here would be that with it."

"Don't be fooled. They all have some medical problem that makes them unable to take care of themselves on their own. In the case of Mabel and Bernice they can't hear much and have trouble moving, but their mental abilities are top notch."

"But you also have a memory unit here as I understand it."

Fred nodded vigorously. "That's right. Some residents are in great physical shape but are suffering from Alzheimer's. That's why we keep the facility locked. We can't have someone with dementia wondering off and getting lost. But back to Daimler. He's putting pressure on me to cut my expenditures by twenty percent. Can you believe it? Twenty percent. Think what that would do to the service we provide. It would be a disaster. I have to figure out some way to keep him off my back."

"I know what you're going through. He sent me out here to turn around Sunny Crest, with marching orders to slash costs. I started doing that, but it backfired. Now I'm trying to focus on a balance of wise expenditures and increasing the occupancy rate. You filling your rooms here, Fred?"

"We're at ninety percent right now." His eyes lit up. "You wouldn't have any residents who are ready for a little more care to send my way, would you? That would really help me."

Reginald tried to picture the Jerry-atrics in a place like this. Nah. They were mobile, could take care of themselves and pitched in to help each other. "None comes to mind right now, but I'll definitely refer people your way when they need the additional care."

Fred pushed a stapler to the side of his desk. "So how do I handle Daimler? He's always threatening that if I don't cut costs he can have this property sold off for residential use."

"He likes that threat. He even spoke to a Realtor and wants me to sell Sunny Crest if I can't turn it around quickly."

Fred lunged across the desk and grabbed Reginald's arm. "Don't let him do that. I'm counting on residents moving from Sunny Crest to Sunny Manor. If you disappear, it will be a disaster for me."

"To say nothing of for my residents and staff. I'm doing everything I can to keep the place open, Fred. But it's going to be a tough sell to Daimler. Our property in Boulder is prime real estate. Daimler has dollar signs in his eyes over what he thinks Cenpolis can get for selling the land."

Fred settled back in his chair. "Our property values aren't as high here in Louisville. If you can fend off Daimler, maybe he won't try to do anything with our less valuable land. I'll have to find a way to balance the cost-cutting pressure while keeping the place solvent."

Reginald stared out the window again. The section of the building on the other side of the courtyard had to be less than ten years old. Solid brick and wood construction. "It would be a waste to pop and scrape this facility, Fred. I think you should keep focusing on occupancy rate as I'm doing. If I'm successful in convincing Daimler to stay with Sunny Crest, together we can keep a good thing going." Reginald hoped that he could persuade Daimler.

"How are you increasing your occupancy?"

Reginald gave a conspiratorial smile. "I have a secret weapon. There are a group of residents at Sunny Crest who greet visitors and put on a magic show. It seems to really appeal to prospects, and we've started getting more signups in the last few days."

"Will you rent them out?"

That was an interesting idea. Put the Jerry-atrics on the road to pitch for other Cenpolis facilities. "I don't know. I think they're pretty busy handling the demand for shows at Sunny Crest. But here's another thought. I also have a very good marketing manager who has some excellent ideas on promotion. Maybe I could put her in touch with your marketing person."

Fred drummed his fingers on his desk. "My marketing manager has all kinds of ideas as well, but they all cost too much. I'm having trouble reconciling his enthusiasm with Daimler's dictate to cut cost."

"I think that always goes with the marketing world. Finding the right balance. Still it wouldn't hurt to have our people talk. My marketing manager is Mimi Hendrix. Have your guy call her. She'd be more than willing to exchange information." Then Reginald remembered the senior triathlon. "She has this idea of sponsoring a sporting event for old people. I don't imagine your residents would be up for that."

"It depends. I have several who are very active physically. Sometimes too active."

Reginald thought how active the Jerry-atrics were. Physically and other ways. "Mimi can describe the concept to your marketing guy and see if he wants to work with her on it, provided I give her the go-ahead."

Fred winked. "Holding the old purse strings tight, Reginald?"

"You better believe it. No way I'll let rampant spending sink us. I'm not ready to pull the trigger on Mimi's triathlon yet. Maybe we could share the expenses."

Fred held up his hand. "Whoa. I'm looking for ways to cut costs not increase them."

"I know, but remember, keeping me going, keeps you going."

"We'll start by having the marketing people put their heads together." Fred jumped from his chair. "Now, let me give you a tour. There's a lot to see in this place."

"Good. Maybe it'll stimulate some more ideas on how we can help each other."

For a pudgy guy, Fred moved quickly, and Reginald had to jog to keep up with him as he shot down the hallway.

"First, let me show you a typical resident's room." Fred knocked on a door.

"Come in," a faint voice answered.

He pushed the door open, and they entered a suite, smaller than the ones at Sunny Crest.

"Hello, Agnes. I have a visitor here who wants to see what a room looks like. I always like showing off your place."

Agnes sat in a rocking chair, knitting. Her gray hair was tied up in a neat bun. She wore a yellow flowered house dress and pink bunny slippers. Her fingers moved constantly as the knitting needles clacked together. Her bed was covered with a pink and gray afghan, and a white doily rested under a lamp by the bedside.

Unlike Sunny Crest, no kitchenette. An open bathroom with hold bars visible from a walk-in shower. No Mrs. Rasputin taking down the safety railings in this place.

"How long have you lived here?" Reginald asked Agnes.

"A little over a year. My legs finally gave out. I moved here from Sunny Crest."

"That's where I'm from."

She peered at him. "You look too young to be living in a retirement home."

"I appreciate the compliment. I'm the executive director there."

She stopped knitting for a moment, her probing eyes watching him like a cat looking at a piece of fish. "You must be new."

"That's right. Two weeks."

"What happened to that jerk, Edwards?"

Reginald flinched. "He. . . uh. . . resigned suddenly. I was asked to take his place."

"That's good. I'm sure you'll do a better job. He was a dipstick."

Fred laughed. "Agnes, you never cease to amaze me. Always telling it as you see it."

"No sense mincing words at my age. If I don't like something, I'm going to speak my mind."

"Thanks for letting me stop by," Reginald said.

They exited as Agnes resumed knitting.

Fred gave him a tour of the dining room, craft room and then led him to a meeting room with folding chairs for concerts, lectures and movies.

"You'll notice the fifty-nine inch flat screen television." Fred pointed to one larger than at Sunny Crest. "We show a DVD movie every night there isn't some other event going on in this room. Usually get quite a turnout."

"Probably show *Cocoon* and *Space Cowboys*." Reginald chuckled.

"No way. This crowd likes *Rambo*, *The Terminator* and *Die Hard*."

Probably on Tom Balboa's list of favorites as well. "What about the people who don't hear so well?"

Fred stepped over and tapped a box sitting next to the TV. "We have earphones and a special transmitting unit here for the hearing impaired. Everyone can enjoy the show without turning up the volume too loud."

"You've thought of everything."

At that moment one of the women from out in the courtyard limped up, leaning on a cane. She held a card deck in her hand, placed it down on the empty table next to them and riffled the deck. "Anyone up for a little friendly game of cards?"

Fred wagged a finger at her. "Now, Mabel, you aren't gambling again, are you?"

She placed a hand to her chest. "Me? I'm only looking for someone who wants a little action." She squinted at Reginald over the top of glasses perched on the bridge of her nose. "You look like a gaming gentleman. Want to play some five card stud?" She reached over, picked up the cards and performed a perfect one-handed cut.

Reginald regarded her warily. "I'm sorry. I didn't bring any cash with me."

"Doesn't matter. I take checks or credit cards." She reached in her purse and whipped out a manual credit card imprinter and set it on the table next to the deck of cards. "Visa or Mastercard?"

Fred grabbed Reginald's arm and dragged him out into the hallway. Once safely out of Mabel's grasp, the tour continued to an exercise room.

"We have our cane fu class going on this afternoon." Fred pointed to half a dozen women and one scrawny man in the middle of a large room. An instructor in what looked like a white karate karategi, stood in front of the group. They all held canes in their hands.

"What's cane fu?" Reginald asked.

Fred chuckled. "It's the latest craze. It's a martial art also referred to as cane fighting. It provides excellent exercise and is a means of self-defense that can come in handy if an older person is ever attacked. You should see some of the moves these people can make with a cane in their hands."

Reginald recalled having to dodge a few canes at Sunny Crest when people weren't sure where to place the darn things. He had never considered a cane as a means of self-defense, but now thinking about it, he realized you could whack someone pretty good with a large solid piece of wood or aluminum. Think what a little mini-bat had done to Willie Pettigrew.

They stepped into the room and stood beside a table covered with half a dozen polished wooden canes. Blue padded mats covered the floor.

"How's the class going, Jason?" Fred called out.

"Great, Mr. Dickinson. Of all the assisted living facilities I visit, this group is the best."

"I'm sure you say that to all your students," an old lady in a long saggy green sweat suit said.

"No, ma'am. I tell everyone they're doing good, but only Sunny Manor is the best. You all rock."

"I didn't hear you, sonny," another wrinkled woman in gray sweat pants and a long white T-shirt said leaning on her cane. "What about rocks?"

"Something about us being solid as rocks," the geezer added, waving his cane in the air. He looked frail enough to fall over from lifting the cane above his head.

"Let's pair up for some sparring," Jason announced. "Find a partner."

They all scrambled into pairs. The woman in the long white T-shirt stood by herself. "How come no one wants to spar with me?" she shouted.

"You knocked me down the last time," the green sweat suit woman replied. "You're too rough."

"You sprained my wrist last week," the geezer added. "I'm not sparring with you again."

"You're all a bunch of wimps." She pointed toward Reginald and Fred. "How about one of you two? I need some competition here."

Fred shook his head vigorously. "Not me. I have a bad back."

Using her cane, the woman in the white T-shirt limped over. She peered at Reginald out of the corner of her eye. "You'll do." She wrapped the crook of her cane around his leg and pulled him out onto one of the blue mats. The lettering on her T-shirt read, "Getting To 100 Isn't for Wusses."

"Wait a minute," Reginald protested. "I've never done this before."

"You'll learn quick, sonny. Do what you're told." She jabbed the bottom end of her cane into his stomach for emphasis.

Reginald let out a burst of air and bent over in pain.

She whacked him on his shin with her cane. "Suck it up and stand tall, sonny. Tough it out."

He stood the best he could before any more bodily harm could be done.

Jason handed him a cane. Reginald turned it over in his hand. It wasn't your typical walking cane. It was solid wood with serrated edges on part of the handle. The crook came to a point. "This thing looks pretty lethal." He hefted it in the air.

Reginald's sparring partner whacked her cane into his. "Keep it down, sonny. Someone could get hurt if you wave that thing around carelessly. Show some control."

"Yes, ma'am."

She wrinkled her nose at him. "Don't ma'am me. My name is Maude. You're not going to give me any trouble, are you, sonny?" She stabbed her cane at him, stopping inches from his chest.

His stomach ached, and his shin hurt. "I wouldn't think of it, Maude."

"Good. Otherwise I'll have to kick your butt."

On that happy note Jason told everyone to face his or her sparring partners. "Now bow."

Maude and Reginald bowed toward each other.

"Now I want one of you in each pair to assume a defensive position like this." He held up his cane with a hand on the handle and the other toward the bottom. "Place it at an angle in front of your face, and when a blow comes from your partner, push upwards."

"You can do defense, sonny."

Reginald copied Jason's move.

Jason stepped over and adjusted Reginald's hands. "You want it so your opponent can't strike your wrists."

Reginald looked over to see Maude tapping her cane on the mat. "Makes sense." He adjusted his hold so Maude wouldn't be able to whack his hands.

"Now I want the other person to assume an attacking position like this." Jason held his cane up to his right with hands placed close together. "Strike with a downward slashing motion." He demonstrated. "Okay, assume positions."

Reginald held his cane in the defensive position, and Maude raised her cane as Jason had shown.

"Now strike."

Maude brought her cane forward, and Reginald thrust upward to fend it off.

Pow. Her cane struck his, and his hands vibrated. He could feel the contact all the way to his teeth.

"Again."

Bam. Reginald stumbled as Maude practically knocked him over.

"Once more."

Wham. Reginald lost his footing and fell. His cane flew into the air, and his head hit the mat.

Maude followed through downward and placed the pointed end of the crook right on his throat. "Gotcha good, sonny. You'd be dead if I wanted you out of the way."

The room was spinning, and Reginald saw two Maudes. One was threatening enough. He could understand why no one wanted to spar with her.

She removed the point from his throat, and he slowly sat up. The room and Maude came into focus. At that moment he heard a familiar voice. "What are you doing to my mother?"

Reginald pulled himself up from the mat and who should be standing there in his orange Bermuda shorts and wizard T-shirt but Jerry Rhine.

"Your mother?"

"Yeah. You were just sparring with my mother." He turned toward Maude. "Hi, Mom."

"Good to see you here, kiddo. Do you know this dufus who can't defend himself?"

"Yeah, Reggie and I are old buddies." Jerry patted him on the back. "You're lucky you didn't end up with more than the wind knocked out of you, Reggie."

"Maybe you should spar with your mom." He handed the cane to Jerry.

Jerry thrust out his index fingers to form a cross. "No way. I'm not getting near her when she has a fighting cane in her hand. You have to be an idiot to do that."

Then the discussion from the night of the family dinner came back to Reginald. "You told me your mother was a hundred-and-one."

"That's right, Reggie. You've just been whupped by a centenarian."

Reginald took stock of all his pains and bruises and decided he would survive. "You come here often, Jerry?"

"Once a week. I visit Mom and we have a cup of java in the dining room. They serve better coffee than at Sunny Crest."

"I'll remember to tell Maurice that he has an opportunity for improvement."

"You do that. Want to join us, Reggie?"

"Thanks, but I think I better stay out of striking range of your mother."

Reginald joined Fred in his office to wrap up for the afternoon.

"Quite a place you have here," Reginald said, rubbing his hip where he had fallen after Maude's attack.

"Yeah, I never know what to expect from one day to the next. Say, Reginald, I heard that you had a strange death at Sunny Crest recently."

Uh-oh. Reginald decided to keep the explanation short and to the point.

"A man who had been scamming some of my residents turned up dead in the loading dock area."

"Accident or someone whack him?"

"The police haven't determined the cause of death for sure yet. They're still investigating." He chose not to mention that Maude's son and his friends might somehow be implicated in a murder.

"Fortunately, we don't have that kind of excitement around here. One of the benefits of having the place locked."

"I'd hate to have to resort to that. I'm hoping that we won't have any more scam artists prowling our corridors. I've increased security and that should help keep the wrong types of people out." Reginald looked at his watch. "I better get out of your hair. I appreciate the tour."

Fred stood up and grasped his hand. "Let's keep in touch. We need to team up to ward off the threats from Cenpolis headquarters."

How true. Reginald had three days to save Sunny Crest or the place would disappear in the dust of a wrecking ball, and he'd be holding a tin cup for donations on the Boulder downtown pedestrian mall.

As Reginald exited the building he saw Jerry and Maude standing next to his Jaguar. Maude rested on her cane. Jerry was waving his hands in the air doing his Italian act.

"What trouble are you two causing?" Reginald asked.

"I was showing Mom that you have one of these fancy cars, but it's missing the thing-a-ma-jig on the hood."

Reginald stared at them both suspiciously. "Yeah, strange how it disappeared."

Maude wrinkled her nose and poked her cane at Reginald. "Stop by any time, and I'll be happy to knock you flat on your tush again, sonny."

Chapter 24

Wednesday morning arrived with an unusual summer gloom and drizzling rain. The workday began no better for Reginald when Mimi crept into his office, her shoulders slumped.

"What's the matter, Mimi?" A small headache began to form over Reginald's eyes.

"I got a call a few minutes ago from the marketing manager at Sunny Manor. He said his boss spoke with you yesterday, and he wanted to discuss the senior triathlon."

"I brought that up when I visited their facility. Why so glum?"

"I thought he might be interested in sharing expenses on the event. He told me he had no money to spend whatsoever."

Figures. Reginald rubbed his temple before answering. "Maybe he can help with the promotional effort."

Her shoulders straightened. "Yeah, that would be useful." She waited a beat. "Are you going to approve it?"

"Not yet. It's still under consideration."

Her bleak look returned. "We have another problem."

Reginald recoiled and almost knocked the pile of requisitions over on his desk. In nearly every discussion with his staff that word "problem" kept popping up. The throb in his head intensified. "What now?"

"Within the last thirty minutes, three prospects cancelled visits for today. People don't want to go out in this bad weather. And we had made such good progress over the last several days."

"Invite them tomorrow for a free dinner or lunch."

"Oh, good idea." She perked up and scampered away.

Attitudes changed around here like the weather.

Reginald lowered his head to his desktop. *Controlled breathing.* He repeated the mantra until his head felt better. One crisis down.

Time to check on the litigation. He called Larry Samuelson. "Did you have a chance to speak with Mrs. Rasputin?"

"I did. She's a straight shooter, not like her useless grandson. She certainly doesn't want to sue you. If we can talk some sense into the little prick, this could be resolved."

"So can we dismiss this travesty?"

"Not yet. Nolan Rasputin still insists that he's going to haul you into court and march you through a full trial."

"Can he do that if his grandmother doesn't want to sue me?"

"He can cause trouble but doesn't have much chance of winning. It could cost you time and money."

Reginald detected a jovial rather than sad tone in Samuelson's voice and replied, "Make this go away, Larry."

*****

Rather than sit there and curse lawyers, Reginald decided to continue his rounds to check for Colorado Rockies mini-bats. He looked up Al Thiebodaux's room number on his cheat sheet and headed for the third floor.

When he knocked on the door, a faint voice moaned, "Come in."

Reginald entered to find Al in bed in the small suite. His room looked as emaciated as he did—other than photographs on the walls and one bookshelf in a corner, the only other things in view were a paperback thriller on the bedside nightstand and an overturned box of tissues on the floor.

"You're not feeling well, Al?"

"It's this damp weather." He rubbed his arm. "My arthritis is acting up. I can hardly move."

"Do you want me to arrange for a twenty-five year old masseuse to come visit you?"

A faint smile creased Al's lips. "That might help. What brings you here?"

"I'm trying to find out if anyone heard anything the night the scam artist died. Since you're on one of the lower floors, I thought you might have."

A momentary glint appeared in Al's eyes. "I was a little preoccupied that night so didn't notice anything." Then he flexed his wrist and grimaced. "I should take my pill. Could you bring me some water? There's a glass in the bathroom."

Reginald got the water and on his return trip, he inspected the photographs—people, street scenes, farms and animals.

"Quite a collection of pictures." He handed the glass to Al.

"I took these photographs during my professional career. I spent twenty years with the Associated Press and then opened my own commercial business in New York."

One picture showed a smiling Dwight D. Eisenhower surrounded by a bevy of young women sporting "I like Ike" buttons.

Reginald pointed to another photograph. "That looks like Houdini."

"That's right. I took it with a Brownie camera when I was a little kid, right after one of his last performances. Jerry's been after me to buy that picture. I told him it's not for sale."

Reginald tapped his fingers on the frame. "I can imagine a magician wanting a picture of the master."

"But I'm going to surprise Jerry one of these days and give it to him." Al chuckled. "I'll catch him unaware. I can't wait to see the expression on his face."

"Do you still take pictures?'

Al shook his head, and his chin drooped. "No, the arthritis in my fingers won't let me."

Reginald's gaze turned to the wooden bookcase. He stepped over, bent down and spotted a mini-bat on the bottom shelf. "You must have gone to a Rockies game recently. I see a souvenir here."

Al gulped down his pill and sat up. "Yeah, we saw quite a game. I felt pretty stiff the next day from sitting so long, but it was worth it."

"I understand all six of you go to these types of events."

He chuckled. "That's right. All the Jerry-atrics. We're quite a group. Always take trips together."

"Anyone else attend the game with you?"

"No. Only the six of us. We couldn't talk any of the others into coming with us. Grandkid visits and such."

After wishing him a speedy recovery, Reginald jaunted back to his office and called Hector Lopez.

"Hector, one of our residents is suffering a lot of pain from arthritis. Do we have any masseuses that we use for all these old achy bodies?"

"Watch your phraseology. We have a massage therapist on call. She's been here several times when we've had a request for massages."

"Line her up this morning to go to Al Thiebodaux's apartment. His arthritis is acting up."

"Given your new policy, he'll have to pay seventy dollars for that."

Reginald sighed at what he had wrought. "I'll cover it, Hector."

"Okay, Boss."

Reginald looked at his watch. Time for one more visit before lunch. Checking his list, he took the elevator to the fifth floor and knocked on Jerry Rhine's door.

"Who the hell is it?"

"Your worst nightmare."

"Hey, that sounds like Reggie's voice. Come on in."

Reginald entered to find the suite decorated like a Chinese opium den. The curtains blocked out any outside light. One dim bulb cast its faint glow on a collection of lacquered boxes. Handcuffs hung from a coat rack. Smoke circled upward from a pot sitting on a white oriental table. Jerry held a deck of cards. The aroma of tea wafted through the room. The only thing missing would have been Jerry dressed in a Manchu ch'ang-fu robe instead of his Bermuda shorts and T-shirt with the word "Wizard" emblazoned over his chest.

Reginald blinked. "You holding a séance or playing solitaire?"

"No. Practicing. Damn, I'm going to wow those new prospects, Reggie. I have some new tricks to try out on the visitors this afternoon."

"I'm sorry, but we may not have that good a turnout today. Rumor has it that we've had some cancellations due to the weather."

"Wimps." Jerry ruffled the card deck. "They'll miss a good show."

After his eyes adjusted to the dim light, Reginald looked around the apartment. "Why do you keep it so gloomy in here?"

"I want to make sure I can do my routine in any lighting. I start with bright lights and then go to the dark side. You caught me doing my dark arts." He winked.

"Something from Harry Potter?"

"Well, I might actually be a wizard. You never can tell." He tapped his chest. Then he reached out and acted like he pulled something from Reginald's ear. A wand rested in his hand.

"Pretty nifty, Jerry."

"You ain't seen nothing yet. By the way, I hear you and the Dragon Lady had a little falling out. You're really having a problem keeping up with her."

Reginald tsked. "We seemed to be getting along so well until I spoke with her mother when Karen's necklace turned up in Henrietta's linen closet."

"You should know better than that, Reggie. You can't be questioning the Dragon Lady's mother, I can tell you that. You don't want to be on the bad side of either of those two women. No siree." He opened his hand. A plastic lizard rested there. He handed it to Reginald. "Think of this as a baby dragon. Practice being nice to it, and maybe the Dragon Lady will be more cooperative. You must have really pissed her off this time."

Reginald dropped the lizard into his pocket and sighed. "The incident with the necklace was only the start of it. To make matters worse, she saw a real estate contract on my desk to sell off Sunny Crest. I tried to explain to her that my boss did that and not me. I want to keep this place open, not turn it into residential homes."

"Sounds like you stepped in it with both feet, Reggie. Since you're such a nice guy, I might put in a good word for you."

"I'd appreciate any help I can get. When Rebecca's mad, she's not the most communicative person. She hangs up or doesn't answer when I call her."

"I have some influence with her mother, and her mother can make the Dragon Lady listen. I'll appeal your case to the higher court."

"It couldn't hurt. I also want to thank you again for the good work you're doing in attracting new residents. That's the most important thing that can be done to keep this place open."

Jerry adjusted a set of metal rings. "Hell, I'd do it for you even if you hadn't removed that corncob wedged up your butt. It's good to see that you've loosened up a little, Reggie."

"With you around, Jerry, I have no choice. Now, are you going to give me a tour of this. . . museum?"

"You like my decor?" He waved his right arm around in an arc.

"It's. . .unusual."

Jerry slapped him on the back. "I call it Magician's Whorehouse Modern. Let me show you a few things. You've heard of the Chinese finger torture?"

"I had one of those when I was a kid. It's the gadget you put on your fingers and the harder you pull the tighter it holds."

"Exactly. Now, I can outdo that. Here's my Siberian hand torture. Looks like a hand muff. Put both hands in." Jerry proffered an object that looked like a dead albino squirrel with holes on both ends.

Reginald's eyes narrowed with suspicion. "You really expect me to put my hands in that?"

"Trust me."

"I don't know."

"Come on Reggie, be a sport."

"Okay." Reluctantly, Reginald inserted his hands in the ragged powder puff.

"Now try to remove your hands."

Reginald tugged, and the damn thing held tight.

"Works on the same principle as handcuffs. You might want to try it on the Dragon Lady if my personal intervention on your behalf doesn't succeed."

"Very funny. Now free my hands."

Jerry scratched his head. "That's the damndest thing. I know how to catch hands in it, but I haven't figured out how to turn it off yet. You may have to wear it a few days until I have someone translate the manual. How's your Russian, Reggie?"

"As good as my Chinese."

"Henrietta has to see this." Jerry picked up the phone and punched in four digits. "I'd like to request the loveliest woman in this establishment to come to my apartment for a sight to behold. . . No, I have my clothes on. It's Reggie. . . No, he has his clothes on too. But you'll never guess what happened. He fell for the Siberian hand muff. . . that's right. . . see you in a moment."

Jerry returned the phone receiver to the cradle. "She'll be right here."

Reginald scowled and struggled with the muff. "You're a piece of work, Jerry."

He opened his hands. "I aim to please. While we're waiting, let me show you around as long as you promise not to interfere with any more of my gadgets."

"I wouldn't think of it."

Jerry pointed to a large upright box in the corner that looked like a mummy coffin. "Here's my ancient Egyptian mystery casket." He opened it to reveal large protruding nails. "I climb in, have someone close it with the nails appearing to pierce my body. Then, poof." He snapped his fingers. "I disappear and re-emerge unscathed."

Through clenched teeth Reginald said, "I wouldn't mind the nails working on you right now."

"Aw, don't be a sore loser, Reggie."

Reginald tried flexing his hands again but couldn't get them out of the contraption. "Okay, what else do you have in this den of iniquity?"

189

"All sorts of interesting puzzles and tricks here. I'd let you try some, but it seems you're preoccupied." He chuckled and pointed toward a bookshelf covered with small containers, vials and boxes.

Reginald looked in the direction indicated and also saw a chunky ornate urn on the floor that held two umbrellas, a cane and a Rockies mini-bat. At least he had accomplished one objective even if he had to undergo personal humiliation. He also noticed a personal computer on a desk. "You use the computer much, Jerry?"

"Yeah. I have a number of magician web sites I check out. I also post a blog on magic tricks. There's all kinds of good magic poop on the Internet."

"You proficient with Adobe Photoshop by any chance?" Reginald asked.

Jerry grinned. "Could be."

"You know, I haven't found my mug shot in the elevators the last couple of days. Strangest thing. I had to suffer the affront from a new and unique poster every day but then magically, poof. No more insulting posters."

"I guess people like what you're doing now compared to how you started out. You can't blame residents for being pissed at you, Reggie. You were a stuffed shirt or should I say stuffed with corncobs for the first few days here."

Reginald grimaced and prepared to defend himself. Then he spotted a collection of automobile hood ornaments on a shelf. He walked over and pointed with his two constrained hands. "Any chance you have a Jaguar leaping cat hood ornament?"

Jerry chuckled. "Nah. If I did I wouldn't keep it here."

At that moment Henrietta burst into the room and directed a long red fingernail at the Siberian muff. "Oh, Reggie. You're the first one to fall for that since Jerry tricked a five-year-old granddaughter of one of the janitors."

"That makes me feel oh, so proud."

Jerry scratched his head. "I can't find the instruction manual, Henrietta. Did you borrow it?"

"No, I think you pitched it when you cleaned up last May."

"Oh, well. Reggie, it does match your shirt. And if your nose gets itchy, you can use it as a giant tissue."

Reginald's nose immediately started itching. He glared at both of them.

"Henrietta, since you've been kind enough to come share Reggie's embarrassment with him, I'd like to ask your help on a very delicate matter."

She arched an eyebrow. "Yes?"

"Reggie here has become enamored with a relative of yours who happens to be giving him the cold shoulder. He has tried to apologize to her, but she won't listen. Now I could try capturing her in intertwining Siberian hand muffs with Reggie or maybe you could convince her to listen to Reggie's side of the story. What do you say?"

"Rebecca hasn't followed anything I've told her to do since she turned thirteen, but I'm willing to try. What crime did you commit, Reggie?"

Reginald rubbed the muff against his nose. "She didn't like that I questioned you concerning the disappearance and reappearance of Karen's necklace."

Henrietta's eyes flared, and she aimed her dangerous, long red nails at Reginald. "That's understandable. I didn't like it either."

Reginald hung his head. "I only tried to gather the facts, not make any judgment."

"That's true. You never actually accused me of stealing it."

Reginald gave her a wan smile. "That's exactly what I've been trying to tell Rebecca, but she won't give me a chance to share my side of the story. She keeps hanging up every time I call her."

Henrietta crossed her arms and stared at Reginald. "Any other transgressions?"

"She saw a real estate document with an offer to buy the Sunny Crest property and to turn it into housing units."

"What?" Henrietta stepped forward and thrust her claws inches from his face. "Are you trying to sell our home right out from under us?"

"Don't rake him with your nails, Henrietta," Jerry said. "That's Rebecca's responsibility."

"May I explain?" Reginald took a step back.

She retracted her talons, and Reginald's pulse returned to only twice the normal rate as visions of being scarred for life subsided.

"Without my knowledge, my boss Armand Daimler hired a real estate agent to sell Sunny Crest. I have until Friday to convince Daimler to keep it open. Rebecca saw the document on my desk and assumed I was responsible for trying to sell the property. I tried to explain to her what I've just told you, but she wouldn't listen to me."

Henrietta studied him thoughtfully. "Two strikes against you, Reggie. I can understand why Rebecca's mad. Still, even a fiscally anal-retentive retirement home director deserves his day in court. Tell you what I'll do. Rebecca is coming to see me at five-thirty this afternoon. Give me fifteen minutes with her alone and then show up at my apartment at five forty-five.

She might get a kick out of you in that muff and forgive you."

"But if I stay in this thing, I'll lose half a day of working to save Sunny Crest. I don't have much time as it is."

"Reggie has a good point, Henrietta. In spite of how much pleasure it gives me to see Reggie suffering, I guess I'll have to figure out some way to free him." Jerry clasped the muff, pushed inward and Reginald's hands popped out. "Hey, look at that. I solved it."

Reginald rubbed his wrists. "Thanks for the entertainment."

"The pleasure was all mine." Jerry chuckled and placed the muff back on the shelf. "One thing. Don't mess with any more of my props, Reggie."

"It would be the farthest thing from my mind."

"I need to finish a letter before lunch," Henrietta said. "Reggie, I'll see you at five-forty-five."

*****

Back in his office, Reginald took the plastic lizard Jerry had given him and put it on his desk to remind him that he had a mission to accomplish—winning back the Dragon Lady. He resumed scanning paperwork until he heard the loud clacking of heels. Business manager, Alicia Renton, charged through the open door. "Have you seen Dex or Hector this morning?"

"No, why?"

"I need information from them and can't find them anywhere. No one knows where they've gone. They're not answering their cell phones."

Reginald dropped a requisition he had been holding onto the desk. "Did they come in this morning?"

"Yes. I saw both of them first thing, but they seem to have disappeared."

"I hope they're not trying to settle their differences like those two geezers in the parking lot yesterday."

Alicia chuckled. "Those two guys were something else. What gets into you men anyway?"

"As with yesterday, it usually has to do with a woman, but I don't know what to make of some of these old fogies. I used to think that once people reached the age of seventy, they merely settled in to die."

"Well, obviously, you've changed that mindset."

He raised his eyes toward the ceiling. "I'll say."

*****

Before lunch Reginald visited the kitchen to check on his work release program and spotted Maurice Casotti and Grayson Younger standing together by the stove.

"How are things going, Grayson?" Reginald asked.

"Good. Mr. Casotti has been teaching me how to make clam chowder." He stirred the contents of a large vat with a long wooden spoon.

"What happened to the dishwashing?"

Maurice stroked his moustache. "Grayson finished his assignment this morning and offered to help with the cooking. He's catching on fast."

"How do you know how much pepper to add?" Grayson asked.

"It depends on the size of the container. Here's how I measure."

Reginald strolled away so as not to interfere with the cooking lesson.

*****

That afternoon Reginald was working on his turnaround plan, when he heard a knock on his door. He looked up to see Dex and Hector standing there. They both looked disheveled, shirts untucked and hair uncombed.

"Alicia was looking for both of you this morning. Where have you been?"

"We got tied up for a while," Dex said.

"Just as long as you weren't fighting."

"Boss, I think we've worked out our differences," Hector said.

Dex nodded. "We had a long talk and figured out how to solve our problems."

"That's good to hear. How did this all happen?"

"Um. . . we happened to spend a little time together," Dex said.

"Yeah," Hector said. "Some extended time to talk."

"People have been looking for you all day," Reginald said. "You haven't even been answering your cell phones."

Hector ventured a glance at Dex. "Uh. . . our cell phones kinda disappeared for a while."

Reginald arched an eyebrow. "What aren't you telling me?"

"Nothing, Chief," Dex said.

After a moment of confusion, a realization struck Reginald. "Does this have something to do with Jerry Rhine?"

They looked at each other with wide eyes.

"We need to get back to our duties," Dex said.

193

"Yeah, we've been gone for most of the day," Hector added. "I have to check in with my people."

They scurried away like frightened rodents being chased by a feline, leaving Reginald with his planning and his plastic lizard.

*****

Late that afternoon, Reginald stroked the plastic lizard for good luck and headed up to room 624. His heart racing, he took a deep breath and knocked on the door.

"Who could that be at this hour?" Henrietta queried. "Come in."

Reginald entered to see Henrietta and Rebecca seated, facing each other in the living room of a neatly decorated apartment, fortunately with no magic paraphernalia in sight. The curtains were open allowing late afternoon sunshine to permeate the elegantly decorated room.

Rebecca jumped to her feet as if her chair had caught fire. "What are you doing here?"

Reginald hung his head, a mannerism he'd learned to use frequently since arriving in Colorado. "I've come to apologize, Rebecca."

Henrietta gave a dismissive flick of her hand in his direction. "I wouldn't believe a word he says."

Reginald's mouth opened, and then he closed it. Was he being set up again? Was this how Henrietta planned to help him?

"Oh, Mother. I guess I should at least hear what he has to say."

Reginald stared in disbelief, and then figured he should strike while he had the opportunity. "Rebecca, I'm sorry for putting your mother through the stress of questioning when Karen's necklace showed up in her linen closet. I only tried to gather all the pertinent information from the parties and meant no disrespect. And I want you to know that I am not trying to sell Sunny Crest. In fact I'm trying to save it."

"I'm sure he's lying," Henrietta said.

"Hush, Mother." She turned toward Reginald. "How are you trying to save Sunny Crest?"

He launched into an explanation of the whole situation with the sleazy real estate agent, Frank Ralston, showing up at the request of his demented boss, and how by increasing the occupancy rate, he hoped to keep Sunny Crest open.

Rebecca nodded and didn't try to slash him with the red daggers on the ends of her fingers.

"Would you join me for dinner tonight?" he asked Rebecca. "I'd like to make amends."

"I wouldn't trust him the length of a corncob," Henrietta said. "Don't do it. Stay away from him. He's no good."

Rebecca's eyes flashed. She glared at her mother and then faced Reginald. "Yes, I will. Now I better go home to change. You can pick me up in an hour."

As Rebecca departed with a swish of her skirt, Henrietta winked at him.

"Thanks, I guess," he said.

Henrietta patted him on the arm. "You have a lot to learn about women."

"That's for sure. I'm definitely in over my head."

"While you're here, I'll show you some pictures of Rebecca when she was a little, snot-nosed tyke. Wait a minute while I get my album from the bedroom."

She dashed into the other room, and Reginald wandered around looking at the bookshelf, knickknacks and several metal sculptures of animals. No Rockies mini-bat visible anywhere.

Henrietta returned, sat down on the couch and patted the cushion next to her for Reginald to join her, which he did.

She squinted at the album. "I can barely see this one, but here's Rebecca at two years old playing in the sprinklers in our front yard."

He looked at a curly-haired urchin in a yellow bathing suit with a big smirk on her puss.

"And here she's playing soccer. . . a vacation in Hawaii. . . high school graduation. Oh look, here's a loose picture. I can't tell clearly what it is." She handed it to him.

"It's a picture of you, Karen, Belinda, Jerry, Tom and Al. You're all wearing Rockies baseball caps."

"That doesn't belong in this album. We asked someone to take this when we went to a baseball game recently."

Reginald figured this presented as good a chance as he would have. "I understand from your friends that you each received a Rockies mini-bat at that game."

"Yes, we did. But I seem to have misplaced mine."

Chapter 25

As Reginald left Henrietta's apartment, a feeling of dread seized him. He had located mini-bats in Al, Tom, Jerry, Karen and Belinda's apartments but not in Henrietta's. And another recollection struck him. The night watchman, Seth Kenyon, had heard a noise the night of the murder coming from the west wing of the sixth floor. Henrietta's apartment rested smack in the middle of the west corridor. Could Henrietta somehow be involved in the death of Willie Pettigrew? She had strength enough to whack him, had once possessed a Rockies mini-bat, now conveniently "misplaced," and had been in the facility the night of the incident. He halted in front of the elevator and rubbed his eyes.

That's all he needed. With Rebecca about to give him a second chance, he now had to face the fact that her mother might be implicated in the death of the scam artist.

After pushing the button to retrieve the slower-than-slow elevator, Reginald thought how Sunny Crest had been completely different than what he had expected. Three weeks ago he had never spent more than an hour at a time in a retirement home. In and out on quick inspection trips or to inform some unlucky director that his place of employment would be acquired by another company or closed.

Also, he had been happily oblivious to the foibles of old fogies. He shook his head at the thought of all he had learned in these two weeks. Old people. You couldn't live with them, you couldn't live without them. These supposedly invisible and innocuous seniors sure knew how to keep him hopping.

He would have to skirt the subject of his suspicions regarding her mother when he had dinner with Rebecca. And he'd have to figure out how to learn more about the missing mini-bat.

On the way down to his office, the elevator stopped on the third floor and who should enter but Al Thiebodaux. He stepped in without a hitch in his giddy-up.

"You're looking spritely," Reginald said.

Al's eyes brimmed with joy. "You remained true to your word, Reggie. A beautiful masseuse showed up today. What a woman. She worked wonders with her hands."

"I hope you acted like a gentleman."

"Of course. I don't want Karen to be jealous. But my back, elbows, wrists, hands and knees feel so much better now. I thought I'd have to spend all day in bed. Now I'm ready to cause some trouble. You want to challenge me to a game of shuffleboard?"

"Maybe you can talk Jerry into it." The door to the elevator hadn't closed yet, so Reginald pushed the button for floor two. "I have some work to do. I have to keep this place running so you have a place to live and so your masseuse can come back and keep you fit."

Al bounced out first on the second floor. Reginald watched as he practically sprinted along the hallway.

Back in the old paper factory, Reginald signed a few more requisitions and added some notes to his folder for the do-or-die discussion with Daimler on Friday. He knew the points he needed to emphasize and hoped he could fill a few more rooms as a result of the Jerry and Henrietta show. He was getting down to the wire. Two days to fix it or fry it.

*****

Reginald called Mimi. "Can you tell me the names of some of the best eating places in town?"

"I have a list here that I use for important visitors. It describes restaurants, types of food served and location. I'll drop it off for you."

Moments later she handed him a sheet of paper, which he read through and committed to memory. One thing you could say for this town. Lots of restaurants.

*****

After a quick shower and change of clothes, Reginald gave his locks one last swipe with a brush and headed out of the building to the parking lot.

Jerry Rhine sat on the low stone wall by the entryway, his bare legs dangling. "Big date, Reggie?"

"Darn right. Rebecca has agreed to see me again."

"Congratulations. I'm glad the Dragon Lady had a change of heart. You two make a fine couple."

"Thanks for your help in turning around the situation."

"All part of the service. But you treat her right." He tapped the bridge of his nose with two fingers and pointed them at Reginald. "Remember, I have my eyes on you."

"You'd make a great father-in-law."

"Been there, done that. My two daughters got married long ago. I had a hell of a good time harassing their boyfriends, fiancés and husbands. I'll have to put all that experience to good use on you, Reggie."

"I'm sure you put the fear of God into each and every one of those poor men."

"Nah. But I did make them watch my magic tricks. I couldn't get any of them to try the Siberian hand muff though. That was my test to determine if they were good enough for my daughters. Pretty bright group of guys my daughters brought home. Maybe that should be part of an IQ test." He waggled his eyebrows at Reginald.

"Are you questioning my intelligence, Jerry?"

"Moi? It's just that not too many people have been suckered in on the old Siberian hand muff trick. You'll just have to watch a few more magic tricks to be better prepared in the future. Here, let me show you a new one."

Jerry extracted a bottle from his pocket, opened it and threw what looked like black ink all over Reginald's clean shirt.

Reginald gasped. "What the hell are you doing?"

Jerry held up a hand. "Take it calm, Reggie." Then he extracted a handkerchief from his pocket and began rubbing the ugly spot on the shirt. Instead of helping, the black splotch turned blood red,

"Stop," Reginald shouted. "Enough. I have to go change."

"Cool your jets, Reggie." Jerry waved his handkerchief over the ravaged shirt as if he were fanning a boxer between rounds. "Now look."

Reginald peered downward and gave a start. His shirt had returned to normal. No spot. Not even a wrinkle.

Jerry tweaked his sleeve. "You up for another trick?"

"No way."

"By the bye, my mom says hi. She also told me that she looks forward to kicking your butt again."

Reginald raced to his car faster than you could say killer bees on the loose. As he slammed the door he realized that in the excitement he hadn't had a chance to question Jerry about the miraculous reconciliation between Dex Hanley and Hector Lopez. He'd have that conversation during their next encounter.

Still angry over the little magic prank, Reginald hightailed it out of the Sunny Crest parking lot before any other experiments could be performed on his body or clothing.

He sped out of the driveway and swerved left onto the street. Brakes screeched and a horn honked. He continued onward a block until he heard a siren behind him and saw the flashing red and blue lights of a police cruiser.

"Damn."

He pulled over. In moments an officer sauntered up to his car and asked to see license, registration and proof of insurance. This routine was growing old.

After relinquishing the well-handled documents, he had to twiddle his thumbs while the policeman checked to see if the computer showed Reginald as an escaped fugitive or wanted felon.

Ten minutes later the police officer returned and handed back the license, registration and insurance slip. "Did you realize you cut off a car and almost caused an accident?"

"I'm in a state of mental anguish," Reginald blurted out, and then decided to keep his yap closed so he wouldn't be tested for DUI. He could just imagine having to walk a straight line or blow into a breath analyzer.

The policeman finished writing, tore off a piece of paper and handed it through the window. "Here's a ticket for not yielding when you turned left and cut in front of a car that had the right of way." He removed his dark glasses and stared at Reginald. "The records indicate you have several outstanding citations over the last two weeks."

"I've never had a ticket in my life until I moved to Boulder two weeks ago. This is all very unusual for me."

"Please drive more carefully." He tapped his fingers on the door. "You could rack up enough points to lose your license."

On that happy note, Reginald departed and drove carefully the rest of the way to retrieve his Dragon Lady.

At Rebecca's door she greeted him in black slacks and a white blouse with a gold vest. "What took you so long?"

He sighed. "I had another run-in with the Boulder traffic enforcement squad. They seem out to get me."

Rebecca arched an eyebrow. "Why have you become such a careless driver?"

"I used to think it was from being around old people, but I can't blame anyone but myself. And I'm actually starting to appreciate some aspects of the older generation."

She touched his chest. "Nice crisp shirt."

"You should have seen it twenty minutes ago. It was a disaster."

She closed her door, and they headed down the hallway. "Oh, you must have encountered Jerry Rhine."

"How'd you know?"

"He told me he had a surprise for you this evening. And knowing Jerry, I'm sure he did something to liven your day."

"With Jerry around, it's never dull."

Rebecca allowed him to take her hand on the way to the car. He squeezed her fingers, and she reciprocated. Things were looking up.

"What kind of food appeals to you tonight?" he asked.

"I think you owe me a huge lobster, Reggie."

He scanned through the mental list he had made of restaurants, thanks to Mimi. "In that case we'll go to Delphi's."

He drove east on Arapahoe, slowed in passing two construction zones—careful not to violate any further city ordinances—and pulled into the parking lot at the restaurant.

Inside, the hostess, wearing a long black dress, led them into the dining room. "Would you prefer a table or a booth?"

"I don't want to sit in the middle of the room," Rebecca said.

"Kind of like Wild Bill Hickok always sitting with his back to a wall," Reginald replied.

They slid into a booth and received menus. He ordered a bottle of Sauvignon Blanc and after due deliberation Rebecca, true to her threat, ordered the largest lobster on the menu. He decided on salmon and then raised his glass in a toast. "To our renewed friendship."

"Friendship, Reggie?"

"Just as long as we're together. I missed you these last three days."

"I was too mad to miss you. But now I'm glad we're here tonight." She reached out her hands and intertwined their fingers.

"Will you be at the Friday night party at Sunny Crest?" he asked.

"I promised my mom I'd come. She said that since you and I didn't work out, there might be some other eligible bachelors coming."

He almost gagged on a piece of bread. "I hope you're not giving up on me that easily."

"We'll see how things go this evening. The lobster will be a good start. Now I want a full explanation of your questionable conduct accompanied by groveling apologies and genuflecting."

He sighed and recounted the complete details of the misplaced necklace being found in her mother's apartment.

She tilted her head to the side and peered at him. "And no one knows how it ended up in Mom's linen cupboard?"

"Exactly. You can understand why I needed to ask some questions. It appeared to be such a bizarre event."

"Karen might even have put it there. You never can tell. With her memory problems anything is possible."

Reginald shook his head recalling his disastrous attempt to interview Karen and Henrietta. "Of course she doesn't remember what happened to it, but you're right. We may never know. I'm just glad the necklace has been found."

Rebecca tapped the table with a red fingernail. "Now on to the second of your misdemeanors. The real estate document?"

"As I told you before, that had nothing to do with me. My boss, Armand Daimler, blindsided me by lining up a real estate agent to sell off the retirement community facility. I've met with the guy and told him to put it on hold. My boss thinks Cenpolis Corporation can make good money by selling the land, but I've tried to convince him to hold onto the property and reap the investment on Sunny Crest in the meantime."

"You make it sound like a meat market rather than my mother's home." She leaned toward him, and her eyes flared.

He raised his hand as if to protect the skin on his face. "That's how Daimler looks at it. He doesn't care if people are impacted. Emotions or other peoples' interests mean nothing to him. As he sees it, Sunny Crest is only a business investment. I can't appeal to his better instincts, because he doesn't have any. I'll need to make a pitch to him based on numbers and benefits to Cenpolis. I have to show him why it's in his best interest to keep Sunny Crest open."

She crossed her arms. "And how are you going to do that?"

"Here's my strategy—I plan to convince him that we have a sustainable occupancy rate that will provide ongoing profitability and positive cash flow. Your mother and Jerry have made a significant contribution this week. She leads a great tour, and Jerry's entertainment has piqued the interest of prospective residents. We've had an increase in the number of signups this week. I'll demonstrate to Daimler that we can hold a high occupancy rate, and then he can have his cake and eat it too—current profitability and the opportunity for the property value to continue to increase."

"And if you're not successful?"

He exhaled hard enough to fog an icy window. "Then I can look for a new job, and two hundred people will need to find a new home."

She grabbed his arm. "My mom and her friends love the place. Don't let that happen, Reggie."

"I'm doing my utmost to keep Sunny Crest alive."

As they consumed fruit tarts and a second bottle of wine, Reginald felt the warmth of the alcohol, and Rebecca's presence lead to visions of things to come. They definitely seemed on track to being more than friends again. He felt giddy and realized he had drunk two-thirds of the bottle.

With his head spinning in a false sense of security, out of nowhere he let slip, "I'm a little worried that your mother might be implicated in the suspicious death of the scam artist." Realizing what the alcohol had said, he clamped his hand over his mouth.

"What?" Rebecca slammed her linen napkin down on the table. "You take that back, Reggie."

Having stepped in it, he tried to explain. "It's just that I. . . I think a Rockies mini-bat could have been used as a weapon to bash the scam artist, and your mother's souvenir bat is missing."

"She had nothing to do with the death of that awful man."

Determined to defend himself, he continued, "And the night guard heard a noise from her floor that night."

"My mother is a sound sleeper. She wouldn't be up in the middle of the night. I've had enough of your implications!" She stood and stomped off.

"Rebecca, I'm only trying to share my concern."

But she had disappeared. He slowly raised his body from the chair and followed her. By the time he reached the front of the restaurant, he saw her climbing into a taxi.

Damn. He'd blown it again. He kicked the door.

A waiter tapped him on the shoulder. "Sir, please don't damage our woodwork. Also, you haven't paid your bill."

"I know. I know."

He returned to the booth and slapped down his credit card. Then he had to wait for the indignity of a large bill and no Rebecca. Under his breath he cursed old people, Dragon Ladies and the unfairness of life in general.

As he drove home, his attention riveted to the place where the hood ornament used to reside. Suddenly, his car didn't seem so important to him. He knew that something else meant the world to him. He wanted Rebecca back.

Chapter 26

On Thursday morning, Reginald considered staying in bed and drowning his sorrows in more sleep. He weighed the option to admit defeat, head back to Chicago and start over without the Dragon Lady. Or he could press on, butt his head against the great white fortress of Sunny Crest and figure out how to redeem himself once again with Rebecca. He gave a deep sigh, feeling as if he had the weight of the Sunny Crest building and all its residents on his shoulders. He couldn't give up. The desire to see Rebecca again and the call to duty to save Sunny Crest won out, so he staggered down to the dining room to nourish his body with coffee and a sweet roll. Finding a corner by himself, he nursed his caffeine and sugar as thoughts surged through his tired brain. He had to find some new ways to get back in Rebecca's good graces and save his crowd of rowdy geezers.

Suddenly, someone whacked him on the back. Startled, he looked up to see Jerry with a big grin on his face.

Jerry plopped down in the other chair at the table. "Was last night your lucky night, Reggie?"

"No, not exactly."

Jerry adjusted his hearing aid. "I didn't hear you."

"Things didn't go well last night with Rebecca."

Jerry's happy countenance changed to a frown. "More problems with the Dragon Lady?"

"You could say that. I shot off my big mouth again and infuriated her."

Jerry shook his head. "You have a real way with the ladies, Reggie. And after I paved the way for a reconciliation. What did you do this time?"

Reginald exhaled as if his lungs were congested with Dragon smoke. "I suggested that her mother might be involved in the death of the scam artist."

A snarl appeared on Jerry's face. "Henrietta had nothing to do with that." He slammed his hand down on the table.

Reginald winced at this reaction. "There is some circumstantial evidence. The night guard heard a noise coming from Henrietta's hallway."

"I can assure you she slept right through that night."

Reginald nodded. "That's right, you mentioned before you were there with her."

"I know what a deep sleeper she is. And you mentioned your concern to the Dragon Lady?"

"Yeah. I hinted at my suspicion."

"You are a dumb cluck, Reggie." With that Jerry stood up and strode out of the dining room.

Groaning over starting the day on such a positive note, Reginald went to his office. He called Larry Samuelson to check on the lawsuit brought by Nolan Rasputin to see if his luck had changed or if he was on another bad roll. "Any progress in ridding ourselves of this nuisance lawsuit?"

"Not yet. I tried to talk some sense into that young Turk, but he still wants to proceed full tilt with the litigation. He seems to have saved a lifetime of anger to spew at you and Sunny Crest."

"Lucky us. Why don't you have his grandmother put a restraining order on him?" Reginald slammed down the phone.

To add to his fun, Maurice Casotti appeared in the doorway, his hands behind his back. "We have a problem."

Visions of salmonella poisoning, carving knife accidents and people choking on food danced in Reginald's head. "What now?"

"Our main freezer conked out."

"Can't you resuscitate it?"

"No can do. It's dead. We need to buy a new one immediately or we'll lose hundreds of dollars of frozen food."

"And you have a plan to deal with this?"

Maurice's face brightened. "Yup. You only need to affix your signature to this." He whisked his hand from behind his back and deposited a purchase requisition on the desk.

"Do you want this signed in black ink or my blood?"

Maurice's face beamed. "Either will do."

Before Reginald could even catch his breath after the exertion of spending thousands more of Daimler's money, Henrietta Marlow charged into the office. "What did you do to my daughter?"

"Unfortunately, nothing."

"She's really angry, but won't tell my why."

"I seem to have this way of making her mad. We had a nice dinner, but then I put my foot in my mouth, and she rushed off to catch a cab home. That's the last I saw of her."

Henrietta pointed a bright red fingernail at him. "You treat her right or else, Reggie."

As she stormed out of the office, he didn't bother to ask what the else would be.

Eyeing the large stack of paperwork on his desk and trying to decide if he should make the effort to dig into it, he heard a knock and looked up to see Karen Landry standing there.

"Something has happened to my diamond necklace. I can't find it."

Not again. Then Reginald looked carefully at Karen and began laughing. Tears filled his eyes, and he couldn't stop.

Karen stomped her foot. "What's so funny, young man?"

He gasped and regained control. "It's been a bad morning. I'm sorry for the outburst, but, Karen, you're wearing your diamond necklace."

She put her hand to her throat. "Oh." Then she flushed. "Thank you so much for finding it." Pivoting, she left his office.

In spite of himself, he couldn't help beginning to like these people. With all his troubles, he appreciated the lighthearted break.

He momentarily thought he should have asked Karen if she remembered anything from the night of the murder, but realized that would be a fruitless exercise. Then he reviewed all he had learned. That night, Al didn't hear anything and still had his mini-bat. Karen had her mini-bat. Tom and Belinda had been locked in carnal bliss and both had their mini-bats. That left Henrietta and Jerry. They had been together in her room. Jerry tended to wander the halls, so he could have been up that night although he claimed that he didn't see anything. And he still had his mini-bat. That left Henrietta, who had the reputation of being a sound sleeper but didn't have her mini-bat.

And giving the slightest hint to Rebecca of suspicion pointing to Henrietta had landed him in the poop pile. He felt like a guy on the rack in a medieval dungeon being pulled in four different directions. Between Rebecca, Jerry, Henrietta and Armand Daimler, they each could tear off one of his limbs.

On this happy thought, his phone rang. He reached for it, wondering which of his many fans had called.

"All set to sign the papers?" Frank Ralston's cheery voice asked.

"No. And I don't think the deal will go through. Save yourself and me a lot of aggravation, Ralston. You can tear up the contract."

"That's funny. Fifteen minutes ago I spoke with Armand Daimler, and he exuded confidence that we could now close the deal."

"He and I have a call scheduled tomorrow afternoon," Reginald replied in his most icy tone. "We'll have a final decision then."

"I'll be happy to stop by on Saturday to complete the paperwork. I'll await the good word, Mr. Bentley."

Yeah, Reginald knew what he'd like to do with Ralston's good word.

When the day's mail arrived, he scanned through a stack of personal bills, several ads for retirement home services and a flyer for a discount pizza. If he couldn't save Sunny Crest, he could always get a job delivering pizza, racing around town in one of those little beat-up cars with a cone on the roof advertising deluxe pepperoni. But with all his traffic citations, he might not be able to do that. Pizza joints insisted on a delivery guy having a valid driver's license. He slapped his cheek, realizing he needed to get a grip on his strange reality.

One envelope caught his eye—an official seal of the city of Boulder. He tore it open to find a ticket for a violation of Section 7-4-3, Obedience to Red Signal Required. Two pictures fell out of the envelope. One displayed the rear license plate of his Jaguar as the car entered an intersection with a red light shown. The other showed his scowling mug as he tensely gripped the steering wheel. He recognized the intersection of Arapahoe and 28th in the picture. *Damn.* The photo radar had nabbed him on Sunday when he had followed Rebecca to her apartment and had run the red light to keep up with her car.

As he continued through the stack of mail, he came across an envelope from Channel 5 News. He tore it open to find a letter that read, "It has come to our attention that your retirement home has been providing poor service to your residents. We have researched a number of complaints and intend to investigate further." The document displayed the signature and title of Charles Moncrief, investigative reporter.

To complete the morning excitement, Reginald received a call from Detective Aranello. "I understand you want to see me."

"That's right. I was informed you'd gone out of town. You attending a detectives' anonymous meeting or on vacation?"

"No way. I'm here in Grand Junction to collect evidence for another case. I'll be back in Boulder tomorrow afternoon."

"Any progress in the Willie Pettigrew case?"

"One piece of information I can tell you. We've located Harold Sykes."

"Is he still a suspect?" Reginald asked, hoping something might change his discovery of the mini-bat.

"Nope. Sykes is in jail in Vancouver, Canada, and has been incarcerated for the last month."

Reginald's stomach turned into a lump of lead. He thought of the mini-bat in the paper bag in his closet and knew what he needed to do. "Any chance you could stop by tomorrow evening? We're having a little party here, and I'd like to speak with you in person."

"Fine. I'll be there around eight."

*****

In the middle of the day, Reginald took a break and went outside to hike in the open space to clear his head. His emotions were in turmoil—the desire to be reconciled with Rebecca, his stupidity in mentioning suspicion concerning her mother, the time clicking away before Daimler intended to fry Sunny Crest, the suspected mini-bat murder weapon and all the other problems that needed his attention. As he trudged along, a gray cat scampered across the path and disappeared in the tall grass. There had been a time when he would have kicked at it. But maybe cats weren't so bad after all. Rebecca's cat, Princess, had accepted him. Too bad he couldn't be back in the good graces of Rebecca herself.

A quarter of a mile along the dirt trail, he paused and looked back at Sunny Crest. Two weeks earlier, the eight-story, white building had only been a place of employment for him. Now it held an interesting cast of characters who relied on him to protect their home and safety. His stomach churned. In less than two weeks, this citadel had harbored a scam artist, a thug intent on kidnapping him, a smoke bomb, a probable murder using a mini-bat, a missing necklace, a lawsuit over a broken hip, a silverware thief, the disappearance of his Jaguar leaping cat hood ornament, a resident with an ankle-attacking Shih Tzu, a battle between staff members Dex and Hector, two old geezers trying to throw punches at each other, his mug shot on posters in the elevators, his backfiring cost-cutting attempts and now an investigative reporter breathing down his neck, but most important an encounter with a woman who meant the world to him even though she didn't want to see him. Into this mix could be thrown the various ailments and intriguing personalities of the Jerry-atrics. He certainly needed some of Jerry's magic to preserve this place and to win Rebecca back.

A cloud passed in front of the sun, leaving the building in shadows. He felt a darker cloud hanging over him. Could he convince Armand Daimler to keep this place open? Could he find a way to convince Rebecca that he wasn't the world's biggest jerk? Would the suspicious death be solved? And what if it turned out to be, as he now suspected, a homicide, and the murderer was someone like Henrietta?

He had today and tomorrow to take action. He needed to do something other than stare off into space.

The cloud blew eastward, and the white building glowed again in the bright sunlight.

Today and tomorrow.

*****

Reginald headed back toward the parking lot and realized that he hadn't recently bothered to wipe down his car with a soft cloth. Amazing how priorities could change. As he passed his gleaming beauty, he glanced at the hood. The Jaguar leaping cat had reappeared. There would have been a time when his heart would have leaped as much as the cat. Now, he just stared at it. Sure, he was glad it had been returned, but its reappearance only added to his sense of foreboding.

*****

That afternoon Reginald called Mimi Hendrix into his office. He showed her the letter from Charles Moncrief.

She visibly paled. "You know who he is, don't you?"

"Some investigative reporter on television."

"He's the one who uncovers all kinds of scams or companies providing poor service. You know, sticking up for the underdogs—people who've been cheated or treated unfairly with no ability to fight back. He does background research and interviews alleged offenders. He's given you his only warning and now will show up unexpectedly with his cameraman, so he can lambaste you on Channel 5 news."

"How do you suppose he became interested in Sunny Crest?"

"That's simple. His grandmother happens to be Mrs. Seneca whose dog you tried to evict."

Reginald smacked his forehead. You never could trust animals or animal owners. Then he paused. "Wait a minute. We did right by Mrs. Seneca."

"Yes, but she made a phone call while we stepped out in the hallway. The wheels had already been set in motion by the time we offered her a solution. If we could only give Charles Moncrief a good impression when he comes, think of the PR boost we'd receive."

Reginald moved a sheet of paper around his desk as if it were a planchette on a Ouija board spelling out a solution. "Maybe we can have his grandmother recount how she's now happy with her ground level apartment. In any case, we'll have to take our chances with Moncrief and his television camera. On another subject, I need a status on the occupancy rate."

Her face brightened. "Good news there. No one died or gave notice this week."

"That's a reasonable start. New occupants?"

"After the poor turnout yesterday, we had a record crowd today. Henrietta gave them a tour this morning, followed by Jerry's show. I had lunch with them and Maurice outdid himself with filet mignon cooked to taste." She gave him a smug grin. "I'm happy to report that as of twenty minutes ago, we have agreements that will put us at ninety-five percent occupancy."

"Excellent. I want a final tally by two p.m. tomorrow. I'll need that for my call with Armand Daimler."

"Two more groups coming in tomorrow, so I'll let you know."

He did some quick calculations. He was getting close. Would that be enough to convince Daimler?

*****

That night Reginald had trouble falling asleep. Finally, he dozed off, only to awaken at two in the morning. Dream remnants of scam artists, murderers, necklace thieves and lawyers swirled in his head. After tossing and turning, he gave up and decided to walk around. Throwing on hiking shorts, a T-shirt and tennis shoes, and grabbing his Sunny Crest badge, he took the stairs down to the first floor. After noticing a man on duty at the reception desk, Reginald decided to head out the back way and pushed open the door to the loading dock.

An ear-shattering ringing ensued followed by the sound of running footsteps. Within seconds, the security guard stood there, pointing a gun at him. Reginald identified himself, showing his Sunny Crest badge.

The guard punched in a code in a box on the wall to stop the alarm.

"I'm sorry," Reginald said. "I forgot we have a new alarm system."

"Please read the sign in the future," the guard said.

Reginald spotted a large placard on the inside of the door to the loading dock indicating that the door was alarm-activated between midnight and six a.m. He hung his head. "I missed the sign. I'm just going out for a little air."

"I'll let you out this way before rearming the door. You'll have to return by the front door. Please don't do this again."

Duly chastised, Reginald stepped out into the cool late summer air and surveyed the loading dock, looking much like it must have the night of Willie Pettigrew's demise. One low wattage bulb cast its dim light ten feet into space. He peered down into the bay where the body had been discovered that fateful morning. Willie Pettigrew had obviously been ready to go into the building or had just left after doing who knows what mischief. He had burglary picks. To avoid detection, this had been his chosen entrance and exit path. He seemed able to cruise through Sunny Crest like a shark swimming through the ocean. But why had he been here in the middle of the night?

Reginald leaned over and viewed the floor of the bay again, remembering the sprawled figure he had seen a week ago Tuesday morning. He half expected to spot one of those police chalk outlines showing where the body had been found.

"Sightseeing, Reggie?"

At that sound of a voice, Reginald almost fell off the dock. He caught himself, looked wildly from side to side and spotted Jerry Rhine sitting at the end of the loading dock, his legs dangling over the side like Huck Finn fishing in the Mississippi.

"I didn't see you there, Jerry. How did you get past the alarm?"

"I know how to deal with those gadgets. It was very peaceful here until you set off the siren. You have a way of disrupting things, Reggie."

"What brings you out here in the wee hours of the morning?"

"I couldn't sleep, so I came out for some fresh air. It's quiet enough to allow me to sit and ponder my existence. Unless someone disturbs my solitude by setting off alarms."

Remembering their previous encounter on the loading dock when Jerry saved his butt from the thug who mistook him for Edwards, Reginald asked,

"Do you come out here often, Jerry?"

He shrugged. "Several times a week. My old body doesn't need as much sleep as it used to. It's a good time to plan new magic tricks." Jerry pulled himself up and ambled over. "Here, you have something sticking out of the back of your shirt." He reached behind Reginald's neck and pulled out a bouquet of artificial roses.

Reginald shook his head in amazement. "You're always prepared, Jerry."

"Yup. I learned that during my Boy Scout years."

"Hey, I've been meaning to ask you something, Jerry. What happened with Dex and Hector? You and I discussed how they didn't get along. Yesterday, they disappeared for most of the day, then later showed up and claimed to be best buddies. You have anything to do with that?"

Jerry chuckled. "Yeah. I provided a little counseling."

"Meaning?"

"You really want all the bloody details?"

Reginald gazed once again into the loading dock bay. "I think I can handle it."

"Pretty simple. After I used a little magic to lift their cell phones, I lured them into the storage room and locked them in. They could have beat on the door all day long, and no one would have heard it. I left them an instruction sheet on what they needed to do. It involved a little sensitivity training, sharing their life stories and agreeing on what they could do to get along better. They had to resolve their differences before being released. I guess after half a day alone together in the storage room, they worked out their problems."

"You never cease to amaze me, Jerry."

"Hey, that's what I'm about."

Reginald looked around the loading dock. "You know, I can't figure out why that scammer, Willie Pettigrew, happened to be here in the middle of the night."

"He was obviously up to no good."

"He'd been conning residents, but everyone's asleep at this time."

"Not everyone," Jerry said.

"Yeah. There might have been a few people wandering around, although the security guard didn't see anyone." Reginald paused and gazed from the loading dock into the darkness. "Pettigrew must have been here to steal something."

"Or kill someone," Jerry said.

Chapter 27

Reginald's gut clenched at Jerry's words. "You're right. Willie Pettigrew might have intended to kill someone. I hadn't thought of that."

"I'd guess that the guy took the next step in his criminal activity and planned to do some real damage," Jerry said. "It's probably just as well that he's no longer in the land of the living. Now if you'll excuse me, I think I'll go back upstairs."

Jerry moved to the door, gave it one of his magical taps and pulled open the door.

"I still don't understand how you do that," Reginald said as Jerry disappeared and the door slammed shut without the alarm going off. He raced over and grabbed the handle. Locked. He tried giving it a tap as Jerry had, but it didn't open. He hammered with his fist, pushed and pulled but couldn't budge the damn door. Finally, he gave up and walked around the building to the main entrance. Passing the guard at the desk, he showed his ID badge and headed back for a few more hours of fitful sleep.

*****

Friday morning Reginald slumped into a chair in the Sunny Crest dining room to munch on a donut with his trusty cup of coffee.

Jerry Rhine stopped by his table. "You resemble regurgitated fish guts, Reggie."

"I don't feel much better."

"Your eyes look bloodshot as if you'd been on a bender. It appears middle-of-the-night strolls don't improve you."

"No. I guess not."

"Hey, you should stop back here at ten. I'm putting on the first of two performances of the day. Henrietta and I will fill this place for you, Reggie."

He rubbed his hands together. "You'll have so many residents, you'll have to give up your own apartment."

"Isn't ten in the morning kind of early for a magic show?"

"Nah. We have to catch the morning people. Then we'll have another performance right after lunch for those who like to sleep in. Just goes to show that Sunny Crest can accommodate all types. Even ex-corncob owners." He slapped Reginald on the back and headed over to join Tom and Al.

Jerry appeared much too cheery for Reginald, not being one of the morning people today.

*****

Reginald spent the morning regaining his focus and reviewing expenditures for the week. Sunny Crest continued to run above budget, given his newfound leniency, but with ninety-five percent occupancy, the run rate resulted in black ink instead of red. If they could add a few more residents, they'd be in excellent shape. He jotted down some numbers and adjusted his message to be delivered to Daimler. Satisfied he had done everything possible to prepare for the showdown with his boss, at ten he entered the dining room to watch the performance.

A group of fifteen people sat in folding chairs facing Henrietta. Two men charged into the dining room. One wore what looked like a Giorgio Armani charcoal wool two-button suit and clutched a microphone. The other man, in jeans, held a television camera.

Uh-oh. The investigative reporter had chosen this time to invade Sunny Crest. The slick-looking guy said into a microphone, "We've had a number of complaints that the Sunny Crest retirement home provides less than stellar service to its residents. This is Charles Moncrief on site to see what residents have to say." The camera panned to the front of the room.

Henrietta launched into her spiel describing the assets of Sunny Crest, why she enjoyed it so much here, the amiable residents and the wide spectrum of activities. Then Jerry strutted out of the kitchen in black tails and top hat like Fred Astaire on steroids. Tom followed behind, pushing a box, and Karen pirouetted along, dressed in her gold-sequined outfit.

"Ladies and gentleman, we have a real treat in store for you today," Henrietta announced. "I present the Jerry-atrics."

Jerry jumped forward with his disarming smile. "It's good to see all of you at Sunny Crest this morning. You've heard of money growing on trees. Well, at Sunny Crest money grows in ears." He reached out and tweaked a man's ear and showed a ten-dollar bill. "Or in fancy hairdos." He touched the coiffeur of a woman and out popped a twenty-dollar bill.

"Sunny Crest happens to be a very lucky place. You've heard of pulling a rabbit out of a hat." Jerry held his hat out to the audience so they could all see that it was empty. He turned it around, tapped it and began extracting a chain of brightly colored silk scarves. Between each scarf dangled a rabbit's foot.

"You're probably aware that some retirement communities try to cut expenses unmercifully. Let me show you how other places do that." He wheeled the box forward. "The lovely Karen will climb inside this box."

Karen entered the box with her feet sticking out one end and her head out the other. Then Jerry closed the box, covering her torso. He grabbed a saw from his prop table and sawed through the middle of the box. "This is how those other places slash costs." He raised a large black cape and had Tom hold it in front of the box.

Jerry pushed part of the cape to the side so only Karen's shoes showed. "They cut a little here." He grabbed one shoe and pulled.

A mannequin leg popped out, which Jerry dropped on the floor. "And they cut there." He grabbed the other shoe and pulled out another mannequin leg. He had Tom move the cape so only Karen's head remained hidden, and he opened the box to show a mannequin torso but no Karen. "At these other places you feel like you have nothing left."

Then he closed the door to the box, and Tom held the cape in front of the whole box again. "But at Sunny Crest we keep you whole." He dropped the cape, opened the door and Karen emerged with a look of contentment on her face.

Jerry, Tom and Karen bowed and everyone clapped.

Charles Moncrief said into his microphone, "Well, this presents a pleasant surprise. You've just heard several of the residents of Sunny Crest tout the advantages of living here. This seems like a retirement home with active seniors who know how to put on an entertaining show. Back to the studio."

Moncrief and his cameraman scurried out the door as Henrietta continued speaking, "This concludes our tour. I'd like to hand out application forms." She passed out sheets to the group. Half a dozen people took pens out of pockets and purses to fill out the paperwork.

Reginald shook his head in amazement. Who would have imagined this?

Jerry really could conjure up prospective customers for Sunny Crest. And the Jerry-atrics had saved his butt from the investigative reporter.

*****

In considerably better spirits, Reginald decided to make a call on Mrs. Rasputin at the Boulder Community Hospital. He drove carefully, making sure to stay within the speed limit, not cut in front of anyone or make any provocative moves to catch the attention of the authorities. Then he parked in a legitimate parking spot, not one reserved for the handicapped. Having dodged any further encounters with the traffic division of the Boulder Police Department, he arrived at Mrs. Rasputin's room and found her watching a soap opera on television.

She looked up and clicked off the TV remote. "I'm tired of these programs. I'm ready to return to my friends at Sunny Crest. You here to spring me, young man?"

"When will the doctor release you?"

"Hopefully this afternoon."

"We're looking forward to your return, Mrs. Rasputin. But what's happening with your grandson who wants to sue us?"

She gave a dismissive wave of her hand. "That's only Nolan being overzealous. He just needs to let off steam."

"Maybe so, but he's causing us a lot of trouble."

At that moment who should burst into the room but Nolan himself.

"Are you harassing my grandmother?" he shouted as he stomped up and thrust his face two inches from Reginald's.

Reginald resisted the urge to stick his fingers in the dweeb's eyes, deciding instead to avoid a lawsuit for assault and battery. "No, I'm checking to see when she'll be returning to Sunny Crest."

Nolan waved his arms in the air like a gooney bird trying to take off. "I'm not going to let her go back to that atrocious place."

Mrs. Rasputin fixed her stare on him. "Nolan, that's not your decision."

He turned toward her. "But. . . but. . . but," he sputtered.

"Stop sounding like a motorboat." She slapped her hand on her bed. "And cut out this nonsense with the lawsuit. I like Sunny Crest, and I'm ready to go home."

"I can't allow that, Grandmother."

"Oh, yes you can. Otherwise I'll have a little talk with that girlfriend of yours and let her know what a jerk you're being."

Nolan turned red. "That place isn't safe. Look what happened with the railing in the bathroom. Who knows what they'll do to you next?"

She glared at him again. "You and I both know I took that safety railing off, so stop being such a twit. Do you understand me? Now withdraw that lawsuit or Phyllis will hear an earful."

He looked wildly around. "I don't think that's the best course of action."

"Nolan!"

He led out a deep sigh. "Yes, Grandmother?"

"No more lawsuit."

"Yes, Grandmother." He turned and slunk out of the room like a dog that had been whipped.

Mrs. Rasputin waited until he had disappeared. "Now, that's taken care of, Mr. Bentley. Will you arrange to get me out of here?"

"I certainly will."

Reginald practically jogged to the nurse's station and verified that Mrs. Rasputin would be released at two p.m. Then he called Hector Lopez.

"Hector, I need some transportation and someone to assist Mrs. Rasputin this afternoon so she can return from Boulder Community Hospital."

"Yes, Boss. I'll set it up."

"And can you order two bouquets of a dozen roses each? Have one put in Mrs. Rasputin's room at Sunny Crest and leave the other in my office. I'll pay for them."

"You got it, Boss."

Back in Mrs. Rasputin's room, Reginald informed her that transportation arrangements had been completed.

"That's good news. Thank you, young man. People at Sunny Crest are always so helpful."

"We try to be. And I wish you a speedy recovery."

With that problem solved, Reginald drove back to Sunny Crest, again paying close attention to his driving. As he entered his office, he found Henrietta, Belinda and Karen waiting there.

He nodded his greeting to them. "What a charming reception group. And Henrietta, thanks for the great tour this morning. You wowed them again."

Her eyes glinted with pleasure. "Jerry was the hit of the program. Five more sign-ups. Jerry even told me you were going to give up your apartment if we needed another room for a paying customer."

"I'd be happy to if that's what it takes to keep Sunny Crest open. But I want to stay here and be around all of you. You keep me entertained night and day."

"You can always buy a sleeping bag and bunk down on the couch in the reception area." Henrietta nudged him. "Now do we have enough residents to keep this place open?"

Reginald did the mental calculation. Two-point-five percent increase in occupancy. "We're in excellent shape." He looked back at the group. "By the way, Belinda, welcome back. Did you have a good trip?"

"Wonderful, but it's nice to return to my own apartment and be with my friends." She squeezed Henrietta's hand.

Reginald dropped into his chair as the others remained standing. "So to what do I owe the pleasure of your visit?"

Belinda wrung her hands. "I'm afraid I caused a little confusion when I left on my trip, and I want to clarify something."

"I sense a confession of some sort."

Belinda lowered her eyes. "Yes. It concerns Karen's necklace."

Karen looked confused. "But I have my necklace right here. See, y'all?" She touched her throat, and the diamonds danced in the reflected light.

Henrietta patted Karen's hand. "Yes, dear, but earlier in the week we thought it was missing."

"This all started when Karen asked me to take care of her necklace," Belinda said.

"Y'all, I don't remember that," Karen said.

"That's part of the problem," Belinda continued. "Anyway, Karen requested that I keep it for her for safekeeping, but when I had to go out of town, I thought it best to not leave it unattended in my room. That's when I decided to have Henrietta keep it. I was running late and when I went to Henrietta's room she wasn't there, but the door was unlocked, so I hid it in her linen closet."

"And that's where one of the maids found it," Reginald said.

"Yes, but I guess along the way Karen realized she didn't have it, couldn't remember that she'd entrusted it to me and since I didn't have time to mention to Henrietta where I left it, things ended up in a tizzy."

Reginald laughed. "You ladies certainly have a way of making things interesting around here. You could give Jerry a run for his money on making things disappear and reappear."

"So, I want to set the record straight on how the necklace ended up in Henrietta's apartment." Belinda hung her head.

"I appreciate the clarification," Reginald replied. "I ended up in hot water with Rebecca because I questioned Henrietta."

"Speaking of which," Henrietta said, "Rebecca's still mad at you. I can't get her to talk about it, but is she ever pissed."

Reginald let out a sad sigh. "I wish I could find some way to get off her blacklist."

"Are you coming to the party tonight?" Henrietta asked.

"Yes, I plan to be there."

"Good. Rebecca's coming as well. I'll put in a bad word for you, and that might help." Henrietta winked at him as the ladies departed.

Reginald felt a sense of relief that the great necklace theft had been resolved. He chuckled. A month ago he had been in a boring job dealing with accountants all day. Now he had the excitement of the unpredictable antics of the Jerry-atrics. What a world.

Next on his to-do list, the all-important meeting with Mimi Hendrix to receive a final report on occupancy progress. At exactly two o'clock Mimi marched into his office with a smug expression on her face.

"You look like you just won the Colorado lottery."

"Well, I do have very good news for you, Mr. Bentley. Once people move in, we will be up to ninety-eight percent occupancy as a result of the commitments from the two groups today."

"Not a hundred percent?"

"It would be if we had an exact match between rooms available and requests. We now have a sizable waiting list, but it's not always possible to meet specific needs with the choices of suites, one-bedroom and two-bedroom apartments. We've filled all the two-bedroom units and have a number of married couples who want to wait for those."

"Can't you have Jerry Rhine conjure up the right type of apartments?"

"Well, he's magically produced a lot of new residents for us, but I don't think even he can turn a suite into a two-bedroom apartment."

"I wouldn't put it past him. Now, Mimi, do you think we can hold this high occupancy rate going forward?"

"I don't know why not. As long as we maintain our excellent service, keep the awareness campaign going in the community and have Henrietta and Jerry help sign up new clients, we should have no problem."

"That's very encouraging. Now I'll add this information to my recommendations to Armand Daimler. Thanks for the update."

After Mimi left, Reginald tapped away on his calculator and finished his final calculations. The easy part of the day had been completed. Now he needed to make the most important phone call of his career.

He stood up, stepped over to his door, shut it and locked it, before returning to his chair. Then with trepidation, he punched in Daimler's number and waited while the admin got him on the line.

"Reginald, what do you have for me?"

"I've done a lot of analysis this week, Mr. Daimler, and have a very positive picture to review with you."

"You going to make me big bucks on that real estate in Colorado?"

Reginald took a deep breath. "Yes, by keeping Sunny Crest open."

"That's not the answer I expect from you, Reginald."

He gripped the phone, ready to make his final appeal. "But it's the best answer for you and Cenpolis Corporation."

"Why do you think that?"

Good. Daimler was engaged.

"First, let me report on the progress at Sunny Crest, and then I'll lay out the strategy for the future."

"Okay, give me the short-term view."

Reginald quickly scanned the notes on his desk. "As you know, you sent me here because of the declining occupancy rate and lack of profitability. I've only been here two weeks, but we've made significant strides in balancing expenses, increasing occupancy rate and turning profitable again."

"Balancing expenses? I told you to slash expenditures."

"And I started doing that when I first arrived, but it backfired. It immediately looked like we would lose rather than gain residents."

"No problem. That would support shutting it down."

Reginald looked around the office, glad he had no spectators. "Yes, but I believe that would have been a short-sighted decision and not in the best interest of Cenpolis."

"Oh?"

"Yes. By reviewing expenses and cutting some and expanding where we can best improve our return on investment, we have now reached the appropriate run rate for a facility this size. I also visited Fred Dickinson at Sunny Manor as you suggested. By keeping Sunny Crest open, it also serves as a feeder into Fred's building when people need more care. Cenpolis gets that additional benefit by Sunny Crest staying in operation. And the key result—we now have signed contracts to achieve a ninety-eight percent occupancy rate. That's higher than any of the other retirement communities owned by Cenpolis." Reginald congratulated himself. His financial experience in corporate headquarters reviewing the results from each of the Cenpolis properties came in handy.

"Yeah. The good ones hit close to ninety-five percent."

"And we have a waiting list of other customers eager to come to Sunny Crest and a plan to sustain the ninety-eight percent occupancy rate. This can be very lucrative for Cenpolis."

Reginald crossed his fingers and waited.

"You think you can maintain that?"

His heartbeat increased. Daimler was still listening.

Reginald could see the dollar signs spinning in his boss's head. "Yes I do. We have an excellent partnership between the staff and residents, and our residents have been instrumental in pulling in new clients."

"That's a new twist."

"Exactly. I think we've developed a sustainable success model that will produce ongoing profitability over the next fiscal year."

"Okay, but why not sell it off and gain higher profits from chopping up the property into individual residential lots?"

Good. This was the question Reginald was prepared to answer. He did a little tap dance with his feet under the desk. "Because now is not the best time to sell the land. Frank Ralston may have painted a rosy picture of what you can get for the property if popped and scraped, but it will take time and considerable investment to turn it into a successful residential community. The bidders know the current city council doesn't support more upscale residential property. They've tempered their bid accordingly. If we wait until a better political climate exists, we'll be able to sell the property for twice as much in current dollars, to say nothing of the increased value over time."

"I thought Frank Ralston's analysis looked pretty good."

Now for the punch line. Reginald hoped his understanding of Daimler held true. "We'd be leaving money on the table. Ralston's numbers look good on the surface, but if his buyers choose to hold onto the property for several years rather than developing it, they'll reap the largest rewards and not Cenpolis."

Reginald had shot his wad. Now he needed to wait to see if he had succeeded.

"Interesting perspective, Reginald. I need to make a decision today."

"I understand. And my recommendation stands. Keep Sunny Crest open, harvest current profits and continue to hold a valuable property that will only become more valuable over time."

"I have a conference call with the Board right now. I'll call you on your cell phone with my decision this evening."

The phone clicked off.

Reginald sat there with his stomach churning. Had he made the best pitch possible? Could there be anything he had overlooked? Had he presented enough evidence? Daimler seemed to get the message. Would he make the right decision? Reginald would have to wait until later to see how his boss responded.

His phone rang, and he picked it up to hear his lawyer Larry Samuelson on the line. "I spoke with Nolan Rasputin moments ago."

"And?"

"He says he has reconsidered and will drop the lawsuit."

"Excellent news."

"Yeah."

Reginald detected disappointment in Larry's voice. Oh, well, he'd have to earn his big bucks some other way, rather than defending Sunny Crest.

"Thanks for your help and send your bill to our business manager, Alicia Renton. She'll take care of it."

"I'll do that." A little more pep sounded in Larry's tone.

After they rang off, Reginald went through his mail and found the usual collection of letters waiting for him. One envelope indicated it was from his medical insurance company, Xbest Medical Service. He decided to open it right then. It informed him that his eye doctor bill that he had inquired about would be paid in full. He pinched himself to make sure he was really awake. Elise had actually resolved his problem without him needing to jump through the hoops of making any further phone calls. He felt like dancing a jig on his desk. Miracles could happen.

Was this a sign that his life might be turning around? He would take anything positive.

He slit open a second envelope, and it contained a letter from the human resources vice president of Cenpolis Corporation informing him that due to his move from Illinois to Colorado, his health insurance would now be covered by Med-Care rather than Xbest Medical Service. *Damn.* After he had finally trained Xbest Medical Service. Now he had a whole new company to battle. He wondered how long it would take their slow-reacting rapid resolution representatives to solve his next problem.

Not wanting to jinx himself further, he refrained from opening any more mail and, instead, stared out the window at the open space. Lawsuit dismissed, necklace issue resolved, Dex and Hector getting along, the dog-owning resident in a happy place, stolen silverware accounted for, the investigative reporter placated and the future of Sunny Crest out of his hands. He still had this little matter of a probable homicide on the premises hanging over his head. He twiddled a pen in his hand. Tonight he'd hand the bat over to Detective Aranello. But what did he really think had happened to the scam artist Willie Pettigrew?

He reviewed all he had learned. Six bats and five of them located. One missing from Henrietta's apartment, most likely the cracked one found in the dumpster. A sound on the sixth floor heard by the night guard, coming from the hall where Henrietta resided—pointing to something happening near Henrietta's room.

Thoughts of the day mingled in with his contemplation. How Nolan Rasputin had finally backed off from his lawsuit after his grandmother had knocked some sense into him. And if the suit hadn't been withdrawn, he would have been stuck with his thumb up an orifice without liability insurance given his idiotic directive to Alicia Renton to reduce insurance costs. And his struggles with his health insurance company.

Something clicked in his brain about the mini-bat in the dumpster.

Insurance.

A partially filled out insurance form with Pettigrew as the beneficiary. He started connecting some of the dots but didn't have the complete picture yet.

He had a nagging suspicion that could only be resolved by a little research.

Tapping on his keyboard, he went on the Internet and Googled the three words "scam" "insurance" and "murder."

Up popped the search results, and he read through six irrelevant entries referencing people who had been convicted of insurance fraud as well as murder. The seventh caused him to sit bolt upright in his chair.

Chapter 28

The entry that filled the screen in front of Reginald referenced a *USA Today* article describing how a pair of women in Los Angeles took out insurance policies on two homeless men, and then ran over each of the men in hit-and-run accidents to collect the insurance. The perpetrators figured that no one would miss the homeless men and that they would be able to collect on the insurance policies with no questions asked. Unfortunately for them, the police made the connection.

Could this California case have been a model for what was about to happen at Sunny Crest? Had the dead scam artist Willie Pettigrew tried to perpetrate a similar fraud by murdering residents at Sunny Crest, figuring no one would miss dead old people who might kick off at any time anyway? Obviously, Willie didn't know the residents of Sunny Crest. In any case, he had certainly gotten the punishment he deserved.

Interesting theory. Reginald would have to share it with Detective Aranello when he turned over the mini-bat and explained his suspicion. He tapped the eraser end of a pencil on his cheek while he thought through the implications. The puzzle continued to whirl in his brain. Then the pieces clicked into place. He snapped his fingers. Of course. That had to be it.

Only one way to get to the bottom of all of this. He picked up the phone and called Jerry Rhine's room.

Jerry's voice came across the line, "Magicians are us."

"Hey, Jerry. Can I borrow you for a while?"

"What do you have in mind, Reggie?"

"I have something I want to discuss with you."

Jerry chuckled. "You upping my cut for all the tenants I'm bringing in? Or do you want to buy me a Jaguar to match yours? Hey, by the way, I noticed that doodad on the hood of your car is back. Must make your heart warm."

"Yeah, my car is in pristine condition again. Can you meet me in the lobby in five minutes?"

"Sure. Maybe you want my advice on women although that requires hazardous duty pay in your case, Reggie."

*****

Reginald dashed down to the lobby and waited as Jerry ambled out of the elevator. He signaled to the magician. "Let's take a little walk into the open space."

Jerry eyed him suspiciously. "You aren't armed and plan to dump my body in the brush?"

"No. But I thought we should have some privacy."

"If it's woman trouble, I'm your man."

Once they had strolled out of earshot of anyone who could hear them, Reginald said, "Something's been on my mind—"

"I know you want to find a way to get Rebecca back."

Reginald came to a stop in the dirt path and held up a hand. "Yes, but there's another subject I want to discuss with you right now. I've been thinking a lot about the death of the scam artist, Willie Pettigrew, whose body turned up in the loading dock bay."

"Ah. A serious conversation. I better turn up my hearing aids." Jerry tweaked the bulges behind each ear. "Okay, now I'm ready, Reggie."

"I won't beat around the bush, Jerry. I don't think Pettigrew died accidentally. I believe someone killed him."

Jerry didn't bat an eyelash.

Reginald pointed his right index finger. "Furthermore, I suspect you caused Pettigrew's death."

Jerry wrinkled his forehead but held a steady gaze. "That's a serious accusation, Reggie."

"Yes. But here's what I've concluded. You were in Henrietta's apartment the night of the murder. You've admitted that."

Jerry nodded. "Can't argue with you."

"I think you left her apartment with her mini-bat, went down to the loading dock and confronted Willie Pettigrew. The night guard heard a sound coming from Henrietta's corridor. I believe that noise came from you prowling around."

Jerry continued to show no emotion. "Go on."

"You hit Pettigrew over the head with the bat, killing him. Then you returned and opened the locked loading dock door with your trick. That way no one else would have seen you."

"Interesting hypothesis, Reggie. In your theory you give me a method and opportunity to knock off Pettigrew. What about motive?"

"That's the challenging part. Here's what I speculate. You yourself gave me that hint the other night when I saw you on the loading dock. Pettigrew planned to murder someone at Sunny Crest. I think Pettigrew had taken out an insurance policy on one of our residents and intended to kill that person to collect the money. Similar to a case in Los Angeles. I think you whacked Pettigrew to save this other person."

Jerry regarded Reginald for a long while as if contemplating a decision. Then he let out a long sigh like a gust of north wind. "Okay, Reggie. Here's the deal. Pettigrew took out an insurance policy for two millions dollars on Karen Landry. She was the perfect victim since she wouldn't remember meeting him. He planned to let himself into Sunny Crest using his burglar picks, sneak up the stairwell, enter Karen's room and suffocate her with a pillow. It would have looked like she died in her sleep. Then he would have collected on the policy, no one the wiser."

A cloud passed in front of the sun, and a cool breeze ruffled the hair on Reginald's arms. He shivered either from the drop in temperature or from what he heard. "How did you find all this out?"

"The result of my wandering around at night. I happened to be sitting in the shadows on the loading dock when Pettigrew showed up. His cell phone must have vibrated because he picked it up and began a conversation. I had to turn up my hearing aids full bore. He spoke to somebody about a London insurance policy that had been activated for Karen. I guess he figured that having a policy through a company in the U.K. would make it more difficult to trace if someone became suspicious."

"But how did you know he planned to kill Karen?"

Jerry kicked a pebble off the path. "The idiot told the person on the other end what he planned to do. I overheard everything. He even bragged that he was starting on a second insurance policy and after the first had been successful, he would repeat the whole scheme again."

"That all fits, but how did you happen to have Henrietta's mini-bat with you?"

Jerry gave a sardonic laugh. "When I woke up in Henrietta's apartment and couldn't get back to sleep, I decided to carve our names on the mini-bat for her. A little love memento. I took my pocketknife and the bat with me when I went to sit on the loading dock. I had just hunkered down to start carving when Pettigrew showed up. Needless to say I never did the carving."

Reginald ran a hand over the goose bumps on his other arm. "So instead of carving on the mini-bat, you used it to deter Pettigrew from killing Karen."

"Yeah. When Pettigrew finished his hushed conversation and put away his cell phone, he was standing in the loading dock bay facing away from me. I knew I didn't have time to call someone to prevent him from killing Karen. I had to take action. I snuck down the stairs behind him. I planned to knock him out and call the cops."

"But you never placed that call."

Jerry frowned and shook his head. "I hit him hard enough that he fell to the floor of the loading dock bay. The blow must have killed him."

"And then you hid the cracked mini-bat until trash day and thought no one would be the wiser."

Jerry's eyes widened. "How did you work that out?"

Reginald shivered involuntarily. "I found the mini-bat, Jerry."

Jerry's mouth dropped open. "You're full of surprises, Reggie."

"And you also hid a partially filled out insurance form that Pettigrew had started. I discovered that with the mini-bat."

"Yeah, I put the form and the mini-bat in a paper bag and stashed them in my magic disappearing box in my apartment. No one can open that contraption except me. Then I threw that stuff into the dumpster early Tuesday morning right before the scheduled trash pickup time." He shook his head. "I never figured anyone would look in the dumpster in the short time before the trash got hauled away. And who would have expected you'd be the one to figure it out?"

"I had a hunch."

Jerry reached over, plucked a stalk of tall prairie grass and let it blow away in the breeze. "Interesting. I never considered intuition your strong suit, Reggie."

"I guess I can surprise as well as you, Jerry."

Jerry stared directly into Reginald's eyes. "So now it's up to you what you're going to do with all this information." He turned and headed back toward Sunny Crest.

Reginald stood there stunned, unable to move. He watched Jerry cross the field, look back once, march up the stairs and disappear into the building.

Reginald's face felt hot, and a dizzy sensation came over him. Yes, he had solved the puzzle, but what would he do? Jerry had saved Karen's life and prevented Pettigrew from harming anyone else.

What had motivated Pettigrew to scam so many people?

Money.

Reginald thought of Armand Daimler. Daimler didn't kill people, only threw them out of their homes if the numbers didn't meet his hurdle rate.

Compared to Daimler, Pettigrew was absolute evil. He had scammed numerous people out of their hard earned money, intended to kill Karen Landry and would have murdered others with his insurance scheme. This guy didn't deserve to live, and the world was better off with him dead.

Jerry's intentions had been right, but he had caused the death of another human being. Two weeks ago, Reginald would have had no dilemma. He would have turned the mini-bat over to Detective Aranello, explained the whole sequence of events and told Aranello to arrest Jerry Rhine. But now he had his doubts. Should Jerry end his years in prison because of his decision to save Karen? Should Sunny Crest be deprived of the wacky, crazy magician? What should he do?

Chapter 29

Back in his office, Reginald rubbed the plastic lizard on his desk for good luck with the Dragon Lady, grabbed the roses that Hector had ordered and took the sluggish elevator up to his room, noticing that no defaming posters had reappeared. Progress. With his leaping cat back on his car and his mug no longer gracing the elevator most-wanted posters, his life would be a breeze. Right. Except for his problems with the murder, Daimler and Rebecca.

Once in his humble abode, his thoughts turned back to the conversation with Jerry. Images of Pettigrew's body, the mini-bat and Jerry's performances to attract new recruits all flashed through his mind.

What to do? What to do?

Reginald paced around his room evaluating alternatives. He didn't know if he still had his job or if Sunny Crest would stay open. It would be a shame after the great progress they had made this last week to shut the place down. They'd built a model for success and could keep it going. And worst of all, if Daimler made the decision to fry it, a number of excellent employees would be out of a job and two-hundred elderly people would need to find new homes, which wouldn't be easy. And Rebecca. He had to find a way to win her back tonight. So much to resolve in so little time.

His life used to be so simple with no attachments, no old fogies to take care of, no Jerry-atrics. . . no Dragon Lady. *Damn.* He had actually come to like these people and this place. He didn't want it all to disappear under a bulldozer's blade.

He considered catching a short nap but knew he was too keyed up to sleep. And even if he could fall asleep, he didn't want to oversleep and miss his command performance. Instead, he took a short stroll around the grounds to inspect his building. His building. Would it be his building for much longer? If Daimler fried the place, Reginald would miss the white behemoth and the denizens within.

He returned to his apartment, took a shower and spruced up for the evening's activities. He removed a sports equipment bag from the closet, loaded it with the paper sack containing the mini-bat and insurance form and carefully rested the roses inside. Now he could launch his two campaigns.

He checked his watch. He wanted to arrive half an hour after the shindig had begun. Make his grand entrance and do whatever he decided would be done.

*****

When Reginald entered the activity room, the party appeared in full swing. A fire burned in the fireplace, creating the perfect atmosphere for an evening of dancing. A small band played live music, and as he moved into the room, Tom Balboa approached him.

Tom whacked him on the back, almost knocking him over. "Great to have the real music back, Reggie. Thanks for seeing the light."

"Yeah, you all convinced me live music makes a better party than resorting to a boom box."

Tom chuckled. "You're learning, Reggie. You're learning."

Reginald saw Jerry Rhine spiking the punch, so he dashed over to gulp some for moral support. Then he placed his equipment bag down in the corner and carefully extracted the roses. He spotted Rebecca speaking with Karen Landry next to a snack table. Maneuvering his way to them, he took a deep breath and handed the roses to Rebecca. "I want to apologize again. Your mother had nothing to do with the suspicious death. I was out of line."

Rebecca's eyes flashed. "You're going to have to do better than that, Reggie."

He reached out and grabbed her hand. "Please forgive me."

Henrietta appeared out of the crowd. "Don't give in, Rebecca. Whatever he's done, he doesn't deserve to be forgiven."

"Mother. Please stay out of this."

"Only trying to give my daughter some helpful advice." Henrietta pointed a sharp red nail at Reginald. "Send this jerk packing."

As Rebecca looked down at the roses, Henrietta winked at him.

Rebecca raised her eyes and met Reginald's plaintive stare. "These *are* beautiful roses, but how do I know you aren't going to insult my family again?"

Reginald opened his hands. "You'll have to trust that I've learned my lesson. Even fools like me can change."

"We'll see. Now if you'll excuse me, there's something I need to discuss with my mother."

Rebecca and Henrietta glided over to the other side of the room. Rebecca still held the roses. At least she hadn't shredded them. Reginald took that as a hopeful sign.

He turned to Karen Landry. "Do you remember signing up for a life insurance policy recently?"

She wrinkled her brow. "No, why would I need life insurance?"

"I thought some man might have had you sign some papers for insurance."

"You must be confusing me with someone else. Now if you'll excuse me, there's Al. We're going to dance."

She waved and pranced off to grab Al's arthritic hand.

Willie Pettigrew's final audacious scam would have worked. Karen would have been the perfect victim. She didn't even remember signing the form. He shuddered at the thought of an arm stuffing a pillow over Karen's head. How fortunate for Karen that Jerry had been on the loading dock that night.

He spotted Alicia Renton speaking with a resident and moved beside her. "Alicia, I've been meaning to ask you. With Belinda back in town, how is the volunteer staff working for you?"

Her eyes lit up. "It's as smooth as clockwork. Karen types like a demon, and Belinda quickly learned how to file effectively. With your suggestion, they both enjoy the work, and my backlog is gone."

Reginald noticed Dex Hanley and Hector Lopez standing by the snack table, talking together. Dex leaned toward Hector and spoke into his ear. Then they both stood up straight and laughed. Hector clapped Dex on the back, and they continued their animated conversation. Reginald shook his head in amazement. Those two really had learned to get along together.

He spied Mrs. Younger and her grandson Grayson, so he went over to greet them. "How are you this evening?"

"Just fine, Mr. Bentley. I'm particularly pleased that my grandson joined me tonight."

"Hello, Grayson," Reginald said.

Grayson's hand shot out to give a firm handshake. "It's a pleasure to see you, Mr. Bentley."

Grayson Younger had dressed in neat dark slacks, a pressed long-sleeved white shirt accompanied by a neatly shaved face below a short haircut. He looked like a real human being.

"And the best news of all. My grandson told me that he has a new interest in his life—gourmet cooking."

Grayson bounced up and down as if he was a little kid again. "I've learned to make lasagna, stuffed peppers, and crème brûlée this week."

Reginald gave a nod. "That's quite an accomplishment."

"And next week Maurice will show me how to prepare chicken Marsala, Waldorf salad, and tiramisu. There he is now." Grayson waved toward Maurice, who stood across the room, and trotted off to greet him.

"I haven't seen my grandson so enthusiastic since he came to Boulder."

"I guess he merely needed a new focus."

Over to the side, Reginald spied Vicki Pearson and her son chatting with Henrietta and Rebecca. He excused himself from Mrs. Younger and joined the foursome. "No babysitter tonight, Vicki?"

"I ran into a problem again. I hope you don't mind that I brought Mason."

"Not at all. But I wouldn't advise letting him drink any of the punch."

She wrinkled her brow.

Mason was nicely dressed and answered Reginald's greeting politely. He could get used to kids who acted like Mason.

"I want to thank you again for staying with Mason the other night, Mr. Bentley," Vicki said.

Before he realized what he was saying, he blurted out, "I'd be happy to watch him any time."

Vicki's and Rebecca's eyes opened wide.

"You. . . you watched Vicki's son?" Rebecca stammered.

"Uh, yes."

"Mr. Bentley and I had a cool evening together. We played video games, did magic tricks and read Harry Potter."

"And Mason makes an amazing sandwich," Reginald added.

"Well, well," Rebecca said, looking at him carefully. "That's a whole new side of you, Reggie."

Figuring he should avoid any setbacks to what seemed promising progress with Rebecca, he had an idea. "Say, we should introduce Mason to Jerry Rhine, since they're both magicians."

"I'll go retrieve him from the snack table," Henrietta said.

"I'm going to have a bite to eat as well," Rebecca said. She gave Reginald a provocative smile and sashayed away.

He admired her backside and hoped that reconciliation might be in process. She was speaking to him again and hadn't raked him with her nails or left any dragon burns on his arms.

Moments later Henrietta returned with Jerry in tow, wiping his hands on his pants.

"Jerry, meet Mason Pearson," Reginald said. "He's auditioning to take over your entertainment of Sunny Crest prospects if you ever get too old and decrepit."

"That'll never happen," Jerry said.

"What, that he can't take over or that you'll never be old and decrepit?" Reginald asked.

"Both." Jerry regarded Mason. "So you like magic tricks?"

"Yes, sir."

"No sir here. You can call me Jerry. Mason, there's something crawling out of your ear." He reached over and extracted a rubber snake. "Better wash your ears when you get home."

"There's something in your shoe, Jerry," Mason said. He reached over and produced a rubber spider.

Jerry chortled. "Not bad, kid."

"Be careful not to try his Siberian hand muff," Reginald interjected.

"It wouldn't work on him," Jerry said. "He's too smart. Hey, look who's here, Reggie."

Reginald turned to see Maude Rhine with her lethal cane in one hand and her other hand held by the skinny guy from the cane fu class.

"What are you youngsters up to?" Maude asked, waving her cane in Jerry's direction.

"Hi, Mom. You remember Reggie here?"

She squinted at him. "You're the wuss who fell to the mat when I gave your cane a little tap."

"Nice seeing you again too, Maude. Who's your friend?"

Maude waved her cane toward the skinny geezer, and he ducked. "This here's my boyfriend, Bradford. Meet Reggie, the wimp."

Bradford reached out a skinny hand, and Reginald took it afraid he might break a bone if he shook it too hard. Instead, Bradford crushed his hand in a vise like grip, and Reginald winced. "Don't take it personal, Reggie. She calls all men wimps. She's some woman, ain't she?"

Maude actually blushed. "Oh, Bradford. You have such a way with words." She leaned over and gave him a kiss on the cheek. "I go for younger men. Bradford's only ninety-six. Come on we need to cut a rug." With that, she grabbed Bradford's hand again and dragged him off to the dance floor, her cane clacking on the floor.

"What happened to your dad?" Reginald asked Jerry.

"He couldn't keep up with Mom. Died four years ago at ninety-eight."

Reginald whistled. "You come from some long-lived stock, Jerry."

"You better believe it. I should be around for another two decades or so to entertain you, Reggie."

Reginald pictured Jerry in prison for the next twenty years performing magic tricks for the guards and other inmates.

Mimi Hendrix came running up. "Mr. Bentley, may I speak with you?"

"Sure, excuse us."

They left Jerry and Mason talking magic and stepped over to a quiet part of the room near a potted fern that looked like it could use a good watering.

"You'll never guess what happened," Mimi said.

"I bet we received some positive PR on Channel 5 news."

She raised her hand to her face. "How did you know?"

"I happened to witness the close encounter of the investigative reporter kind today. The Jerry-atrics wowed him."

"They certainly did. I've never heard Charles Moncrief give a positive report from one of his investigations before. He went on to say that his grandmother particularly likes living here and gave Sunny Crest a resounding endorsement."

"Fortunately, he fell under a magic spell cast by our own Jerry Rhine."

"One other thing, Mr. Bentley. Have you decided if we can hold our Sunny Crest senior triathlon?"

Mimi's eager expression reminded him of a kid asking for an ice cream cone. Then he thought of the Jerry-atrics swimming, biking and jostling each other as they walked to the finish line. He didn't know if Daimler would allow him to keep the place open or not but what the heck. "I like the idea. I'll give you a final answer by the end of the evening."

Mimi pranced off with a contented look on her face. It felt good to see someone so happy. Reginald only wished he had a video of Moncrief's report for Armand Daimler to watch. Not that it would necessarily have done any good unless Daimler thought it would make him more money.

Reginald observed Tom Balboa holding Belinda's hand and headed over to them. "I have something to discuss with the two of you."

They both blinked with surprise.

Glad he had their attention, Reginald proceeded. "I have a confession and an accusation to make."

Now they both squinted at him as if he had just arrived from planet dingbat with a giant ham sandwich on his head.

"First, the confession. Belinda, I broke the glass in a photo frame in your apartment. I shouldn't have gone into your place while you were gone, and I'll pay for a replacement."

She clicked her tongue at him. "You don't need to do that, Reggie, but I appreciate your honesty."

"I. . . I should punch you in the nose and stomp you into the ground," Tom said, waving his right fist in the air.

Reginald held up his hand. "Tom, that won't be necessary. With your demolition background and the evidence I saw in your apartment the day I visited you, I know you planted the stink bomb in my office. Since Belinda has agreed to let me off the hook, I'll do the same for you. I won't have the gendarme toss you out on your ear. Just don't set off any more stink bombs in our building." He grabbed Tom's hand and shook it. "But it did provide a wakeup call for me. Thanks."

Tom froze in place, stunned.

Reginald released his hand and moseyed over to the punchbowl to add to his resolve for the major confrontation of the evening.

"Drinking a lot of punch, are we, Reggie?" Jerry sidled up to him.

"Yes. I have a lot on my mind."

"Just make sure you don't have to go to the little boys' room every ten minutes."

"I still can't get over how things have been resolved between Dex and Hector. Do you have any ability to fix traffic tickets, Jerry?"

"Never tried that, but you never know."

Reginald grabbed another cup of punch and downed it in one gulp.

"You nervous, Reggie?"

"Yeah, I guess I am."

Jerry gave him a long, searching look. "I imagine you have a big decision to make."

He met Jerry's eyes directly. "Yes, I do."

Jerry cocked an eyebrow. "Must be quite a burden for an ex-corncob holder."

At that moment, Detective Aranello approached. "Mr. Bentley, I've been looking for you. You wanted to speak with me?"

"Yes. First, let me introduce Jerry Rhine, Detective Aranello."

Jerry grabbed the detective's hand in both of his. "Hey, you have something in there." He extracted of bouquet of artificial flowers. "This is for you to give to your lady of choice."

"Jerry is our resident magician," Reginald explained to Aranello. "Always making things pop up or disappear."

The detective held the bouquet at arm's length as if he expected it to explode.

"Now if you gentlemen will excuse me, there's a little lady who expects to be twirled around the dance floor." Jerry waved and scooted away.

Aranello dropped the bouquet to his side as if to shake off any artificial insects that accompanied it. "What did you want to talk about, Mr. Bentley?"

"The death of Willie Pettigrew. Any further information on whether it was a homicide or an accident?"

"Nothing conclusive yet. None of the interviews turned up anything suspicious from any of your staff or residents. The coroner's report isn't completed yet, but I expect it will be classified an undetermined death."

"Anything new on the cause of death?"

"Same as we observed at the outset. Blunt trauma to the head."

"Which could be from a blow to the head or hitting the cement loading bay floor."

He regarded Reginald as if tutoring a third grader. "That's correct, Mr. Bentley."

"And if someone dealt a blow to his head before he hit the pavement, there would have to be a weapon of some sort."

Aranello tapped his foot impatiently and glared at him. "Where are you headed with this, Mr. Bentley?"

At that moment, Reginald's cell phone rang. He pulled it out and saw Armand Daimler's number. "If you'll excuse me for a moment, I have to take this call."

Reginald stepped over to an empty corner of the room, his heart racing. Would Daimler tell him to fry it or let him keep fixing it?

"Bentley here."

"Reginald. I'm glad I caught you. I'm heading to the airport and will be in Singapore for the next week. I've been thinking over what we discussed earlier —"

"I have too, Mr. Daimler. And I'm even more confident than ever that keeping Sunny Crest open remains the best course of action for Cenpolis."

"I'm not a hundred percent convinced, Reginald, but I admire your conviction and enthusiasm. Tear up the contract with Ralston. I'll give you a year to keep the place running. We'll reassess then."

The phone clicked off.

Reginald stood there, taking in what he had heard. He felt warmth spreading throughout his body. Sunny Crest had life! He wouldn't have to kick the Jerry-atrics into the street.

Detective Aranello came over, looking at his watch. "Mr. Bentley, I need to meet someone else shortly. Anything else we need to cover?"

Reginald took a deep breath. "We were discussing whether a weapon might have been used on Willie Pettigrew. I take it if you discovered a weapon, that would point to a homicide, but without a weapon it was most likely an accident." He tried not to look over toward his equipment bag resting along the wall. Out of the corner of his eye he saw it there, seeming to grow larger, practically dancing up and down in his peripheral vision.

"That's correct, Mr. Bentley."

"And with no weapon, what will be your next step, Detective?"

He shrugged. "We'll close the case, pending further information or investigative leads. There's not much more we can do at the present time."

"Thank you, Detective. I appreciate all your efforts here at Sunny Crest. I won't keep you any longer."

As Aranello strode away, Reginald looked out on the dance floor. Jerry and Henrietta swayed to a jazz beat, reminding him of two randy teenagers. Tom and Belinda stomped around together like two tanks in combat. Al leaned on Karen, the weak body and weak mind making one complete person. Then he noticed two other couples. Pete and Henry of the parking lot altercation each held old ladies in their arms. They spun their partners around, stopping to talk momentarily before resuming the dance. Reginald shook his head in amazement at their change. Maude and Bradford popped out of the crowd of dancers. She leaned on him, and he steered her as if he were flying a biplane. Rebecca stood on the side watching the dancers.

Reginald wove his way through a group of geezers and geezerettes, making sure not to trip over any walkers or become impaled by any weapons wielded by cane fu disciples. He reached his equipment bag and lifted out the paper sack holding the mini-bat and insurance form. Navigating over to the fireplace, he glanced over his shoulder briefly to see Jerry frozen on the dance floor, eyes riveted on the paper sack. With no one near him, Reginald slowly removed the insurance form and dropped it into the fire. Then he tossed the brown paper bag in. He turned around to see Jerry still watching. Reginald nodded at Jerry, flung the mini-bat into the fire and stared as the flames consumed it.

Suddenly, Reginald felt as light as a feather. He thought back over the recent past. What an incredible two weeks. He had survived, surrounded by old fogies, had even learned to like a little kid, had been accepted by Rebecca's cat and might some day learn to tame dragons in order to stay permanently in Rebecca's good graces. With a light, jaunty step he headed over to Rebecca, grabbed her hand and led her toward the dance floor. Along the way he passed Mimi, gave her a thumbs up and said, "The senior triathlon is a go."

He was rewarded by the sight of her beaming face.

Reginald continued to run through his mind all that had happened in his short tenure at Sunny Crest. He might lose his driver's license given all the accumulated traffic violations, but even his silver Jaguar didn't mean that much to him anymore. Life held all sorts of possibilities again. As he grasped Rebecca tightly, he watched Jerry twirl Henrietta. Maude Rhine wouldn't have to visit her son in prison after all. Yes, he definitely had begun to like old people. Rebecca put her cheek to his, and electricity shot through his body.

About the Author

Mike Befeler is author of six novels in the Paul Jacobson Geezer-lit Mystery Series: *Retirement Homes Are Murder, Living with Your Kids Is Murder* (a finalist for The Lefty Award for best humorous mystery of 2009), *Senior Moments Are Murder, Cruising in Your Eighties Is Murder* (a finalist for The Lefty Award for best humorous mystery of 2012), *Care Homes Are Murder* and *Nursing Homes Are Murder*. He has six other published novels: *The Tesla Legacy, The V V Agency, The Back Wing, Mystery of the Dinner Playhouse, Murder on the Switzerland Trail* and *Court Trouble: A Platform Tennis Mystery;* and a non-fiction biography, *For Liberty: A World War II Soldier's Inspiring Life Story of Courage, Sacrifice, Survival and Resilience (The Best Chicken Thief in All of Europe)*. Mike is past-president of the Rocky Mountain Chapter of Mystery Writers of America. He grew up in Honolulu, Hawaii, lived for many years in Boulder, Colorado, and now resides in Southern California, with his wife, Wendy. If you are interested in having the author speak to your book club, contact Mike Befeler at mikebef@aol.com. His web site is http://www.mikebefeler.com.

Other Books by Mike Befeler

Paul Jacobson Geezer-Lit Mystery Series
Retirement Homes Are Murder
Living with Your Kids Is Murder
Senior Moments Are Murder
Cruising in Your Eighties Is Murder
Care Homes Are Murder
Nursing Homes Are Murder

Paranormal Mysteries
The VV Agency
The Back Wing

Theater Mysteries
Mystery of the Dinner Playhouse

Historical Mysteries
Murder on the Switzerland Trail

Sports Mysteries
Court Trouble: A Platform Tennis Mystery

International Thrillers
The Tesla Legacy

Non-fiction
*For Liberty: A World War II Soldier's Inspiring Life Story of Courage,
Sacrifice, Survival and Resilience (The Best Chicken Thief in All of
Europe)*

CPSIA information can be obtained
at www.ICGtesting.com
Printed in the USA
LVOW11s0410070917
547834LV00001B/96/P